Light From the Shadows
Modern Traditional Witchcraft

Gwyn

Light From the Shadows
Modern Traditional Witchcraft

©1999 Gwyn

ISBN 186163 0638

ALL RIGHTS RESERVED

Cover design by Paul Mason

Published by:

Capall Bann Publishing
Freshfields
Chieveley
Berks
RG20 8TF

Contents

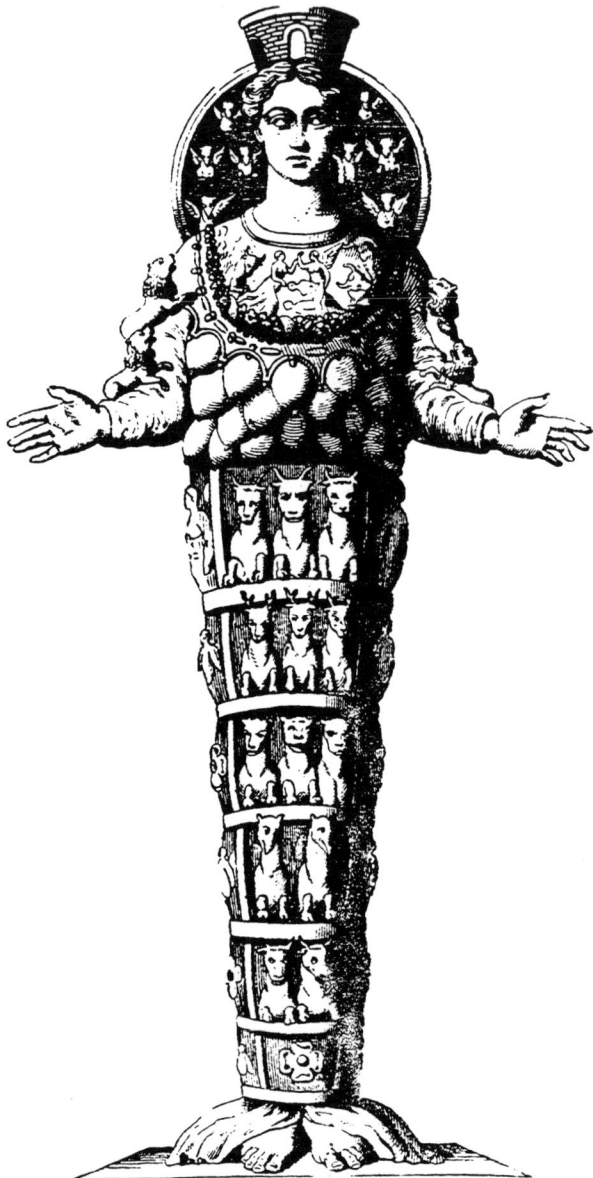

Diana of Ephesus.

Introduction

The purpose of this book is to offer the reader access to the beliefs and practices of a traditional form of witchcraft. It does not offer a manufactured 'granny story', for there is none to tell, or an ancient tradition based on a hereditary pedigree dating back many centuries, for none exists here. Unlike so many other books recently, especially American ones, it has not been written to create a new tradition with a fantasy history.

Instead this book is a practical and theoretical introduction to a modern form of traditional Craft relevant to the dawning of the 21st century. It contains mythic themes, symbolism, theology and archetypal imagery that are common to the beliefs and practices of a number of individuals, groups and traditions of the Craft across the country. It does not claim to represent all those who regard themselves as 'traditional'. Indeed there are many who will disagree with what is written here and that is their right. They can write their own books about what they do and believe in, and no doubt will do so in the future.

The central Mythic Theme of this book, and many of the images and symbols throughout its pages, are firmly based on ancient myths, images and symbols which are as old as humankind. No claims are made that they represent any kind of ancient historical continuity or unbroken tradition extending from the distant past to today, beyond the natural continuity and evolution of ideas preserved in folk memory, or the collective unconsciousness of the human race, or in some (not all) of the folk rituals celebrating the cycle of the seasons. It is the essence on the inner level, not their origin on the outer level, of the material in this book which is important.

The book has thirteen chapters of varying length, once for each of the thirteen moons of the old lunar calendar. The first of these chapters is a general historical overview attempting to define what traditional witchcraft is, or perhaps is not. It also describes the role of witches in the classical world and the medieval period. Chapters Two and Three are an introduction to the uniqueness of the witch god and goddess, with descriptions of their many attributes taken from mythology, legends and fairy tales.

Chapter Four deals with the so-called 'working tools' of the traditional witch and their use in the circle. Chapter Five covers initiation and the 'passing of the power'. Chapters Six to Eleven provide the reader with a comprehensive guide to the Wheel of the Year and its Mythic Theme. However this is not a Book of Shadows, and those expecting recipes for Sabbat cakes will be disappointed. This section of the book does cover the festivals of the turning year and their esoteric meaning and inner symbolism in a conventional format similar to other titles on the market.

Chapter Twelve discusses the operative or practical side of the Craft including magickal rituals and workings. This chapter does not ignore the darker side of the Craft and contains material that is controversial. Finally, Chapter Thirteen examines the contemporary revival of interest in traditional witchcraft and the influence it may have on modern Wicca and neo-paganism. It also analyses the Mythic Theme's significance and relevance for the 21st century and the coming Aquarian Age.

The book ends with a glossary of terms, notes and references, and a reading list for those who wish to take their studies further.

Gwyn

Chapter One
Defining Traditional Witchcraft

It is possible that the heading to this chapter should be 'Attempting to Define Traditional Witchcraft', because of the difficulty in deciding exactly what the term means today. In fact it is used to describe and define a number of disparate and distinct groups and traditions within the modern witchcraft revival of the last sixty years. The term itself means different things depending upon both your cultural understanding and geographical location.

In the United States and Canada the term is used almost exclusively to describe any form of organised witchcraft based on a formal ritual initiation into an established system of covens ruled by a hierarchal priesthood and offering a formal system of training and promotion through degrees.

British 'Traditional' is a term specifically used to describe the modern Gardnerian and Alexandrian forms of the Craft founded by Gerald Gardner in the 1940s and Alex Sanders in the 1960s. In both the cases above, the word 'traditional' is used to separate organised modern Wicca from the solitary witches (who may also confusingly call themselves Wiccans), neo-pagans, and followers of other forms of modern eclectic Craft.

In contrast to the Northern American use of the word, in Britain (with a few exceptions) the term 'traditional' is used to describe any non- Gardnerian, non-Alexandrian or non-neo-pagan, or pre-modern form of witchcraft. In this context, 'pre-modern' may refer to before 1939, when Gerald Gardner was initiated into a 'traditional' coven in the New Forest area of southern England, or before 1920 when Dr. Margaret Murray wrote her seminal book *The Witch Cult in Western Europe.*

It can also refer to those witches, mostly Hereditaries, who claim to follow traditions that are allegedly survivals of the historical witchcraft of the Persecution period. It should also be clearly understood that there have been several revivals of witchcraft and neo-paganism in the last two hundred years. Many examples of modern 'traditional Craft' may only date their origins from after 1800, even though they may claim to be older. Some may be less than a hundred years old.

As a starting point to a complex and sometimes confusing subject we should go to the dictionary and there we find that 'tradition' is defined as 'an opinion or belief or custom handed down from ancestors to prosperity especially orally or by practice.' It can also mean 'artistic or literary principles based on accumulated experience and traditional usage', The term 'traditional' in the last sentence means 'something based on or obtained by tradition, or resembling that of an earlier period of history.' Therefore we have rituals, knowledge and beliefs either passed down through a hereditary lineage or based on experience over an established period of time.

In the context of witchcraft and its practice the above refers to beliefs and practices which may have been passed down through generations and inherited within a family tradition. This is what is known as Hereditary Craft or, mostly in the USA, famtrad or family traditions, Alternatively, it also refers to beliefs and practices which have existed within an established group or tradition spanning a lengthy period of time. This could be fifty or five hundred years.

In the case of 'resembling that of an earlier period of history' this refers either to a revival of historical witchcraft in modern times or, more controversially, the claim of a surviving tradition dating back to historical witchcraft, to earlier Saxon or Celtic times, or even the pre-Christian period. Obviously such claims are more easily made then proved. Any pre- 1800 provenance claimed by a

4

modern group is often regarded as highly suspect even by fellow Crafters.

In many cases of this type it is often found that the claimants are Walter Mitty figures with less then a firm grip on reality and hopelessly lost in a fantasy world of their own creation. The other possibility, rejected by those historians with an interest in the subject, is that in isolated rural areas ancient beliefs and practices may have survived the witch hunts, the Industrial Revolution, two World Wars and the technological explosion of the late 20th century intact. Unfortunately concrete proof for this is seldom offered or to be found, and we are left with only speculation and instinct to guide us in judging such claims.

The word 'witchcraft' itself is of comparatively recent origin, dating back to the early medieval period and Anglo-Saxon England, although the concept is probably as old as humanity. The word comes originally from the Old English wicche (plural) and the Anglo-Saxon *wicca* (masculine) and *wicce* (female). It has variously been related to *wician*, to cast a spell, and *witega*, meaning a wise man prophet or seer. It has been said to derive from the Indo-European root word *weik*, relating to both sorcery and the practice of religious rites [1]. Other, more contentious. derivatives are said to be *witte*, or wise, *wittan*, to be wise, but these have been challenged in recent years. In other Indo-European languages we can find *wikkerie*, or witchery (Old German), *wika*, or to bend (Swedish), *vikja*, or turn aside, conjure away or exorcise, vita, to know, and *vitki*, a wizard (Icelandic) [2]. All these words and definitions link witches with magick, religious rites, wisdom, seership, knowledge and the deflection, or turning away, of evil spirits.

An alternative and controversial view of the definition of the word 'witch' was given by the late William G. Gray, the author of several books on ceremonial magick and the Qabalah. Gray rejected the origin of the word as coming from *witte* or *witega*. Instead he quoted from the *Anglo-Saxon Dictionary* (no date or publisher given) and its entry for witches that defines them in the historical sense as those who make love potions or practice incantations. Gray specifically associated these attributes with the Latin term *malificus*, evil doer, *venificus*, a poisoner, and *prestigias*, a trickster. The latter term being more common in the Middle Ages to describe court jesters.

Gray also linked the word 'witch' with the Anglo-Saxon *wikken*, to make evil. This is the root of the modern word wicked or to be evil. Therefore, argued Gray, a witch was by definition a wicked person of weak character, easily bent or twisted, a poisoner, evil doer and trickster. He concluded: 'By strict interpretation witches cannot be other than malicious and anti-social people' [3].

There is no doubt that a Catholic Inquisitor or Protestant witch-finder would have agreed with Gray's conclusion. Neither can there be any doubt from the folklore and historical records that among the ranks of those who claimed to be, or were popularly believed to be, witches in the past (and in the present) can be found 'malicious and anti-social people'. After all, that is human nature. Occult wisdom and magickal knowledge has often been used and abused for anti-social and evil purposes. The old-time witches were also realists who could curse as well as cure, harm as well as heal. They also had a wide knowledge of natural poisons and they were not subscribers to the modern Wiccan principle 'An ye harm none' As the late Robert Cochrane, the Magister of a traditional coven in the 1960s, once famously said: "There are four types of witch - black, grey, white and publicity. "

Despite William Gray's strong public views on the evil represented by witchcraft he was it seems far more tolerant in his private life. In recent years following his death it has been revealed that Gray worked during his magickal career with several well-known witches, including the late Sybil Leek, Patricia Crowther and Robert Cochrane. Gray's book *The Rollright Rituals* (Helios Books 1975) impressed many by its atmospheric invocation of a form of natural magick which was very similar to Traditional Craft. Gray had a special affinity with the Rollright Stones in Oxfordshire, a witches meeting place since at least the 16th century.

In his book Gray describes a simple ritual to contact the guardians of the stones using invocations of the powers of earth, fire and water. During the ceremony various ritual working tools are employed - a forked staff or stang, a rod or wand, a sword of Celtic design, a drinking horn, a cord, and a shield engraved with a runic inscription. In the Rollright Ritual these represent a standing stone (earth), a fire, a cave (water), the field (earth) and the circle (spirit). This symbolism and ritual form are instantly recognizable to most traditional witches.

While we have the trusty dictionary to hand, and we are attempting to define the nature of witchcraft, it might be a good idea to look at some other common or popular words associated with the Craft e.g. coven, Sabbath or Sabbat, and esbat. The word 'coven' has come to mean a group of thirteen witches, although its original meaning was an assembly or gathering. It is a variation on covent or convent, and the Latin *conventus*, meaning a religious community, usually female. It may also be related to coventicle, a clandestine religious meeting, convention or a formal assembly, convaction or calling together an assembly, and convene meaning to assemble. Traditional witches still speak of convening together. In *Canterbury Tales* Chaucer uses the word 'covent' to describe a meeting of thirteen people. It also survives in London's Covent Garden as the former fruit and vegetable market was built on the site of a nunnery.

Coven may also be linked with 'covenant', meaning an agreement or contract between the worshipper and his or her Gods. In Christian propaganda this covenant became a Faustian pact between the diabolical witch and Satan. As a result of this pact it was commonly believed the witch exchanged her soul for magickal power and material wealth. This was in fact a perverted and debased version of the 'passing of the power' that occurred when the witch was initiated into the Craft. There is an ongoing debate in both historical and Craft circles as to how widespread the coven system was, especially in England and Wales. It is suggested that the majority of witches were loners or solitaries who met only infrequently, if at all, with other practitioners.

Sabbath or Sabbat, as in the medieval witches' sabbath, is a term that seems to have been borrowed directly from Judaism. It may relate back to the period when the Church persecuted Jews. They were accused of eating babies, poisoning wells, defacing Christian symbols and images and the worship of Satan. Almost identical charges were made against Christian heretics like the Cathars, and against the 'witches' when the Persecution began in earnest at the end of the 15th century. The actual word 'Sabbath' comes from the Hebrew *sabat*, meaning to rest (on the seventh day)'. A more controversial, and fanciful, origin for the word derives it from the Arabic *Azabat*, or forceful occasion. This links with the theory held by some Crafters that the medieval witch cult in Europe was influenced by the Two Horned Cult of North Africa. [4]

A popular term used by modern Wiccans today is esbat, meaning a meeting of a coven or individual witches at the new or, usually, full moon. The term esbat was derived by Dr Margaret Murray from the French *s'essbattre*, meaning to frolic. She also saw this word as the non-Jewish form of Sabbath or Sabbat. The word esbat is recorded in the trial of a 16th century witch who refers to *'les petit assembles'* - According to Dr Murray, the esbat was a business meeting and the business was the practice of magic for the benefit of a client or for harming an enemy.' [5]

Today many witches, especially those following a solitary path, call themselves 'hedgewitches'. In its modern form this term comes from the title of a popular book written in the 1980s by Rae Beth. In modern usage it has come to mean a country witch, or somebody interested in herbalism and communing with nature, who does not belong to a coven, and who has taken on the persona of the old-time village wise woman.

In traditional circles it has a more specific meaning. The actual term 'hedgewitch' comes from the Old German *hagarvssa*, 'the one riding on the hedge or fence'. This refers to the liminal boundary between the medieval village and the forest or wilderness outside. It was an old folk tradition that the witch always lived in the last cottage in the village before the "outside'

On an esoteric level, it was symbolic of the boundary between this world and the Otherworld, spanned by the witch in her role as the *mirkryder*, the 'rider in the dark' or 'night rider'. It was popularly said that the hereditary witch was 'born on the boundary'. The term 'hedge witch' is therefore an archaic reference to the gate-keeper or hedge-keeper. This is somebody who guards the barrier, boundary or gateway between this world and the Other. The hedge or wall represents the 'bridge' between the worlds, the material and the spirit, with the gap, gate or stile in the wall or hedge the means of stepping from this side to the Other Side, from this place to another place. [6]

As we have seen, the words 'witch' and 'witchcraft' are of Anglo-Saxon origin. Modern commentators however have projected these terms back into the pre-Christian past to describe the activities of magicians and sorcerers of that period. There is little doubt that the medieval witch-hunters and our Anglo-Saxon ancestors would have instantly recognized the 'witches' of classical Rome and Greece. Indeed the use of sympathetic magick, spells, curses, wax images etc can be dated back to Ancient Egypt, Assyria, and even before then to the hunting rituals performed by the Neolithic shamans in their ritual caves. Although we should be careful in our use of the King James version of the Bible, for the king was a witch-hater, in Biblical times people consulted seers like the Witch of Endor, who practising necromancy or communion with the dead, and other practitioners of the magical arts who allegedly could summon up spirits. There were also Hebrew women who were believed to possess the power to shapeshift into the form of animals and cause disease and death by magick. These women had allegedly made a pact with the Seirim, the goat demons who followed the fallen angel Azazel. If discovered these women were tried by the rabbis and stoned to death. [7]

In classical Greece and Rome sorcerers and magicians were popularly said to meet in graveyards and at crossroads. These were both places sacred to the goddess of the dark moon, Hecate. In folk belief she was the patron of witchcraft and the deity who ruled the underworld. Hecate was one of a triplicity of lunar goddesses with Selene and Artemis. Virgil refers in one of his poems to the lovesick Queen of Carthage in North Africa who consulted a 'woman of occult power'. This woman, described as a priestess, cast love spells and called up 'those spirits that wander at night'. She did this with 'her hair unbound' by evoking the moon goddess three times using invocations to the 'threefold Hecate' and 'the three Dianas' (8)

In the first century BCE the Roman poet Horace linked witches, or female sorcerers, with the Roman goddess of hunting and the moon, Diana. In his opinion, the witch was the stereotypical old hag with long wild hair who casts spells on all who have offended her. He claimed that Diana and Proserpine, daughter of the earth goddess Demeter and Queen of Hades, granted magickal powers to the witches who worshipped them. He also claims,

Shrine of Ethelbert, King of the East Saxons

predating the medieval witches' sabbaths by 1500 years, that the Roman witches gathered together in secret to perform their mysteries. At these meetings they used a 'book of incantations' and performed a ritual to 'draw the moon down from the sky'.

One of the most famous accounts of witchcraft in the classical world is given by Apuleius in his novel *The Golden Ass*. This contains scenes of shapeshifting into the form of an owl using a 'flying ointment' which would not be out of place in the records of a witch trial in the 17th century. The novel also includes evocations of the 'goblin dead' and references to the dark and bright aspects of the witch goddess, represented in the story by Isis and Proserpine. Although the story is fictional it is said to have been based on the writer's own experiences and his initiation into the Mysteries of Isis.

Laws against witchcraft and malefic magick in ancient Rome were severe. As in Later historical periods, the witch was seen as very much an outlaw and social outcast. She is depicted as someone who opposes the established religion and social order, dedicated to cthonic deities whose time has past and who are feared by most people, and intent on causing harm to the moral fabric of society. The conflict between new and old forms of religion has always been a cause of social friction and it has created the fear of demonic forces and malefic magick in the popular mind. It has been suggested that the folk image of the 'evil witch' or sorceress of Greek mythology, Medea and Circe, may originally have been 'goddesses of a former religion or priestesses of the Mother Earth cult. Their knowledge of roots, herbs and mushrooms - gifts of the Earth - may have been part of their priestly training'.[9] Even as far back as the ancient Greeks and Romans the mythic pattern of the gods of the old religion becoming the devils of the new divine order was firmly established.

This process continued apace with the emergence of the Christian Church as a political force after the fall of the Roman Empire in the early 5th century CE. It is a common fallacy that Christianity replaced and eradicated paganism within a short period of time. The historical and archaeological evidence instead offers a picture of a long period of 'dual faith' lasting many centuries. During this period the Church struggled to gain spiritual supremacy over the old pagan beliefs, with the ruling class and missionaries trying to force their new beliefs on an unwilling population who clung to their ancient ways.

Although pockets of Christianity had been established in Roman Britain, mostly among the wealthier city dwellers, with the withdrawal of the Roman legions around 410 CE the south of what is now England was occupied over a period of years by Angles, Jutes and Saxons from southern Scandinavia and northern Germany. These people were initially pagans and it was not until 597 CE, nearly one hundred years after the Roman occupation ended, that Pope Gregory sent a mission led by Bishop Augustine to Kent to convert the pagan English. This first mission had a limited success and in fact, after the death of Augustine, his colleagues had to temporarily flee across the Channel to Gaul (France) when paganism was revived among the English tribes.

Forty years after the mission landed, King Eorcenberht of Kent was forced to outlaw pagan idols among his people and he ordered their destruction. In the same year (640) St Eligius condemned those who placed lights at stones, springs and trees and where three ways met (crossroads). He also condemned the use of sacrifice, the 'enchanting' of herbs or the 'consecrating of flocks to the Devil' by passing them through a hollow tree or an aperture in the earth. These early laws were not successful, for at the end of the 7th century King Wihfred was forced to forbid his subjects from making offerings to 'devils' (pagan gods).

The earliest laws against witchcraft in Britain were clerical prohibitions used to suppress the survival of pagan rites and beliefs in Saxon times. Theodore the Greek, who was Archbishop of Canterbury from 668 to 698 CE, issued decrees stating that any woman who practised witchcraft should do a year's penance. Anyone who destroyed another by 'evil spells' was to spend seven years fasting and praying. These same decrees also outlawed the wearing of animal masks and costumes in the pagan custom at the midwinter celebrations.

Theodore decreed: 'If anyone at the kalends of January walks as a stag or a little old woman, that is to say, if they change themselves into the likeness of wild animals or clothe themselves in the skins of cattle and wear the heads of beasts, those who in fact transform themselves in such wise into a kind of wild animal shall do penance for three years, for this is devilish.'

On the Continent, Roman Catholic missionaries such as St Martin and St Boniface were waging their own private wars on paganism and witchcraft as early as the 5th and 6th centuries. Martin, an ex-pagan and ex-Roman soldier, used to ride around the countryside with his cronies burning down nemetons or sacred groves. He comdemned the local peasants in Gaul who 'lit candles for devils at the crossroads'. Irish laws from the same period, and credited to St Patrick, denounced those who consulted sooth-sayers who claimed to be able to see spirits in mirrors.

In the 8th century the Archbishop of York decreed that anyone found practising the magickal arts, witch craft or 'evil spells' should fast until they repented. If the spells resulted in the death of the victim then the fast should last seven years. In the same decree the Archbishop condemned offerings to devils (the pagan gods), divination by 'heathen methods', vows made at wells, trees and stones, and the gathering of herbs using any prayer other than a Christian one. At the same time the clergy in Northumbria were laying down laws fining people who still performed sacrifices, worshipped idols and 'loved witchcraft'.

At the end of the 9th century, in 890 to be precise, the Pope was forced to write to his English bishops complaining that 'the nefarious rites of the pagan have sprouted again in your parts'. The laws of King Alfred condemned anyone who made sacrifices to the pagan gods to death. In the reign of King Edward (899-925) harsher laws were made against the *wicca* (male witch) and the *wiglaer* (diviner). These laws incurred either banishment from the realm or death if they refused to be exiled. Causing death by bewitchment became a capital offence during the reign of King Aethalstan (925-940). In 959 King Edgar issued an edict instructing all priests to promote Christianity and destroy pagan survivals. This edict specifically mentioned the practice of necromancy, well-worship, divination, enchantment, spell casting and rituals at trees and stones

The Danish King Canute, who ruled England from 1016 to 1035, also passed laws against witchcraft and, significantly, connected it to the making of offerings to idols. The Danish laws against witchcraft also banned pagan practices such as worshipping trees, stones, fire, water, the sun and moon. In 1014 Wulfstan, the Archbishop of York, preached a sermon condemning the activities of 'wizards and sorceresses' in England. He metaphorically described these 'sorceresses' as *waelcyrge*, or Valkyries, in the Saxon sense as spirits of the underworld, and he denounced from the pulpit the continuing worship of the moon stars, water, fire and the Earth itself as pagan gods.

From the evidence of these laws we can be confident in saying that Anglo-Saxon England was only nominally Christian, and that pagan beliefs and practices not only survived but thrived for at least 400 years after the arrival of Augustine and his papal mission. To put this into a modern perspective, this is the same period of time from the Tudor age to the present day.

It was not until the Norman Conquest in 1066, and the mayhem and disruption it caused to Anglo-Saxon society, that the Church began to take the upper hand. William I organised a massive church and castle building programme to subdue the native population both spiritually and physically. That paganism still survived under the surface even in early Norman England is evident from the supernatural and pre-Christian elements to be found in the folk legends of popular heroes like Edric the Wild, Hereward the Wake, Robin Hood and Owen Glyndwr who for several hundred years led the resistance to the French-Normans and later the Anglo-Normans.

William the Conqueror repealed the death penalty for witchcraft, but anyone using poison or the magickal arts to kill was outlawed and banished from the kingdom. For centuries afterwards these two crimes would be linked, indicating the herbal knowledge of the witch and its potential use for malefic purposes. Passing these laws however did not stop William from employing a witch to cast a death spell against the rebel army of Hereward the Wake in the East Anglian fens.

Henry I (1100-1135) made the use of wax images to cause harm illegal, and in the reign of King John the first court case involving accusations of black witchcraft was heard. In 1209 Agnes, the wife of a merchant called Odo, accused another woman of sorcery. However the woman was acquitted after successfully passing the 'ordeal with red-hot iron'. In the early 14th century, possibly as the result of European influence, magicians and witches were classified under English law as both heathens and heretics. The laws of Edward I (1272-1307) ruled that anyone found guilty of sorcery should be burnt at the stake. Most of the major trials in the 14th and 15th century involved the use of sorcery, or malefic magick, in political plots and conspiracies among royalty, the nobility and Church officials Those convicted faced death at the stake for treason.

In the 16th century the Archbishop of Canterbury issued orders to his priests that they should inquire into allegations of 'the use of enchantments, witchcraft and soothsaying'. During the reign of Henry VIII (1509-1547) an Act had been passed declaring witchcraft to be a felony or violent crime. This legislation referred to those who practised witchcraft, e.g. conjured up spirits, divined for lost property and 'made images of beasts and devils'. A new Witchcraft Act was introduced by Elizabeth I in 1563 with the death penalty by hanging. This followed advice to the queen from her bishops that witchcraft was widely practised in her realm and an attempt on her life using a wax image. It is perhaps slightly ironic that the worst of the English witch-hunts were led by Protestants. In 1604 James I introduced a new Act, again with the death penalty. This was not replaced until 1735, when it was made a crime to pretend to practice witchcraft. This law was finally repealed in 1951 and replaced with the present Fraudulent Mediums Act.

During the period of the 1604 Act the definition of witchcraft and witches was laid down in a treatise on the subject written in 1594 by a lawyer called William West. Magicians were classed as those who conjured up the shades of the dead or 'show things, either secret or far off'. Soothsayers divined the future, raised evil spirits to answer questions and used rings, mirrors and crystals. Diviners found lost property and jugglers healed humans and animals using charms and spells. Enchanters and charmers used 'words, herbs, characters and images', while the witch proper was a person who had made a pact with the Devil. They were believed to cast spells to kill animals and humans, blast crops and raise storms, and were carried off by a familiar spirit or on a staff to spend the night 'dancing and in diverse other devilish lusts and lewd disports'.

Three 17th century witches (note the different ritual staves)

In addition to these, for lack of a better term, black witches, people also consulted the 'white witches', 'wise women' and 'cunning men'. These practioners of the occult were seldom prosecuted under the Witchcraft Act because they were believed to be, rightly or wrongly, only practising magick for beneficial purposes. These cunning folk, charmers and pellars (healers) were tolerated because before the National Health Service the wise woman or cunning man was often consulted for healing by the poor people of the parish.

These cunning folk used their psychic powers and herbal remedies to cure illnesses and they often used Christian prayers and symbols to aid their spells. The belief in the countryside that certain people possessed supernatural powers, could heal or harm, and controlled ghosts and nature spirits (faeries) was widespread until recent times. In some remote areas it still lingers on. This type of witch can still be found in rural areas of Germany, France, Italy, Spain, Corsica, Finland, Hungary and Russia.

The cunning man or woman was not called upon because he or she was regarded as the source of all wisdom, but because it was believed that they had the power to entreat or trick the dead, evil spirits and the faeries who were all commonly accepted as responsible for bad luck or misfortune. This in essence was a pre-Christian concept dating back to the making of sacrifices and offerings to the pagan gods and goddesses in return for their help, even though many of the cunning folk worked their magick within a Christian context. The word 'cunning' comes from the Old Norse 'kunna', or know, and it means someone skilled in deceit and evasion, artful, crafty and ingenious. These were all attributes possessed by the cunning man or wise woman and expressed in their dealings with both their clients and the spirit world.

Today there is some confusion between the cunning folk and witches, especially with the popularity of so-called hedgewitches and 'village wise women' as titles used by modern witches. It should be noted that in many cases, especially in the case of the

Witches dancing in circle (Note the 'magic mushroom' Faery mound and Green Man in tree)

cunning men, these rural practitioners of the magickal arts acted, officially or non-officially, as witch-finders. They were also often consulted by people who believed they were under psychic attack wanting counter-spells to combat the malefic magick of witches.

Many of the cunning folk were practising Christians who would not have recognized a pagan god if it bit them. Others seem to have been aware of surviving pagan beliefs and customs. One example were the white witches or pellars called in by a 19th century Cornish farmer suffering from bad luck. They carried flaming torches around his fields in a nocturnal ritual and drove his cattle through a bonfire in an old Celtic pagan rite to exorcise the evil from his land.[10]

Some of the 18th and 19th century cunning men and wizards were educated men who could read Latin and Greek. Some were doctors and others were astrologers with a knowledge of mathematics and astronomy. They used grimoires, or grammers of magick, including volumes purchased by mail-order from London booksellers. It has also been claimed that a few of the famous cunning men were also Magisters or leaders of witch covens.

One of these was a wise man called Old Jenkins who lived at Weobley Marsh in Herefordshire in the late 19th century. He used to boast that forty witches in the surrounding villages were known to him and he was their 'master'. When he was brought before a court and repeated his claim to the magistrate he was told that witches did not exist. [11]

Another 19th century cunning man who it is alleged was also a 'witch master' was Old George Pickingill. He lived the last years of his life in the Essex village of Canewdon and it is said he was the Magister of the local coven that allegedly dated its origin back to the 15th century. Pickingill also founded nine covens in East Anglia and southern England. These were led by specially selected priestesses of the 'witch blood' and practised Pickingill's unique form of traditional witchcraft [12].

Most of the early cunning men who operated in the 16th and 17th centuries escaped persecution because they received public patronage from their rural communities, or because they did a good job hunting down black witches and casting counter-spells against malefic magick. After the official Persecution came to an end with the 1735 Act the situation becomes more confused. After this date there were several revivals of 'witchcraft' and these drew on many influences including the contemporary resurgence of interest in classical paganism, ceremonial magick, Rosicrucianism, neo-druidism and Freemasonry, as well as elements of the folk magic of the cunning people.

The fact that these pre-20th century witchcraft revivals were influenced by theosophical occultism, Freemasonry and ceremonial magick is clearly seen in the genesis of the modern form of Craft known as Wicca. The revival of witchcraft before the Second World War, and the subsequent creation of modern Wicca by Gerald Gardner, was influenced by Freemasonry, Rosicrucianism and the Hermetic Order of the Golden Dawn. It was also influenced by the works of Sir James Frazer and Dr Margaret Murray published from the 1900s through to the 1930s. It appears that Dr Murray's works specifically were one, but not the only, of the influences on the New Forest coven founded in the 1920s into which Gerald Gardner was initiated.[13]

Of course, the modern history of witchcraft is dominated and overshadowed by the complex and enigmatic figure of Gerald Gardner and the reforms or inventions, depending upon your viewpoint, he introduced in the 1940s. The membership of his parent coven in the New Forest was an odd mixture of Rosicrucian-Masonic occultists and local country folk. It has been claimed that this coven was descended from one of the Nine Covens founded by George Pickingill in the mid-19th century. It had ceased to convene during the First World War and was revived again in the early 1920s.

The New Forest coven worked on 'traditional' lines; worshipping the Horned God exclusively, using the fly agaric 'sacred mushroom' for trance work and a version of the medieval *sabbati ungeunti* [15] However, it had also been heavily influenced by the middle-class occultists who joined it in the 1930s.

By the late 1940s Gardner had left the traditional path and created his own version of modern witchcraft. This was largely based on material he had cobbled together from the works of Aleister Crowley, Charles Leland and the Golden Dawn. Some traditional concepts, such as ecstatic circle dancing to raise the power, were retained. Justifying this reformation, one traditional witch has said: "Gardner wanted to popularise the worship of the Old Gods, thus liberating people from the repressive and inhibiting ways of patriarchal organised religion. He wanted to quickly promote a religion of love, pleasure and excitement."

Following Gardner's passing to the spirit world in 1964 all types of 'Hereditary' and 'Traditional' claimants appeared. Many seemed to have taken their inspiration from Robert Graves' *The White Goddess* or from the medieval anthology of Welsh myths and legends known as *The Mabinogion*. Some of these claimants had even been members of Gardner's coven at Brickett Wood in Hertfordshire. When this fact was revealed, as it often was, they claimed to have infiltrated the coven on behalf of their tradition 'to find out what was going on'.

At least one member of Gardner's coven may have been a genuine Traditional. She was a talented artist called Monica English and a drawing by her of Pan can be found in Cottie Burland's book *The Magical Arts* (1967). English was the wife of the master of a local hunt in Norfolk and she belonged to a small coven in the area that had been practising for over 200 years. It seems that English joined Gardner's coven because her parent group were worried that his publicity might expose the Traditional Craft and they wanted to be forewarned.

What are the main differences between Wicca and traditional witchcraft? To answer that question we must generalize and risk upsetting those in the traditionalist camp whose beliefs and practices do not conform to what is written here. In general traditional ways of working are based on a more informal and

Frontispiece of Charles Leland's book on Italian witchcraft
'Aradia or the Gospel of the Witches'

improvised structure then Wicca. There is less emphasis on the written word and 'doing it by numbers'. Traditionalists say that too many flowery words and theatrical ritual get in the way of the real business of communing with Gods and the spirit world.

The Traditional Craft also rejects the suburban sitting room as a suitable place to perform its rites. As far as is feasible in our unpredictable British climate, they hold their meetings outdoors. For this reason robes or everyday clothes are worn and it is the reason why traditional groups are sometimes popularly referred to as 'robed covens' As you would expect from a tradition of working outdoors, the genius loci or 'spirit of place' is important, as is the concept of the 'sacred landscape'. There is also an emphasis on the use of 'earth energies' at sacred sites or power centres, contact with the elemental forces and Elfame, the realm of Faerie, and communion with the spirit world.

There are several elements in the modern Traditional Craft which could be classified by today's neo-pagans as 'shamanic'. These include the use of hallucinogenic natural drugs, techniques of psychic vision, trance and mediumship to contact the Otherworld, the summoning of elemental spirits, the use of familiars and spirit guides and wortcunning or herbalism.

Obviously such elements can be found, to a lesser extent usually, in modern Wicca, but it must be stressed that the approach and whole ambience of traditional ways is very different. It is exemplified in a belief system which gives prominence to personal contact with the spirit world, the dark aspects of the God and Goddess, the Horned God as both Green Lord of the Wildwood and Lord of the Wild Hunt, and contact with the elemental and faery realm.

It is also true to say that Hereditary and Traditionals are more reluctant to seek publicity then Wiccans. They are unlikely to be spotted at pagan conferences draped in occult jewellry, wearing embroidered robes and carrying ceremonial swords. They are also unlikely to appear on *This Morning* with Richard and Judy. In fact they often look very ordinary, wear ordinary clothes and 'have a great fund of knowledge of unwitchy things like the stars and the trees and the ancient sites in the area, and people seem to think they are just interested in 'folklore'.[16]

In the old days it is said that many of the witches attended the village church and were regarded as respectable pillars of the community. What they might have done in the woods at full moon was unknown to their neighbours. This is how, it is said, the Craft survived the dark days of the Persecution. To be non-Christian or anti-Christian in rural areas singled you out for criticism or worse. In some villages in the early part of this century if the squire did not see you in church on Sunday you were out of a job on Monday. In 1910 in East Anglia a vicar's wife struck one of his parishioners across the face with her riding crop because he did not lift his cap to her. [17]

It has been noted earlier how the word 'witch' took on a negative meaning and image in common usage. Discussing the Craft in East Anglia, modern practitioner Nigel Pennick has said: 'Like all folk traditions it (the Craft) has no definite name for itself, being referred to by outsiders by more or less generic terms like 'magic', 'wizardry', 'sorcery' or 'witchcraft' '. [18] Over the years many names have been created by insiders to describe the path of traditional witchcraft and its practitioners. They include the Nameless Art, the People, the Elder Faith, the Old Craft, the Crooked Path, the Old Path, the Old Tradition, the Old Ways, the Way of Night, or simply the Faith.

In addition specific names and titles have been created by traditions and groups associated with either their beliefs or geographical locations. Some of the publically known ones are the Cultus Sabbati in Essex, The Way of the Eight Winds in East Anglia, Whitestone in Surrey and Sussex, The Covenant of the Spirit Hunt in Cheshire, the Derwent Amber Wove in Staffordshire, the Tuatha de Cornovii, the Clan of Tubal Cain, the 1734 Tradition. Although they do not claim to be witches per se, there are also the Sons of Gwyddon in North Wales and the Guardians in the Peak District of Derbyshire. Both these groups claim to be following family traditions handed down from Celtic times and their beliefs and practices are very similar to traditional forms of witchcraft.

What then is Traditional Craft? As one witch has put it: 'The Craft is a simple way of life. It involves tuning into Mother Earth at every opportunity in her natural environment. It means a sacred communion with all living things, inner and outer, exploration of ancient sites, and a 'joyous celebration of the changing patterns of the seasons'.

Herne the Hunter

Chapter Two
The Horned One

Humankind's concept of Divinity or the Divine is limited due to the confirment of the soul in the physical body. Therefore throughout history surrogate images have been used to personify the abstract concept of the Absolute and, quite literally, bring it down to earth so it can be more easily understood. Because such images are, by necessity, individual in nature and cultural by design, there has always been the tendency to criticize, condemn or even persecute those who possess a different image of the Divine to one's own.

This misunderstanding about the nature of Divinity is a fact of life and it is root cause of human conflict at the present time. This is because, at our present stage of spiritual development, the true nature of the Divine is beyond our grasp. The spiritual mysteries cannot be communicated at a conscious level. They can only be understood at the deeper level of gnosis or knowing, and this form of perception is clouded in the minds of the ignorant, the prejudiced and the bigoted.

Witchcraft is often spoken of as a dualistic faith i.e. it worships two divine forces personified as a God and Goddess. Most of the ancient pagan cultures also recognized the existence of a Supreme Creator or creative principle who existed beyond the gods and goddesses. This principle could be either male or female or it transcended gender and sexuality altogether, being either androgynous or asexual. It was sometimes known simply as the Life Force, with many names such as prana, ch'i and od, which created, sustains and permeates the universe. This belief is still held by many traditional witches and the Supreme Principle is variously known as the Ancient Providence, the Dryhten and All-That-is.

Some witches regard this Supreme Being as the Ultimate Goddess with No Name. She is 'the unnamed Goddess, the progenetrix of all creation' and 'the old Gods and Goddesses are nothing more than manifestations of the same awesome power of creation, destruction and re-creation we call the Infinite Goddess'.[1]

The term 'Providence' used by some witches to describe this universal and supreme divine power or force is also feminine. It comes from the Latin *orovideo*, meaning 'to foresee', and refers to the personification of female prophetic power. It was a word used in ancient times to refer to the female oracles who were able to provide' for the tribe or the community through their fore-knowledge of the movement of the stars, the passing of the seasons and weather lore.[2] It can also refer to Fate, which was represented by a trinity of goddesses in pan-European mythology.

This universal creative principle, by whatever name or title it is known, manifests in witchcraft as two Powers or Forces imagised as a God or Goddess. In the broadest of terms they personify the 'masculine' and 'feminine' aspects of nature and humankind. In Northern European mythology they are the principles of Fire and Ice and in the East they are known as Yin and Yang.

At our present stage of development archetypal images are used to represent and personify these twin divine forces. In this context, archetypal images are forms of the Goddess and the God imprinted in the human psyche and the collective unconscious as deities, racial heroes and cultural exemplars of myth, legend and fairy-tale. As one modern Wiccan describes them, these 'humanoid images are ways for us to approach and understand a greater mystery - that the different images we have worshipped over the aeons are creations of the human mind. They are ways for us to approach the ineffable mystery - the one Great Spirit that gives life to the universe.'[3]

Modern pagans and witches share with the followers of other world religions the archetypal image of the Divine. In many ways it is an inadequate and immature model of the Godhead and eventually it will be discarded as humans evolve and progress spiritually. In the meantime witches work quite happily with the archetypes because they are an integral part of the collective human unconsciousness, are deeply rooted in folk memory and the myths of our race, and can be accessed or invoked for both magickal purposes and spiritual development.

The Swiss psychologist Carl Jung described these archetypes as promordial images representing fundamental human qualities which appear in myths, folk-lore, dreams and psychic visions. However, in defiance of popular theory and belief among psychologists, it should also be understood that the archetypes are 'real' images of the Gods i.e. the personified aspects of natural forces or the creative principle. They can, and do, possess a separate reality outside the artificial realm of the human imagination and mythology. The occultist Dion Fortune summed up this, apparent, contradiction by saying: 'The different Gods and Goddesses.... are the creation of the created....fashioned in astral substance and ensouled by cosmic forces'.[4] This is something that those who think the Gods are only aspects of their own psyche should meditate upon.

To summarize the paragraphs above; the Creative Principle can be visualised or experienced in human terms as either a 'masculine' or 'feminine' power represented by archetypal images drawn from the culture of choice. These images will in practice usually reflect the personal religious beliefs of the believer and the culture in which he or she is incarnated. Taken to its logical conclusion, we have a holistic spiritual view that can encompass such apparently contradictory archetypal images as the materialisation of the goddess Isis in a magician's temple and the vision of the Virgin Mary to a pilgrim at Lourdes. They are both manifestations of the feminine principle experienced within the cultural and religious framework of two differing, and conflicting, belief systems and world views.

In its Witchcraft Information Pack supplied to new enquirers the Pagan Federation boldly states: 'Witches worship principally the

Goddess of Earth and the Triple Moon and her consort the Horned God; but all Gods and Goddesses, including those of other faiths, are honoured as different aspects of the one Divine Power.' Many traditionalists would query the last sentence as they consider the God and Goddess to be unique to Western and Northern Europe as we shall see.

Even as this is written, the Pagan Federation is discussing the relevance of its Three Principles of belief introduced in the 1970s. The third of these asks prospective members to 'Honour the totality of Divine Reality, which transcends gender, without suppressing the female or male aspect of deity'. The majority of PF members have managed to live with that statement for over 25 years, but an editorial article in the PF's journal, *Pagan Dawn*, has pointed out that many members apparently 'worship a genderless 'Spirit of the Land', and Dianic groups worship the female almost to the exclusion of the male. It therefore claims these pagans could not currently join the PF because they would not be able to accept the third of the Three Principles. (5)

Although the PF document quoted above says that in the Craft 'all Gods and Goddesses, including those of other faiths, are honoured...', in traditional terms the witch god and goddess are specific deities. Some witches refer to them by their names or titles in Celtic, Germanic or Norse mythology. other traditionalists will refer to them simply as the Lord and Lady, the Old Ones, the Old Man and the Old Woman, or even just as Him and Her. The reluctance to actually give 'proper' mythological names to the God and Goddess is a hallmark of the Traditional Craft.

A description of the sophisticated relationship to the Gods is given in the following comments by a modern traditional witch whose established coven 'believed in a single Supreme Spiritual Being who is literally Everything, As such humans cannot conceive this Being and it is necessary to consider the entity being, for our purposes, male and female, positive and negative The Father and Mother principles. However, being of one entity, they each had some aspect of the other. The masculine more dominant in the male, the feminine in the female. The sun, harsh and burning, but life sustaining, represented the God. The other, less blinding light, the moon, represented the Goddess. Nature, Mother Earth, was basically female, the winds, clouds, space were basically male. But in some cases, e.g. rocks, there may be changes. Mudstones, soapstones, siltstones and limestones were feminine, as part of Mother Earth, but basalt, granite, obsidian were seen as having harsher, masculine, aspects. The God and Goddess were seen in all things and were thought of as a Lord and Lady, although not especially visualized in human form. If they were, the Goddess was seen as a plump, motherly figure, the God as a tall, broad, bearded man.' [6]

It has to be remembered that the Celts originally had a very abstract idea of the numerous gods and goddesses they worshipped, often just on a local basis. It was not until the Roman era, when the conquerors compared the Celtic deities to their own pantheon, that anthromorphic images of the Gods were created. Previous to that the Celtic gods had been represented by pillars or crudely hewn blocks of wood carved with abstract symbols or heavily stylised faces.

This abstract concept of the Gods dates back to ancient animistic beliefs that everything in the universe is 'alive'. Our ancestors firmly believed that every stream, river, lake, hill, tree and stone was inhabited by its own individual nature spirit or minor god. In reality what they were saying is that the Life Force, or the creative energy which created and permeates the universe, could manifest at a localised level using an archetypal image that could be recognized by the human brain. These genii loci, or 'spirits of place', were often worshipped as gods or as manifestations of the Old Ones by our ancestors.

In their purest form some of the beliefs of traditional witchcraft are similar to those expressed through the highest levels of Native North American religion. In their world view everything is sacred and 'every-thing that exists, no matter how large or small, is part of the whole, a part of the sacred essence of all existence. Nothing is separate from anything else. Everything is part of creation. Whilst individual thing may have a physical existence that makes them appear separate according to our concepts of time and space, the very concepts of physical dimension and of separate time and space are themselves really an illusion.' [7]

In the traditional form of modern Craft in this book the twin bright and dark aspects of the God are represented by two powerful images the Lord of the Greenwood and the Lord of the Wild Hunt. Traditionally, the Lord of the Woods or the Green Man rules the year from May Eve until the autumn equinox, while the Lord of the Wild Hunt rules the dark season of the year from Hallowe'en or Hallows to the vernal equinox in the spring.

Shiva-Pasupati - the Horned God of the Indus Valley

In some traditions they are known as the Oak King and the Holly King respectively and they are the gods of the waxing and waning year. In this myth, which is possibly Welsh in origin, the Oak King rules from midwinter to midsummer and the Holly King from midsummer to midwinter. According to one Wiccan interpretation they are the light and dark twins who meet in ritual combat twice a year. The defeated twin, it is said, withdraws into Caer Sidi, the Castle of the Silver Wheel, for the six months he is not in power[8]. The symbolism is very similar to the Lords of the Greenwood and Wildwood.

The god of the witches has many faces which are reflected in myth and legend. He is first and foremost the consort of the Goddess as her lover and/or son. In the creation myth of the Italian witches the witch god, in the form of Lucifer, is the lover, son and brother of the moon goddess Diana and he represents the sun [9]. The God is also the sacred king, the vegetation god, who dies a sacrificial death at either midsummer or harvest time, descends to the underworld to learn the wisdom of the Goddess, and is reborn at the winter solstice or the vernal equinox. In his solar aspect his death and rebirth parallels the waxing and waning of the sun through the year.

The following mytho-poetic journey of the God around the Wheel of the Year comes from a neo-traditionalist source. It describes the God's twin aspects as the Lord of Light and Darkness, and his changing role at each of the seasonal festivals in relation to the Goddess.

The Sacred Journey of the Horned God

The Old God walks the solar path of the Wheel of the Year, following the changing cycle of the seasons and the weaving pattern in the sky of the sun, moon and stars.

At Yule, the midwinter solstice, the time between time when the sun stands still at the Bull's noon and the clock chimes thirteen, the God is *sol invictus*, the Lord of Light. At this magickal time of the year he is born anew from the womb of the Great Mother as the Horn Child of promise, the once and future king, the Lightbearer. In the cold midwinter darkness of the longest night of the year, as the Old Year is dying and the New Year waits to be born, his light shines brightly among the stars as a sign of redemption for humankind.

When Candlemas draws nigh, with snowdrops and snow-flakes, the God is the young stag who bears the rising sun between his antlers. As the cold mist and icy frost are melted in dawn's early rays, he is initiated into the mysteries of warriorhood by the Goddess. It is she, as sovereignty of the land, who instructs the young God in the mysteries of sacred kingship and the rulership of the land and its people.

At the vernal equinox, as the earth stirs from its winter slumber, the young God accepts the Goddess in her aspect as the Maiden as his bride. This partnership is sealed in the maze dance at Beltane when he becomes the Oak King, wearing his foliate mask and cloak of green leaves. He is the Green King, the Jack-in-the-Green, the Green Man. He is also Puck and the Lord of the Animals. In his sylvan guise he celebrates the Great Rite in the greenwood with the Lady, she who is the May Queen, Queen of Elfame, the ancient goddess of the land who has granted him kingship in the sacred marriage.

At Midsummer, the time of owl feathers and elderflowers, the Bright God is at the zenith of his solar power. His image at this time is the virile King Stag on the hill, yet the red poppies flowering in the corn field are an omen of his waning power and his wyrd or fate as harvest time approaches.

By Lammastide his powers are already wilting in the summer heat. As the harvest is gathered in and the days begin to shorten, the God is tied to the tau cross of oak branches with willow withies. His sacred blood, red as the poppies in the corn field, is spilled by the Mother with her silver sickle to re-vitalise the land. The Old King is dead! Long live the King!

Harvest Home is in the fall when the Horned God descends through the portals of the dolmen by the mound. He travels to the dark domain of the Snow Queen, Old Mother Goose herself, the Old Queen who is the dark witch goddess of fate, death and transformation, crone guardian of the Cauldron of Inspiration and Regeneration.

As the dry leaves fall from the trees heralding the onset of winter, the God makes his last journey in Our Lady's crescent moon barge to the Hollow Hill beyond the setting sun. On the Isle of the Dead he crosses over the alder bridge to the Castle of Roses beyond the grave. As winter approaches, the God prepares to don the silver mask and starry cloak of the Holly King, who is Jack O' Lantern, Jack Frost and Old Father Yule.

On Hallows, or Winter's Night, when black candles flicker in turnip masks, the transformation is complete. The Old God, Lord of the Wildwood, is now Herne, the Wild Hunter, the dread Guardian of the Dead, the Grim Reaper, Master of Misrule, the Hooded and Masked one who brings the terror by night. In his dark aspect he wears a cloak of shadows and the goblin mask of the Lord of the Wild Hunt, the hunter of souls, with his faery hounds who howl at the gibbous moon and ride the north wind. He is the dark ruler of the Mighty Dead, the Hidden Company, the Watchers and the Primal Ancestors from Gabriel's Wain.

The Wheel of the Year turns anew at Yule and the Morning Star is born once more from the stygian darkness of midwinter. On the longest night of the year the God arises reborn from the Cauldron as the Horn Child and the sun shines at midnight.

In the spring and early summer, as is seen above, the god of the witches is identified with the Green Man. This term was first used in 1939 by the folklorist Lady Raglan to describe the, often sinister looking foliate masks found carved in pre-Reformation churches. These masks are male faces with oak, ivy and hawthorn leaves and branches sprouting from their mouths, nostrils or ears. Sometimes the leaves form a beard or totally encircle the face.

Although this image was adopted by the Church in medieval times, probably as a symbol of resurrection, the foliate mask dates back to classical Roman times and represents Silvanus, the god of the woods. In the modern pagan revival the old image of the Green Man as god of the woods has become a powerful totem. It represents the masculine aspect of the Earth Spirit as the guardian of animals and the protector of nature.

A traditional Craft ritual, probably derived from English folklore, combines the aspects of the Old God as Lord of the Greenwood and the Wild Hunt. It is called the Rite of the Wish Maid and involves a men's dance miming the agricultural cycle of the year from ploughing, to the sowing of seeds, to the harvest. A priestess, taking the role of the Wish Maid, seeks to seduce the men from their daily labour, but fails in her efforts. The 'Upright Man' presents her with gifts of flowers, a spray of oak leaves, a finch (symbol of an oracle), and a taper to light the balefire on the beacon hill. He then reveals himself as Hran or Herne, the Lord of the Wild Hunt and the Greenwood, and the master of the Wish Hounds. The Great Rite between the Hunter and the Maid ends the ritual. [10]

In the Traditional Craft Herne is a popular name for the witch god, especially in his winter aspect. In the legend Herne the Hunter is a ghostly huntsman who haunts Windsor Great Park in Berkshire with his pack of spectral hounds. He is mentioned by William Shakespeare in *The Merry Wives of Windsor* and the legend is said to have been based on the true story of Richard Herne, a gamekeeper or steward in the reign of either Richard II, Henry VII or Henry VIII. The legend is confused about the right date.

Herne was out hunting with the king one day and he wounded a stag. Enraged with pain the stag charged at the king and would have killed him, but Herne threw himself in front of the animal. The king was saved, but the huntsman was mortally injured and shortly died. A wizard suddenly appeared and told the king his steward could be saved by cutting off the stag's antlers and fixing them to the dead man's head. As soon as this was done Herne came back from the dead and was healed of his fatal wound. Shortly afterwards the huntsman was caught poaching and the king, not wanting to show favour, was forced to dismiss him from his service. The depressed gamekeeper hanged himself from a 'blasted oak' in the forest and ever since then his spirit has haunted the place.

It is obvious that the above legend contains elements of an ancient myth far older then its historical setting. In the story Herne sacrifices his life to save the king. By this brave act he becomes a substitute victim instead of the king. Herne is killed by a stag, the sacred beast and animal form taken by the Horned God of the witches. The mysterious 'wizard' then resurrects Herne by crowning him with the antlers of the dead stag.

Later in the tale Herne is made an outcast and hangs himself from an oak tree that has been struck by lightning. The oak is the sacred tree of the Indo-European sky god whose weapon is the thunderbolt. In folklore king stags are associated with 'blasted trees' because when without leaves in the winter their branches resemble antlers. In fact, oaks with many twisted and dead branches were known as 'stag headed'.

Many witches and folklorists claim the legend of Herne is a folk memory of the ancient worship of the Celtic stag god Cernunnos in Windsor Forest. From the symbolism in the legend it seems more likely that Herne represents the Norse god Odin, who was known as the Hanged Man. To the Anglo-Saxons he was known as Woden and was the leader of the Wild Hunt.

Odin hung himself on the World Tree to gain the wisdom of the runes and human and animal sacrifices were made to him by hanging the victims on trees. When Woden appeared in human form to his followers on Middle Earth he often took the persona of a wizard. The Saxon kings of the House of Wessex claimed descent from Woden and this may explain why the appearances of Herne the Hunter at Windsor are said to be bad omens for the royal family.

Since the 1970s, when Goddess monotheism unduly influenced the modern pagan movement, the Old God has been making a comeback. He is very popular in his form as the Green Man and appears on mugs, t-shirts, posters, greeting cards and wall plaques which are on sale in the High Street. In this form he has also been adopted as an eco-totem by those protesting at the destruction of the countryside by new roads and housing estates.

Many witches realise that a belief system based on matriarchy and female monotheism is just as much a spiritual contradiction as one based on patriarchy and male monotheism. In our male dominated society the resurgence of the feminine principle has been needed to restore the balance. Despite this, especially in the Traditional Craft, there is still a powerful role for the Horned God and a balance between the Lord and Lady. In fact in some traditional covens the Horned God is worshipped exclusively.

Those branches of the modern Craft that have kept alive the emphasis on the Horned God are unlikely to to be acceptable to the politically correct New Age Wiccans we see around us today. He is a powerful and potent force who is still feared by many. His presence can bring 'great terror and fearful dread' in its wake even to his followers. The late Robert Cochrane described how he once had a vision of the Old God as 'a being vastly ancient, massive like some great and ancient tree in a dark forest, brooding yet all-sentient, smelling of dead leaves and newly turned earth.' Cochrane says he was not frightened, but awed because 'He was so old, old from the beginning of the world'. [11]

The old Horned God therefore is not a New Age wimp or even a 'new man'. Yet, paradoxically, his feral nature and raw virility can empower women if they can relate to him as a protective figure. If they can consider the God as a link to the male energies within their own psyche then his natural feralness becomes something to enjoy and delight in, rather then something to be feared. This is especially true for those 'wounded women' who find it difficult, for whatever reason, to relate properly to men other then as potential rapists, wife-beaters and child molesters.

On a personal level the God can also allow men to come to terms with their aggressive, destructive, shadow sides and learn how to use male energy in creative and constructive ways. In his roles as Lord of the Animals and Guardian of the Greenwood he can teach men to be strong and protective without resorting to the macho stereotypes of senseless, uncontrolled violence which is the product of patriarchal conditioning since childhood.

The multi-faceted God force in witchcraft represents many different types of masculine energy and divine power. He is a solar deity, a god of vegetation, fertility and the seasonal cycle, the co-ruler of the underworld, a guide to the dead, master of animals, ruler of the faery folk, guardian of forbidden wisdom, cultural exemplar and cosmic trickster.

At his most elementary level, the Horned One is the god of death and resurrection symbolised by the phallus at Beltane and the skull and crossbones at Hallowe'en. He is the dying god who is eternally reborn and this initiatory experience of life, death and rebirth is represented symbolically by the annual cycle of growth, decay and renewal in nature. The God's initiation by the Dark Lady of Knowledge in the underworld is reflected in the inner mysteries of the Craft.

Chapter Three

The Witch Goddess

In modern Wicca the Goddess is the centre and focus of attention, with the Horned God taking a secondary role and position as her consort. In modern traditional witchcraft, as we have seen, the God takes a more important role and there is a balance between the male and female divine forces. The God is the ruler of fertility and death, while the Goddess rules birth, fate and the renewal of creation. In essence they are both fertility deities; to incarnate on Middle Earth you must be born into a physical body, and to be born you must first be conceived. Life cannot begin without the impregnation of the female egg by the male seed, and the initiation of a soul into the physical world is the nine month period of female pregnancy.

As was mentioned in the last chapter, many traditional witches believe that the Goddess is the Supreme Creator who gives birth to the universe, the Gods and humanity. One Traditional Craft source states: 'The Goddess represents the creative element in the universe. Above all She represents it in totality - seen and unseen. As such She embodies the Greater Mysteries. The Goddess is the Great Mother from whom all life arises. The Goddess is the unifying spirit in all creation, because from Her all things come and to her all things return.' [1]

Because of the propaganda of the medieval Church and the works of modern writers like Dr Margaret Murray, the belief has arisen and been widely accepted that historical witchcraft was centred on the worship of a male deity in the form of the Devil or the Horned God. This is a false impression that needs correcting. As discussed in Chapter One, in the classical world witches were associated with the goddesses Hecate and Diana-Artemis.

In her Roman form Diana was a goddess of the moon and hunting and in her Greek form, Artemis, she was the Lady of Animals. With the Roman occupation of Western Europe Diana's cult spread out to all corners of the Empire. In fact in 5th century Gaul she was regarded as the supreme deity. During the 5th and 6th centuries, despite the emergence of the early Church, there was a flourishing Diana cult among peasants all over Europe who regarded her as the goddess of the woods and fields. (2)

In the 4th century CE the Church's Council of Aycra denounced those heretics who belonged to 'the Society of Diana'. The council believed that these people had been deceived by the Devil who had taken the form of the pagan Goddess. Three hundred years later, St Barbato converted the Duke of Benevento in Italy to Christianity. At her bidding he cut down a tree on his estate which was used as a meeting place by local witches who worshipped Diana.

One of the most important medieval references to the witches worshipping the Goddess, and specifically Diana, was the clerical document known as the *Canon Episcopi*. This 10th century document claimed that witches could fly on broom-sticks and shapeshift into animal form, but that such events were diabolical delusions. The *Canon* said that the witches imagined they did these things in spirit (sic) and were deluded by the Devil and his demons.

The key passage in the *Canon*, often quoted, reads: '....some wicked women, perverted by the Devil, seduced by illusions and phantoms of demons believe and profess themselves in the hours of the night, to ride upon certain beasts with Diana, the goddess of the pagans, and an innumerable multitude of women, and in the silence of the dead of night to traverse great distances of the Earth, and to obey her commands as their mistress, and to be summoned to her service on certain nights.'

This passage established the concept of a female leader of the Wild Hunt who was a pagan goddess and the belief that a company of women known as witches, 'Good Ladies', 'sybils', 'night riders' and 'hedge riders' travelled in spirit to nocturnal meetings. It also blurred the division between the pagan gods and the Church's myth of Satan or the Devil.

In the 12th century John of Salisbury wrote about witches who held feasts presided over by Herodias, the wife of Herod the Great, who seems to have been one of the names used to describe the witch goddess at the time. A common medieval term for the witches' sabbath was 'the game of Diana'. One 16th century source claimed: 'they (the witches) adore the Lady of the Games and sacrifice to her as a god'.

Artemis, or Diana

Other Southern European names for the witch goddess included Dame Habondia, Abundia, Sybille, Bensozia, Zobiana, Bona Domina and Herodiana (combining Herodias and Diana). Sybille was said to fly through the night sky in a fiery chariot drawn by cats. She was possibly a version of the Norse goddess Freyja. In the early 16th century the Spanish Inquisition reported that the peasants in the Basque region worshipped a female deity known simply as La Dama or The Lady. She was described as a beautiful woman who flew through the air surrounded by fire. It has been claimed that as the Persecution became more widespread, and the idea that witchcraft was a Satanic conspiracy spread further, the old pagan goddesses dwindled in status to the Queen of the Fairies, or the Queen of Elphame (Elfane) and the Maiden of the coven was given the name of the goddess and also known as the Queen of Elphame...' (3)

From his investigations of the Italian witch cult surviving in Tuscany at the end of the 19th century the American folklorist Charles Godfrey Leland associated Herodias with the Hebrew goddess of the dark moon, Lilith (4). It is interesting that in the cathedral of St Bertrand-Conmiges in south-west France there is a carving of a bird-footed woman, known locally as Lilith, giving birth to a Green Man. In France, and other parts of Europe, the witch goddess was depicted with goose feet and she survives in fairy tales as Old Mother Goose. Here we have the witch god and goddess clearly represented as mother and son. Incidentally, the historical Herodias is said to have emigrated to this part of France and her tomb allegedly stands in the cathedral.

The belief that Diana was the leader of the 'good women', or witches, survived into the 15th century. The sermons of a Dominican preacher published in Cologne in 1474 refer to Diana 'who goes about at night with her army' (5). In the second half of the 16th century trials were held in rural Sicily of 'companies of women who met to worship a female divinity known variously as the Matron, the Teacher, the Greek Mistress (Hecate?), the Wise Sybil, the Mother or the Queen of the Fairies, who was accompanied by a male consort' (6)

There were also references in these trials to entities known as 'the women outside', 'the beautiful ladies', 'the night women' or 'those who travel by night', who may have been names for witches, minor deities or faeries. These 'companies' of witches consisted of seven women and were named after towns,e.g. the Company of Parlemo, or by other titles such as the Company of the Mother or the Company of the Distaff and the Table. In Croatia (former Yugoslavia) similar companies existed and were

The Fate Goddess

led by a male leader, described as 'Devil and priest', and a female leader known as The Lady or the Old Mother. She held the rites under an oak tree or at a crossroads [6].

The Sicilian witches were said to assemble once a month in the woods. There they worshipped a human 'king' and 'queen' known as God and Our Lady. After an act of worship a communal meal was eaten and the Great Rite was performed by all present. Before the assembly ended the leaders handed out herbal remedies which were taken home and used to heal the sick. In one case an elderly fortuneteller said she had been made the queen for the evening and everyone had to bow to her and do as she said. According to the myths of the Sicilian witches their goddess came from Babylon. She was the sister of King Solomon or the Virgin Mary. This links her with both Lilith (who is said to have been the Queen of Sheba) and with Diana who became associated with the Virgin Mary.

The imagery of the ancient moon goddesses was transferred to the Virgin Mary. She adopted their blue robe, representing the heavens and the sea, their crown of stars, their symbols of the rose, crescent and Morning Star, and their title of Queen of Heaven. As virgin, mother and widow Mary also has their triple aspects associated with the lunar phases. The three Marys mourning at the foot of the cross for their lover/son correspond to the triple moon goddess and the trinity of Fate goddesses whose role we shall examine later.

Many pagan aspects were transferred to the mythical life of Jesus. For instance, when he was reborn from the cave he was greeted as a gardener by Mary Magdalene, and this is a term used to describe the sacrificed vegetation god, as was the term 'Shepherd'. It was the Magdalene, a 'fallen woman', who anointed the feet of Jesus with balm before his pre-ordained death, as the sacrificial victims were anointed by the priestesses of the Goddess in ancient times. It is no coincidence that Jesus is called the sun of righteousness, the Light of the World and is compared to the Morning Star (Revelations 22:16).

Unfortunately, in many medieval images the Virgin Mary is standing on the moon, not crowned with it, Sometimes it is not the moon, but the serpent-dragon, which in Christian mythology is the symbol of the Devil.

Diana was also associated with Dame Venus who was said to haunt the mountain of Venusberg in Germany. In the 14th century legend of Tannhauser and Venus it is said that moaning, cries of pleasure and diabolical laughter were heard by travellers coming from a cave beneath the mount. There were also reports of beautiful females standing at the cave mouth like sirens trying to entice travellers underground. Unearthly music could be heard playing in the background.

Tannhauser, whose name means 'forest dweller', was a minstrel and Christian knight who fell under the spell of one of these beautiful Otherworldly women while passing by the Venusberg at night. He followed her into the heart of the hollow hill where, as Dame Venus, she ruled a faery realm of revelry and debauchery. After seven years of this hell, the knight begged Venus to release him, but she refused. He then called upon the Virgin Mary to save him and immediately a rift appeared in the mountainside through which he was able to escape to the outside world.

As a good Christian, Tannhauser was ashamed of his life in the mountain. He set off to Rome to get absolution from the Pope himself. Unfortunately when he arrived at the Holy City the Pope refused to see him. Disillusioned with his religion, the knight eventually returned to Venusberg and the welcoming arms of his goddess lover.

In this tale Venusberg is the sacred mountain or the World Mountain which appears in many ancient myths and in shamanism. In the Traditional Craft it is the Hollow Hill and is one of the entrances to the Otherworld or the spirit world. Symbolically it is the womb-tomb of the Great Mother or Mother Earth - the underworld to which the dead pass along the death road or ghost path led by the Wild Hunt. In British mythology it is the hollow hill of Glastonbury Tor wherein dwell Morgan Le Fay and Gwynn ap Nudd.

The story of Tannhauser and Venus seems to blend the southern European version of the witch goddess, Diana-Artemis, as the Queen of Love, with the Central and Northern European versions known as Holda and Freyja. Frau or Dame Holda is the female leader of the Furious Host or Wild Hunt in Central European folklore. She is also the 'archaic underworld Earth Mother, mistress of death, initiation and rebirth who rules over the cthonic realm...' [7]

In 1630 a German sorcerer confessed that he had travelled to the Venusberg and was taught the secrets of herbal lore by Dame Holda. He described the goddess as a fair woman from the front, but at the back she was like a rotting hollow tree, black with decay. This bizarre description signifies the dark and bright aspects of the Goddess. At Salzburg in 1582 the wife of the Archbishop's counsellor was arrested and charged with visiting Herodias at Venusberg with other night travellers. There they had met the female spirits and dwarves who formed her retinue. One of these was a grey bearded dwarf called Eckhart, who was also the servant of St Nicholas or Santa Claus.

A 16th century woman from Bern in Switzerland also admitted that she had ridden with the Wild Hunt and that it had been led by Holda. In common parlance 'to ride with Holle' (Holda) meant to convene with the witches. In the 13th century clerics had complained that young people would rather pray to Perchta (Holda) then to the Virgin Mary. During the Christmas and New Year period they left offerings for her on the roofs of their houses. She collected these as the Wild Hunt passed by and left gifts for her human worshippers in their place.

Holda is both a 'Hag goddess of winter, and a vibrant queen of sexuality who is the bestower of gifts' [8]. Some folklorists believe that, with Diana and Artemis, she originated from the divine female guardians of animals and nature found among the hunting cultures of prehistoric Europe [9]. As described by the

German wizard above, Holda could appear as both dark and bright in her aspect. She was either a young girl, veiled and crowned in a shining white dress, or a hunchbacked, wizened old crone with long grey hair and dressed in a tattered shroud.

As the so-called 'White Lady' Holda was associated by the peasants with the fertility of the fields and she also brought good luck to the household. If she was ignored or insulted then Holda transformed herself into the Old Hag. Then her gifts were misfortune, crop failure, illness and death. In this form she was responsible for the winter snows and the fog. One of her sacred animals was the goose and the snow was said to fall from her wings as she flew over the countryside in that form.

Holda's other sacred animals included wolves, dogs, cats, pigs, goats, horses, bears and bird of preys. These all animals associated with the hunting goddesses of ancient Europe. Holda was also a goddess of the forest and wildwood. While she was seldom linked to a male god figure, in the southern Tyrol her husband is the arboreal 'Wood Man'. In common with this male woodland spirit, Holda was invoked as the protector and guardian of the forest animals and their habitat.   Holda's role as a goddess of death and destiny is related to her patronship of spinning and weaving. She protected spinners, weavers and spinsters, but also punished anyone who failed at this craft or who produced bad work. During the Twelve Days of Yule, which was her annual holiday, any woman who still carried out spinning would suffer bad luck in the coming year or was even struck blind. At this time the goddess also bestowed gifts on children, but if they had been naughty during the year she punished them instead. Again we have evidence of her dual nature.

Folk memories of Holda survive in European fairy tales. Stories of faery godmothers, wicked stepmothers with spinning wheels, the Good Faery, and old witches living in cottages in the forest or wildwood all reflect her attributes. Popular fairy tales and nursery rhymes such as *Snow White, Sleeping Beauty, Hansel & Gretel, Little Red Riding Hood* and *Cinderella* all contain elements that are derived from folk tales about Holda as the witch goddess. That 'grand old dame' of fairy tales and pantomimes, Old Mother Goose, is another folk version of Holda.

In the 18th and 19th century bowlderisations of these fairy tales Old Mother Goose became a comic figure, a foolish old woman who told 'old wives tales'. Originally she was the 'wise old woman', the 'wise crone' or sybil who taught morality to the young, could foresee the future and had the knowledge of the world [10]. Eventually Mother Goose, who laid the golden eggs of wisdom and knowledge, became the stereotyped witch with a conical cap, pointed nose, lantern jaw and walking stick (wand). The wise woman had been transformed into a wicked, child killer - the dark shadow of the faery godmother or gossip who blessed and protected the new born.

Holda is a powerful goddess and not one to be invoked lightly. One of her modern devotees has said of her: 'Although a winter goddess, Holda is no dainty, pink cheeked china doll'. She has a 'raunchy presence, luxurious shock of wild, dark hair and gypsy-like appearance. She is definitely not the Goddess for blokes who like docile little women in Laura Ashley dresses who do not mind being called silly little girls'[11].

Folklorists have said that because the Church identified Holda with Diana, some historians have assumed that the cult of the Roman goddess was imported into Austria, Switzerland and Germany. An alternative view suggests the image of a hunting goddess ruling winter, death and fertility arose independently in those areas, was influenced by beliefs from Northern Europe, and eventually became the goddess of the medieval witch cult. This goddess had the common features of the Mistress of Wild Things represented by Diana-Artemis 'who represents...the force of nature which is both life-giving and life-taking' [12].

Holda in fact shares many attributes with the Norse goddess Freyja, who was a patron of magick and sexuality. Freyja's position in Northern European mythology is as 'the dark queen of enchantment ruling magickal spells, shimmering (shapeshifting or shapechanging) and the sending of the fetch or astral body in spirit travel' [13]. Her priestesses were known as volvas, or "she who can see into the future', and they had a primary role in Norse society as seers.

The volva was seen by some writers as the prototype of the medieval witch. Dr Brian Bates, director of the Shamanic Research Project at the University of Sussex, has said that the role of the volva 'Sometimes went beyond divination, and mediated the power that created new life and brought increase into the fields, among the animals and in the home. They brought also the power to link people with the unseen world. Besides divining concerning the fruits of the earth and the baby in the cradle, they also offered wise counsel granted through divination concerning worldly events' (Bates 1996: 154).

Freyja riding a Siberian tiger (12th century)

It has been suggested that Freya is the Northern European version of the witch goddess and a medieval mural in a German cathedral depicts her naked except for a cloak riding a distaff as if it were a broomstick. Although she is renowned for her sexual prowess, Freyja is also a goddess of death and the dead. With her Valkyries she claims half of the slain from the battlefield from Odin. One writer discussing this dark side of Freyja, and linking her with Holda, says: 'She was not only the goddess of life, but also of death. But death was not to her worshippers a ghastly grinning skeleton, but a loving mother recalling her tired children to sleep in her bosom'. [14]

Freyja's mother was said to be the primeval earth goddess Nerthus. This Germanic deity relates back to the Bronze Age representations of the Goddess or her priestesses, in Northern Europe as long haired, naked women or women wearing short kilts with their breasts bared. Some wear large round earrings and ritual necklaces of amber (the traditional witch's necklace), or display their breasts with their cupped hands in a classic gesture of fecundity. They are sometimes accompanied by a stag god and are associated with the spring and harvest festivals, the fertility of the land, and the journey to the underworld.

The image of Nerthus was kept in a shrine in a nemeton or sacred grove on an island in a lake. At special times of the year, in spring and before the harvest usually, this image was placed on a wagon or cart and it was processed around the countryside to bring fertility to the land. When the image was returned to the lake shrine the slaves who had pulled the cart and attended the goddess were sacrificed by drowning. At least one existing English witch tradition still worships Freyja and Nerthus - but without the human sacrifices! [15]

It has often been said that modern Wiccans are obsessed with 'pretty little moon goddesses in Laura Ashley frocks'. This may or may not be correct, but to many Wiccans the traditional image of the witch as an old crone on a broomstick is no longer acceptable. In newspaper articles and television interviews the publicity witches bend over backwards to disassociate themselves from this historical image. In doing so they are turning their backs on one of the most important and powerful images and aspects of the witch goddess.

In Scotland this hag witch goddess was known as Nicnevin and Sir Walter Scott described her as a Northern European version of Hecate 'who rode on the storm and marshalled her rambling host of wanderers under her banner'. He also compared her to Diana, who he described writing sixty years before the publication of Leland's book, as the goddess of the Italian witches [16].

Nicnevin was both the Queen of Elfame and the Mistress of the Witches' Sabbat. Predictably perhaps, she owned a spinning wheel and granted any human brave enough to pray to her the gifts of spinning and weaving. However she could only be asked this boon between Candlemas and Shrove Tuesday, when she wandered Middle Earth disguised as an old woman. At Hallows she rode out of the faery mound with her Wild Host to collect the souls of the dead.

She wore a long grey cloak, carried a wand and could appear in human form as either a young woman or an old crone. For obvious reasons she has been compared to the Cailleach, the 'winter hag' who hands over to the bright spring maiden Brigit on Candlemas Day. Some folklorists have suggested that Nicnevin was a Northern European winter goddess imported into Scotland by Norse settlers and grafted onto a native goddess of winter and darkness.

In both Scotland and Ireland the *bean sidhe* or banshee (faery woman) has been interpreted as a folklore survival of the dark aspect of the Goddess. Again she also had the bright aspect, as she could manifest as either a young woman of unearthly beauty or as an old hag with fangs and webbed feet. Sometimes known as the 'washerwoman', she was seen near fords washing the armour or shrouds of those who had fallen in battle. Fords are typical 'inbetween' places and they are symbolic of the boundary between this world and the Other. The banshee also only appeared at the liminal times of dusk and dawn.

The banshee is often regarded as a version of the Morrigan or Great Queen, the triple Irish goddess described by one writer as 'the phantom queen of death, sexuality and conflict, ruling night and winter' [17]. This same writer connects the Morrigan with the Celtic goddess Andraste, the hare goddess of the forests and woods. She was worshipped by Queen Boudicca of the Iceni tribe, and is still revered today by one branch of the traditional Craft in East Anglia. The Morrigan was a warrior goddess who flew over the battlefield in the shape of a crow feeding on the souls of the dead. In this respect she has similarities with Freyja and the Norns or Nornir, the triple fate goddesses in Norse mythology.

The banshee is often seen as the guardian spirit and messenger of death to old families in Ireland and Scotland. In this role she is a debased version of Sovereignty, the ancient goddess of the land. In Irish folk tradition the banshee appears as the person-ification of fate who foretells the death of heroes or compels them to break the taboos that affect their wyrd or destiny. She will also the kingmaker who selected the ruler of the land. In a medieval legend of Robin Hood, an aspect of the witch god, his death is foretold by an old woman standing on a bridge who is wailing and crying. She is a typical personification of a banshee or 'washer at the ford' warning the hero of his wyrd or fate.

In fairy tales we find accounts of knights who meet old hags and are asked for a kiss. If they comply the hag turns into a beautiful princess who grants the knight the keys of the kingdom. This is a bastardised version of the anointing of the chosen king by the goddess of the land. In the patriarchal version, it is a princess who kisses an ugly frog and it turns into a handsome prince. One famous example of this sacred kingmaking in Irish folklore is the story of Niall. As a young man he is tested to see whether or not he has the qualities for kingship. He meets a hideous old hag at a well and only when she is kissed by him does she reveal herself as Eriu, the goddess of the land. She is transformed into a beautiful young woman by his embrace and when they marry he becomes king, for she is the land itself which all rulers must serve.

Frigga-Freyja riding a distaff (12th century)

It has been said that 'The foundation of Celtic religion is the sacred quality of the land, symbolised by a potent Goddess of Sovereignty. From this potent figure, who is often associated with love, death and sexuality, all other mythical figures derive. The Great Heroes, often found with solar and underworld attributes are her sons; the culture goddesses, who assist, enable and sometimes transform human development, are her daughters'. [18]

The final, and most important, aspect of the witch goddess, heavily hinted at already, is the personification of fate or wyrd. The latter word is Old English and it derives from the Old Saxon *wurt*, the Old German *wurd*, the Old Norse *urter*, and the Germanic *werth* (worth) meaning 'to become'. It is also associated with the Old German *wirt*, meaning a spindle and suggesting the metaphorical process of spinning or weaving fate. Hence the popular modern term of 'the web of Wyrd'. Fundamentally, it refers to the worth of a person and the potential for what they will become or achieve during their life. Fate comes from the Latin *fatum* and it means 'that which is spoken' or 'the power determining events'.

In Norse mythology the wyrd was controlled by the three fate goddesses known collectively as the Nornir or Norns. Originally they were Mother Earth known as Urtur or Urdr, sometimes known as Hertha and one of the German names for the witch goddess. Later they divided into three separate goddesses known as Urd, Verdanti and Skuld representing past, present and future. The Norns weave the threads of life on their spinning wheel and, like the Greek Fates, one spins the thread (birth), one measures it (life) and the third cuts it (death).

The weaving and spinning of the Norns is important because it was believed they not only wove the fate of humanity on their spindles, but also the whole fabric of the universe. The spider is their totem animal and the image of the helpless victim trapped in a spider's web on one level alludes to the use of nooses, snares and ropes to drag the spirits of the dead down to the underworld. It should be noted that the so- called 'bog bodies' unearthed all over Northern Europe were found with nooses or halters around their necks and most had been strangled. The noose is the traditional sign of subjection to Hecate as the End and the Beginning of Life, which of course makes it the umbilical cord and hangman's noose in one.' [19] Web comes from the German *webh* meaning 'to weave' and therefore the Web of Wyrd refers to the matrix or mould from which life in the universe originated.

Matrix comes from the Latin *mater matris*, or 'womb of the mother' and brings us neatly back to the primal earth goddess as the creatrix of life and the symbolism of her womb cave and the Cauldron of Creation and Rebirth. This reminds us of the archetypal world of the Platonists, where the pattern of creation was formed before it was transferred to the physical plane, and the holographic theory of the universe proposed by radical

Freija.

quantum physicists. Scientists talk today of 'superstrings' and 'wormholes' connecting parallel universes and of a web of sub-atomic material which connects everything in the cosmos. The superstrings allegedly connect all matter together and create an energy matrix which gives the universe its structure.

The Norns also survived the advent of Christianity as faery godmothers with spinning wheels who granted wealth, health and happiness on babies, or bad luck and disaster depending on the child's wyrd. They also appear in Shakespeare's Scottish play as the three witches an the blasted heath. They are the Weird or Wyrd Sisters who foretell the future of the prince. Shakespeare based his version of the hag witches on an earlier account where

56

they are described as 'creatures from the elder world' and 'goddesses of destinie'. In this context 'elder' does not mean older, but refers to the Otherworld and the faery realm, from the Old English *eldritch*.

A modern traditional witch has described the Three Ladies or Wyrd as 'the Goddess who to us is as old as time, and Her face is as white and as cold as newly fallen snow. Her brow is as smooth and as white as alabaster,....Her hair is as black as ebony, parted in the middle and hanging down to just below her shoulders.. Beneath thick black curving eyebrows are a pair of ice cold, vivid blue eyes.. The nose is..long,thin and slightly hooked, while the mouth is large and generous with blood red lips' [20].

Finally, we end this chapter on the Goddess with a quotation from another traditional witch, this time describing how her followers should relate to her: 'It is not enough to see The Lady, it is better to serve Her and Her will by being involved in humanity and the process of Fate....In Fate, and the overcoming of Fate, is the true Grail, for from this inspiration comes, and death is defeated'. [21]

Chapter Four

Tools of the Trade

In the first chapter it was noted that traditional witchcraft has been influenced by ceremonial magick and Freemasonry during the 18th and 19th centuries. It is in the 'tools of the trade', the ritual working tools and ritual objects used in the religious ceremonies and magickal rites of the Craft, that this influence can be seen. Yet we can also see differences between the modern usages and more traditional customs.

The principal ritual tools used by modern Wiccans are based on Golden Dawn-type magick. They are the athame, or black handled knife, used to cast the circle, evoke the the four quarters and direct magickal energy; the white handled knife, used for practical purposes such as collecting herbs, carving runes etc.; the cup or chalice; the wand; the pentacle; the censer; cords; and the coven sword.

In Wicca each of these working tools is presented to the neophyte at their first degree initiation and their meaning and use is explained. At the elevation to the second degree the witch has to demonstrate their mastery of the tools in the circle.

In various branches of the Traditional Craft, allowing for variations, the principal working tools are the stang or staff, the blasting rod or conjuring stick, the besom or broomstick, the cauldron, the stone, the drinking horn, and the cords. Additional ritual objects such as crystals, scrying mirrors, the witches' cradle etc. may be used for magickal and psychic purposes.

The Stang

The stang is the primary working tool of the traditional witch. Its name comes from the Old Norse *stong* and the Middle English *stange* meaning 'pole'. This tool may have originated with the crude wooden pitchforks used on farms since the Middle Ages and before. Today it is made from yew, oak or ash and this forked staff, sometimes carved with a mask of the Horned God, represents his presence in the circle. It also, in some traditions, is a symbol of the phallus of the sky god fertilising Mother Earth.

As a symbol of the Horned One it usually stands in the north of the circle. In some traditions it is moved around the quarters at each festival to symbolise the journey of the God in his solar aspect around the Wheel of the Year. One modern traditional witch describes the role of the stang in the circle as follows: 'In the mysteries of the Craft the stang is set in the north to symbolise the presence of the Horned Master as guardian of the portals of Anwynn and opener of the 'ghost road' into his underworld kingdom' [1].

When the stang moves around the circle it is often garlanded with the seasonal flowers proper to each of the festivals of the year. At Yule, for instance, it stands in the north at the 'midnight' position as a guide to the Horn Child who is born at this time. It will be decorated with holly and ivy (the Lord and Lady) and red ribbons as a symbol of the sacred blood and the life force. At Candlemas in early February, the stang is in the north-east of the circle and is decorated with snowdrops. At Eostre or the spring equinox, the stang is placed in the east facing the rising sun. It is decorated with daffodils and primroses. On May Eve, or Beltane, it can be found in the south-east section of the circle. It is garlanded with the hawthorn blossom of the May Queen and twigs of birch, hazel and willow.

In the southern quarter on Midsummer's Eve, the summer solstice, the stang is decorated with St John's Wort and oak leaves to represent the Lord of Light at the zenith of his power. At Lammastide, in early August, red poppies and barley ears garland the stang in the south-west. When Harvest Home is celebrated at the autumn equinox, the stang is in the west and is decorated with wild berries, acorns and pine cones. Finally, at Hallowe'en, it is in the north-west with yew leaves as a garland [2].

The stang also represents the old tau cross, made from oak branches, used to sacrifice the Lord of Light at midsummer or Lammas. When it takes this role two crossed arrows are placed on its shaft and a sickle at the base. Sometimes the sickle is joined by a skull and crossbones symbol to signify death and resurrection. A lighted candle (indoors) or a lantern (outdoors) is placed between the 'horns' of the stang. This is a symbol of the gnostic wisdom, illumination and enlightenment granted by the God.

It is recorded in the accounts of the medieval witches' sabbat that the Devil who presided over the rituals wore a lighted candle or torch between his horns. In those forms of English Traditional Craft influenced by the Norse myths and traditions, the stang is Yggdrasil. the World Tree upon which Odin sacrificed himself. In this branch of the Craft it is the gateway from Middle Earth to the higher realms of the Gods and the pathway to the Mysteries. [3]

In the Northern tradition generally, the priestesses of Freyja, the volva, carried a staff or rod as a symbol of their office as seers. These staves had a knob on one end with precious stones set below it encircling the shaft and bound with brass. It has been suggested that this staff of office was also a symbol of the World Tree. This is supported by the fact that one of the alternative names for Yggdrasil is 'the Mighty Staff'. It is a name which relates to the *axis mundi*, or World Pillar, which reaches up into the heavens to the North or Pole Star, around which all the other stars appear to revolve in the northern night sky. One writer has suggested that the knob on the volva's staff is the Pole star, the stones are the circumpolar stars, and the brass decoration is the metal associated with the World Pillar of Eurasian mythology [4].

The Wand

In many ways the wand is a smaller version of the stang, except that it has a more practical and intimate use in the circle to channel, project and direct the power that is raised. Depending on the use of the wand it can be made of various woods. For instance, hazel for dowsing, birch for healing and fertility, willow for clairvoyance, yew for necromancy, and blackthorn is the traditional wood for a 'blasting rod'. Some wands are phallic tipped, have a pine cone at the end, or are forked like a miniature version of the stang.

Traditionally any wood used for the making of wands or stangs should be gathered at the special liminal 'inbetween times' of dusk and dawn when the mistgates between Middle Earth and the Otherworld are open. If possible fallen wood should be used, especially from storm damaged or lightning struck trees. If it has to be cut then permission should be asked first from the dryad or tree spirit. A small offering of a silver coin, a libation of alcohol, some food or a few drops of your own blood should be made to the arboreal spirit in exchange for taking the wood.

Two wands or conjuring sticks belonging to an 18th century witch from Finchingfield in Essex were re-discovered in the 1940s. In 1780 a local school teacher named Goofy Mumford was accused of witchcraft and beaten to death by a mob. Sixty years ago one of her relatives, Dan Peddar, inherited her cottage. While doing some alterations he discovered what he called a 'witch stick' hidden in a wall. It was about three and a half feet long and was carved with intertwined snakes. It was made of rosewood and, according to local folklore, was an implement used to beat witches. The snakes, it was said, were charms against the evil powers of darkness.

When the cottage was re-thatched some years later a second 'witch stick' was found concealed in the roof. This was shorter than the first and about the length of an average walking stick. Burnt into it were designs of a bull and cow, a family of rabbits, butterflies, birds and flowers. Peddar described this stick as one used in witchcraft 'for fertility' [5]. In 1992 a psychic who examined the stick with the snakes on it declared that it had been used for healing and this is suggested by its symbolism.

The Besom

The popular folk image of the witch depicts her as flying through the night sky with her black cat as pillion passenger. One of the earliest references to witches 'riding the wind' comes from a 13th century source. This tells how the 'good women' attending Dame Habondia rode on sticks to her meetings. Obviously, witches could not physically fly through the air, but in hereditary Scottish witchcraft the expression 'to ride the wind' is used to describe spirit travel or astral projection [6]. 'Riding the broomstick' is therefore the ability of the witch to leave her body and travel to any geographical location in Middle Earth or to the Otherworld.

Medieval witches, it is believed, used narcotic plants in the form of the sabbati ungeunti, lifting balm, 'flying ointment' or 'Devil's salve', as a short-cult to facilitate spirit travel. The witch then projected her astral body or fetch, sometimes in the form of a small animal like a mouse, weasel, hare or cat, or she actually experienced the sensation of flying through the air. The witch hunters interpreted this astral journey as a delusion or dream in which the accused person believed they flew to the witches' sabbath and consorted with the Devil. The more gullible, faced with something which was beyond their normal understanding, actually believed witches could fly using broomsticks and other bizarre modes of transport.

The traditional woods used to make the witches' besom are ash, birch and willow. These woods are representative of the feminine elements of earth, air and water. Ash, the World Tree, is used for the stake or handle; birch twigs, symbolising fertility form the brush; and willow withies bind the brush to the stake, representing the moon. In parts of East Anglia the traditional witch's besom has an ash handle, but the brush is made of a mixture of hazel, birch and rowan twigs. In this instance hazel is wisdom and initiation, birch is for purification, and rowan is for healing and protection from evil [7]. Sometimes the broom handle is a stang, with the forked end hidden in the brush, or it could be phallic tipped.

In ritual use the besom sweeps the circle or meeting ground before the rites begin. This action symbolically purifies the area of any negative influences and creates a 'sacred space' for working in. In some traditions the circle or ground can only be entered by stepping over the broom laid on the earth, or a crossed sword and besom. This emphasises the role of the besom as a magickal vehicle for travelling from one world to the next and as a gateway or bridge 'between the worlds'

In folk magick the besom could be used for sweeping good or bad luck into a house. Ordinary dust was used for good luck, but if there was an evil intent graveyard dust or a powder made from cremated animal or human bones was used instead. The sweeping action was accompanied by a muttered spell for good or evil depending upon the circumstances of the ritual.

There is a story from the last century on the Isle of Man of a local man who encountered a witch early on May Day by the old calendar (May 12th) performing a ritual at a crossroads. The man warned the witch that if he saw her again that day she would get a good kicking. Some time later in the day he met the witch again at another crossroads. This time she had swept clean a large circle around herself using her besom. As he had promised, the man kicked her, confiscated her broomstick and burnt it [8].

Strange enough, for what is supposed to have been an imaginary practice, several recipes for the flying ointment were collected by the witch hunters and other interested parties. These recipes contain highly poisonous and hallucinogenic plants such as mandrake, deadly nightshade, wolfsbane, henbane. opium and hemlock, as well as more horrific additions such as bay's fat and bat's blood added by the Inquisitors. The witch either smeared this ointment on her naked body or on the handle of her broomstick which she then rode like a horse. The purpose of this

63

was to rub the anointed handle against the perineum, the site of the most important psychic centre in the human body. It was then ingested into the skin and the narcotic elements in the ointment produced a sensation of flying and helped the release of the spirit body.

The Cauldron

Although not used by all traditionals, the cauldron has an important symbolic position in the Craft. Originally it was probably the communal cooking pot of the family or tribe and eventually it took on a deeper and more esoteric meaning. It became a symbol of the Goddess, of new life, fertility, plenty and the regeneration of the spirit. It indeed became 'the mystical cauldron in the underworld cave...all nourishing vessel of the Goddess..the source of all birth, regeneration and becoming. It is both the womb of the Mother and the well which restores the dead to life'. [9] At its most potent and mysterious it is the cave or cavern, the 'womb of stars' of Dame Holda, the faery mound or Hallow Hill beyond the setting sun, the underworld ruled by the Old Queen.

In the old myths and legends from Wales contained in *The Mabinogion* a famous cauldron is owned by the witch Ceridwen. In the story she left a small boy called Gwion to tend this vessel and the brew of herbs simmering inside it. By a quirk of fate, three drops of the brew are splashed on the boy's and when he sucks it dry he becomes divinely inspired. Ceridwen, taking the role of the death goddess of transformation and regeneration, chases after Gwion to reverse the spell.

In a series of shapeshifts, representing stages of initiation, the huntress and her prey change into different animal forms as the chase progresses. Finally, Gwion evades capture and is re-born as the bard Taliesin, 'the bright browed one'. So it is her Cauldron that through time 'the Hag brews her alchemical mixture of magical herbs, which give the ability to change shape, to travel between the worlds, to know the past, present and future'. [10]

The cauldron in the mysteries of the Craft is symbolic of the Grail, the sacred vessel quested after by pure knights and found in the castle of the Goddess. She is the underworld keeper and guardian of the Cauldron of Inspiration and Rebirth wherein 'past, present and future are one and the same thing, and it is always in a constant state of flux, always forming and reforming and never still. It holds all the knowledge of the past and present...over and over creating what is yet to come.. it is full of life past and life to come as symbolized in the concept of death and rebirth' [11].

In the 1960s an article was published by the late Robert Cochrane in the now long defunct magazine *New Dimensions* describing the traditional use of the cauldron by his group. In this article the cauldron was used by a small group of witches in a cave ritual. First a tripod was set up over the fire that had been lit and the cauldron was suspended over it. The Lady of the group then poured some wine into the brass cauldron and added herbs and apples. Then the hooded and robed witches perform a maze dance in front of the simmering pot. The Lady then dips a ladle into the cauldron and this is passed around so all can participate of its contents - 'the fruits of life'. There is more dancing around the fire, and then the summoner takes the cauldron and empties its contents into a ditch which has been dug around the circle. In Cochrane's words: 'Steam rises around us and the red liquid floods through and forms a completed circuit, washing the ash aside, whirling around the willow and rowan twigs' [12]. The rite is ended.

The Stone

Stones can be used for several purposes in the Craft and in many forms. Sometimes a large stone can be the centrepiece of the circle in the form of an altar stone. In Celtic influenced traditions it is an actual stone head carved to represent the Godhead and known as the Godstone.

These Godstones can also be prehistoric standing stones, like the King Stone at the Rollrights or the Hele Stone at Stonehenge, used as a focus of the rites when they are held outdoors. These stones represent the phallic energy of the Horned God.

In Celtic belief, probably inherited from the earlier Bronze Age and Neolithic peoples of these islands, the head was the site of the human soul and the Divine could be contacted through it. The Celts prized the heads of their enemies and they collected them from the battlefield. These heads were kept as oracles or placed at gateways or above doorways as protective devices to ward off evil.

In parts of Yorkshire and Derbyshire, where it is rumoured old Celtic ways still survive, there is a folk craft of producing stone heads. Although these are of modern origin, some of them have been associated with poltergeist activity and even the mani-festation of half-human and half-elementals. In one famous case a stone head was sent to the archaeologist Dr Anne Ross for examination as initially it was believed to be of Celtic origin and date. During its stay in her house both Dr Ross and her daughter experienced encounters with a 'werewolf' type entity. When the stone was returned the hauntings ceased.

In some traditions of the modern Craft the stone is in fact a whetstone of the type used to sharpen agricultural tools and the swords of warriors. This type of stone was highly prized in ancient times and a famous one was found buried with a pagan Saxon king at Sutton Hoo in Suffolk. The whetstone is symbolically linked with smith gods like Vulcan, Weyland and Tubal Cain and the forging of weapons for the Gods. It also, of course, appears in the Arthurian myths as the sword-in-the stone used to test and select the new king.

In general however, it can safely be said that the stone dates back to the severed head cult of the Celts. This is indicated by the fact that the stone head is sometimes substituted by an actual human skull. In common with the stang, this is a symbol of the God's presence in the circle. As such it can be used in oracular and necromantic rites as we shall see later. [13]

The other use of stones in the Traditional Craft is for magick and gaining the Second Sight. These can either be crystals used for healing or scrying, hag-stones (flat round stones with a hole in the centre) for protection and psychic self-defence, or the so-called Troy stones. The latter are flattish stones or pebbles carved or painted with a spiral. This is meditated on by tracing the finger of the left hand around the spiral or by just gazing at it. This action creates a light trance state enabling the practitioner to contact the spirit world. Stones in general can be used as powerful power objects and psychic batteries filled with magickal energy.

The Cords

The cord or *cingillum*, sometimes known as the witch's girdle, is often used in a coven situation to mark the rank or grade of the wearer. In those traditional groups where the degree system has been borrowed from Wicca, the colour of the cord is used to denote the progress of the initiate. The usual colours for the cords are white, red and black as they represent the triple aspect of the Goddess recognized by many traditions.

In some cases the cord is tied with nine or thirteen knots relating to the phases of the moon, the Celtic calendar of thirteen moons, or the traditional number of witches in a coven. As we saw earlier, the cord has a sinister meaning as the noose or garrote used to strangle the sacrificial victims of the Goddess in ancient times.

In practical use the cord can be used, with an athame and the stang, to mark out the dimensions of the circle. In magick cords are used to weave spells. The knots tied in the cord can be used to bind a spell or when untied to let spirit forces loose. In its knotted form the cord can also act as a type of 'witches' rosary' for meditation and trance work.

Robes

It has been noted before that the Traditional Craft groupings are sometimes called 'robed covens'. One tongue-in-cheek description of a modern traditional witch begins: ' These can usually be recognized by their boots. They are good, thick, really serious boots that make the average fell walker look like a rank amateur' It goes on to say: 'Another mark of the traditional school is the tendency to thick woollen sweaters and really heavy skirts (in the female variety), and thick woollen socks to go with the boots'. (14)

Although this is amusing it does bear some resemblance to the truth. Robed covens weather permitting, like to hold their gatherings out of doors so they can experience and work with the elements. In the unpredictable British climate anyone who goes skyclad or naked outdoors, unless it is very hot summer weather, must be very brave. The traditional will either wear sensible, warm outdoor gear or a thick robe or cloak over ordinary clothes. Indoors lighter robes can be worn with nothing underneath, with ritual nudity, if practised at all, reserved for special rituals.

The robe is usually of a simple tabard or kaftan design with a hood that can be pulled up and over the face during meditation or trance work. Again usually the robe is plain black although some groups do colour code, with the leaders in red and blue and other members in brown or green. Green is the faery colour of Mother Nature and red symbolises the God, blood and the life force. Blue is, of course, the colour of the Goddess.

Other Ritual Tools

Many traditionals will not allow metal into their circles because they believe it interferes with the flow of 'earth energy' and disturbs the guardians' who watch over sacred sites. Iron, for instance, has always been regarded in folk tradition as a metal which can banish and control faeries. For this reason the circle or meeting ground may be marked out with old style wooden farm tools. The circle is drawn with the stang, a wand or an implement made of horn or stone. It is said that some Hereditary groups have adopted the practice of using a wooden or bone handled ritual dagger with a flint blade for this purpose. [16]

Other branches of the Traditional Craft have no reservations about using a ritual knife or a sword to trace the circle and direct power. They liken the knife's use to mark the boundaries of the circle to the sacred plough used to destroy boundaries in pagan times [16]. Other traditionalists see the modern athame as a legitimate survival of the sacrificial weapons of the past [17].

Some of the cunning folk deliberately used iron knives so they could control and banish elementals and nature spirits. Iron was used because it was both an 'offensive' and 'defensive' metal and could conjure spirits and exorcise ghosts and demons. Country people in East Anglia placed iron blades under their doormats to keep the witches and faeries away as late as the 1950s [18]. In Sussex a sickle or scythe blade was laid across windowsills on summer nights when the windows were left open as a charm against 'witch hares' [19].

In Surrey and Buckinghamshire the peasants embedded small pieces of ironstone into wall pointings to protect their homes from witchcraft and evil spirits. This practice was known as harneting and was later used by the famous Edwardian gardener Gertrude Jekyll in her garden designs.

Most traditionals agree that the idea of a coven sword is a fairly recent innovation borrowed from ceremonial magick. In the Middle Ages few ordinary people could afford swords and it was regarded as the weapon of choice of a knight or gentleman. It is possible that where the Magister was a landowner or lord of the manor he may have introduced a sword into the working tools of his coven. If a sword is used in a modern setting then it is as a 'bridge' into the circle, to banish wayward members, or direct curses.

The scourge was widely used in Wicca during the 1950s and it is still used to a lesser extent today. It has been said that scourging was a practice introduced into the Craft by Gerald Gardner to satisfy his sexual needs. This idea has been firmly rejected by all those who worked with him in his Brickett Wood coven. It has also been suggested that the scourge was introduced into some branches of the Traditional Craft in the 18th or 19th centuries. This was possibly as a result of the interest in classical paganism and the Egyptian Mysteries by the educated occultists who promoted revivals of witchcraft in those periods. In the Greek Mysteries a scourge was used to purify the candidate before initiation, and in Ancient Egypt the scourge or flail of Osiris was a symbol of his rulership of the underworld and the dead. It is also possible that the scourge originated with the threshing flail, although the more cynical point out that the 'English vice' of flagellation was popular in 18th and 19th century brothels.

In modern Wicca the 'officers' of the coven are the High Priest and Priestess, the Maiden, and sometimes a Summoner - a role borrowed from the traditional side. In the Traditional Craft there is the Magister or Grand Master, sometimes known as the Man in Black; the Lady, Mistress or Dame; the Maid or Maiden; and the Summoner. The Lady takes the role of priestess and is the channel through which the power and authority of the Goddess flows into the circle. Sometimes she is called the Queen of the Sabbat and in some traditional groups takes a secondary position to the male leader. In other traditions the Lady rules alone, with the male officers taking secondary positions, or the Magister and Lady preside together.

The Summoner, also confusingly known as the Man in Black, is the record-keeper, scribe and go-between with other covens and traditions. As his title suggests, he is responsible for summoning the other members to meetings. He ensures that they convene at the right place at the right time and date. His symbol of office is the blackthorn staff or 'Black Rod' and in those covens dedicated to the Horned God he is the Magister's deputy.

The Maid or Maiden is a younger version of the Lady and stands in for her when she is not present. One of the Maid's tasks is to be the guardian of the sacred hearth. She tends the balefire and this role recognizes the importance of the fire and the hearth as the central focus of the household in ancient times. In some traditions the Maid may cast the circle before handing over to the Master or Lady. She may also hold the office of coven seer or oracle.

In some traditions there is a third female officer known as the Crone. This role is usually taken up by an ex-Lady who has attained the rank of Elder. In practice this is a woman over sixty years of Age with many years of experience in the Craft. It is said that in those covens which concentrate on knowledge and power, the Lady or high priestess holds little or no executive power. She sits at the Magister's right hand during the feasts, leads some of the dances and ceremonies, and on occasion performs the task of seer or spiristic medium under the Magister's control' [20].

Among progressive traditionals, the Master and Lady have equal control of the coven as the human representatives of the God and Goddess. There are few modern traditions that follow the old medieval system of six female witches and a male leader. In the Pickingill Craft, still practised to day in East Anglia, all the rituals are led by a woman. This allegedly dates back to pagan Northern Europe when women served and honoured the God for 'the fertility religion of Scandinavia deemed the priestess was the wife and consort of the God' [21].

Some traditional and Hereditary witches have claimed that the casting of a circle as an enclosed magickal space was inherited by the Craft in comparatively recent times from ceremonial magick. Others point to the use of a circle for magick in Anglo-Saxon times and to the stone circles of our prehistoric ancestors. Old-time witches, it is said, did not dance in circles that had been cast using the working tools, but at stone circles, earthworks, around standing stones and burial mounds. However as a symbol of psychic wholeness and spiritual unity the symbol of the circle has been sacred since the megalithic culture.

There has been an ongoing debate about whether or not the circle is cast to keep the power raised during rituals in, or to protect those inside it from evil forces. This debate completely misses the point that the primary function of the circle is to be 'the space between the worlds of men and the Gods'. It is an artificially created 'inbetween place' in the sense of an invisible liminal boundary between the material and the spiritual. In this sense 'the compass (circle) is a temple, a sanctuary and a cosmogram in whose bounds the witch is projected into sacred time where all words and acts become archetypal and primordial in their power (22).

In Wicca the four points of the compass or quarters of the circle are designated to the control of the elements in accordance with the magickal correspondences of Golden Dawn-type magick i.e. north = earth, east = air. south = fire and west = water. In some traditional forms of the Craft the west stays with water, but the north = air, east = fire and the south = earth. Most of the progressive traditionals ignore convention and work with the elemental forces in the circle in the places where it feels 'right'. It is not a matter of dogma.

The circle is cast or raised using the rod or a knife. It is consecrated with water, fire (a candle) and air (incense). While the circle is being cast those present will visualize it as a physical barrier of blue light enclosing the group or individual. In some groups this is reinforced by an actual physical barrier of tree branches, ash or soot. When working outdoors sometimes an actual ditch is dug marking the boundary of the circle or meeting ground.

Some traditions call upon watchers or guardians, either at the four quarters or generally, and the Old Ones, the Lord and Lady, are asked politely to attend the rites. Candles (indoors) or lanterns (outdoors) are lit at each of the quarters. If a balefire is lit then it is in the centre of the circle and all participants should be within the circle before it is ignited. In Wicca and Traditional Craft entry to the circle is by crossing a symbolic bridge or entering a gateway. The symbolism of this simple act brings us back to the significance of the boundary and the doorway, gate, stile and 'gap in the hedge' through which the 'night rider' steps 'between the worlds'.

Chapter Five

Entering the Circle

Initiation is defined in the dictionary as the admission of a person into a mystery or society, usually within a religious, or at least a ritual, context. the actual word initiate means 'to begin' or 'to originate'. In common exoteric parlance it refers to a new start or beginning. In the esoteric, arcane sense it means less of a formal acceptance into a social, cultural or religious elite, although obviously it also has that meaning, then a deliberate act marking a fundamental change in the life of the initiate and their consciousness. In spiritual terms, if correctly done, initiation should lead to a heightened state of awareness. One effect, if not already manifest in the initiate, would be a realisation of the existence of other realities or dimensions beyond the physical.

Seen in the above terms, initiation is a symbolic act ritually performed on the outer level and representing a desire by the candidate to transform their perception of the universe. There initiation into the Craft is a rite of passage and the first step on the inner quest for the psychic integration of mind, body and spirit. This will ultimately lead to the mystical experience of direct contact or gnosis (knowledge) of the Godhead. As one traditional has put it: 'the Faith is finally concerned with Truth, total Truth. It is one of the oldest religions, and also one of the most potent, bringing as it does man into contact with the Gods and man into contact with self.' [1].

The connection between the ritual of initiation and rites of passage relates both to the stages in a person's life, e.g. birth, childhood, puberty, adulthood, marriage, retirement, death etc, in the sense of passing boundaries in space and time which create a change in status. Put into simple terms; one moment the candidate is a cowan, an outsider, standing outside the circle. The next moment he or she has entered the circle and what follows will change them forever. A threshold or boundary has been crossed or breached and the candidate is no longer the same person. By accepting initiation into the Craft, the initiate has taken their first step on the Path. It is a path that not all humans will take in this lifetime. The Craft is for the few, not the many, and it represents the path of the Mysteries within the popular pagan movement. That is not snobbishness or elitism, but fact and the way things are.

The 'crossing the boundary' metaphor is as important in the initiation process as it is in any other aspect of the Craft. When the candidate is initiated or inducted into the Craft he or she links with the group mind of the coven and the thought forms, or 'guardians' associated with its tradition. This is why if a person has been initiated and moves to another area to join another coven, or decides to join another tradition, they will be asked to undergo another initiation ceremony. This does not invalidate what has gone before, but connects the newcomer to his or her new coven and/or tradition.

Traditionally there has always been an accepted form of initiation into the Mysteries which has been practised by occult societies down through the ages. It is based on historical precedents and features graduated stages of involvement and evolvement. These stages will include a probationary, purification, tests or ordeals, an oath of secrecy, the transmission from teacher to pupil of oral or written teachings and instructions, the display and explanation of sacred objects, the re-enactment of cultural myths, a symbolic journey to the underworld, and a ritualistic death and rebirth.

Depending on which Craft tradition the neophyte encounters these aspects of initiation will be present to a lesser or greater extent. Some of the more cloak-and-daggerish elements may be a leftover from the occult and Masonic secret societies of the past who influenced the 18th and 19th century Craft revivals. Some romantics claim they may even be remnants of practice from the days of the Persecution when blood- curdling oaths of allegiance, elaborate secrecy and terrifying ordeals were allegedly used to safeguard the Craft from infiltration by Christian spies and informers.

In Traditional Craft circles the candidate may have to spend a probationary period, usually a year and a day, or sometimes longer, prior to entering the coven. In this period they are taught by the officers. The actual entry into the Craft or the coven in this sense is more of an induction or rite of admission then an initiation proper. Induction means to formally introduce or install a candidate after a period of learning or training. This enables the prospective candidate to be tested and have a fair grounding in Craft ways before they are officially accepted into the group.

In the Whitestone group, founded in the 1970s by 'rebels' from a network of old Craft covens in Surrey and Sussex, the process of initiation takes three years. In the first year the probationer finds and consecrates their magickal tools and works simple rituals with a cord. At the end of this period an initiation takes place and the student becomes a working novice in the coven. During the second year the tools are charged and used in circle work. This results in a First Rite of passage if it is successfully completed. Finally, at the end of the third year of teaching and instruction the novice becomes a fully-fledged witch. Further stages can follow eventually, if the initiate is suitable, so that they can become the Master or Mistress of their own coven. Such a procedure compares well against the 'conveyer belt' system of many Wiccan covens where the candidate can pass through the three degrees in as many months, or sometimes in even a shorter period. It is also true to say that in the more traditional branches of the Craft the ritual of induction is regarded as the welcoming back into the circle, perhaps after many incarnations, of an initiate of the 'witch blood' who has been separated from other members of the Craft by both space and time.

The 'ordeal' is also an aspect of the traditional type initiation and it can take many forms depending on the group and the tradition. For instance, in olden times, in Wales initiates were dragged through a blazing hoop. This was popularly called "sacrificing to the Devil' and its purpose was to 'continue the succession of the wise'. Such practices are a throwback to the 'death and rebirth' rituals of ancient times where the shaman travels in spirit to the underworld, is ritually 'killed' and dismembered, and is then reborn in a new body. This motif is to be found in the old pagan Mysteries of the classical world and Egypt, and it can even be recognized in the myth of the crucifixion and resurrection of Jesus after three days in the tomb (womb).

In practical terms the ordeal may take the form of an all-night vigil in a wood or cave. Although such vigils are well-known from the vision quests of the Native Americans, they were also a feature of druidic initiations, and there is no doubt they inherited them from earlier examples. It has been claimed that prehistoric burial mounds and fougus may have been used for this purpose as well as burying the dead. There is archaeological evidence that some burial mounds were used for rituals as well as internments. The Pentre Ifan cromlech in Pembrokeshire. West Wales, for instance, is known locally as 'the Womb of Ceridwen' and folklore says it was used for initiations by the druids in Celtic times.

An interesting example of a modern form of ordeal is given in an account of an initiation ceremony carried out in a West Country wood dedicated to the Celtic goddess Annis. The following account has been edited from the original: 'the wood is used mainly as a spot for initiations when aspirant members of this hereditary group are deemed ready to learn something of the mysteries... The aspirant, after being prepared mentally by his or her sponsor, and drinking of the potion, is left alone to spend the night by the three stones that stand overgrown in the wood...The inquisition on the following day by experienced Elders will determine whether the aspirant will stay permanently on the fringe of the group or assumes his heritage' [2]. It should be added that the potion mentioned is made from hallucinogenic plants. Although this account was written over thirty years ago, similar rituals are still practised within traditionary and hereditary circles.

Another, more controversial, way of preparing a candidate for initiation was given some years ago in a popular book of the time on witchcraft. It caused some controversy among Wiccans who had not encountered it before.[3] It was suggested that the neophyte should recite the Lord's Prayer backwards. This was not an act of disrespect to Christianity or the Church, but part of a process of weaning the entrant away from their previous religious affiliations and conditioning which affects most of us from childhood. This may be an extreme example, but some traditional initiations do require the candidate to renounce their previous religion and dedicate themselves to the Old Ones and the Craft. There is nothing 'Satanic' about such an undertaking. All it does is ensure that the person is 100% sincere in dedicating themselves to their new beliefs.

There are also very good practical reasons for asking an initiate to take an oath of secrecy to keep what they see and hear at coven meetings confidential. The old magickal maxim 'dare to know, dare to will, and dare to keep silent' comes into play here. Many practitioners believe that the efficacy of magickal workings will be destroyed if they are talked about, especially to cowans. Traditionals and Hereditaries will not invite television or film crews to their meetings! The oath of secrecy is not based on covering up sinister activities, but on plain commonsense and ethical considerations.

The traditional initiation takes many practical forms, again depending on the group or tradition. The following description is a composite based on several versions known to the author. Following the ordeal or vigil to test the candidate's sincerity and resolve, he or she is led to the edge of the circle with their hands tied and hoodwinked or blindfolded. They are given a final challenge before they enter the circle or step over the boundary of 'the space between the worlds'. Their motives for wanting to join the Craft are questioned once more. If their answers are acceptable to those present then they are invited into the circle.

Usually they will symbolically step over a broom or sword, or both, to gain entry.

The candidate then kneels at the altar or in the circle's centre if no altar is present. The Master or Mistress may ask them to renounce their former religious beliefs (if any) and to dedicate themselves to the Old Faith and its Gods. An Oath of Allegiance is then taken which commits the initiate to the coven tradition, or the family. If a sword is used in the coven, this may be pointed at the initiate during the taking of the oath, or he or she may be asked to kiss its blade afterwards.

The blindfold is then removed and the hands are untied. This is symbolic of the rebirth of the initiate from the darkness of the womb into the light of the circle. Sometimes the first thing the initiate will see when he or she removes the blindfold is the animal mask of the Magister as the human representative of the Horned God. The other coveners may be hooded at first to conceal their faces and then they will symbolically reveal them.

The initiate's finger is then pricked and they are asked to sign their name in their own blood in the Black Book of the coven if one is in use. Some traditional groups will use a ritual tattoo to make the old Devil's Mark. This may be in the form of a spider, its web, a bat, a footprint of a hare or frog, or even the 'Mark of Cain'. In some traditions a thread may be used to take the measure of the initiate. These were supposed to be kept in the old days and if the member needed to be disciplined or punished, or even banished from the circle, it would be used against them magickally.

Following the above, the Magister or the Lady then 'passes the power' to the initiate. This can either be done by placing one hand on the crown of the head and one on the sole of the foot, or by sexual induction which we will discuss later. A new 'witch name' may be given to the initiate for use in the circle, they are introduced to the four quarters and given their ritual robe. The initiate may also be presented with a lighted candle which has been lit from the balefire. This represents their new life, the inner light within them and the illumination of the divine gnosis. Finally, the initiate will join in a 'welcoming dance', partake of 'cake and wine', and the feast with the other members of the coven when the circle is closed.

Compare this modern account of a traditional initiation with the following account from folk tradition of the admission of Welsh witches into the Craft in the 19th century. The would-be witch had to sign a pact in blood with the Devil and was then marked with the diablo stigmata, or Devil's Mark with a needle or a thorn. The witch then had to kiss a toad and renounce Christianity. This sounds bizarre, but 'kissing the toad' was a cryptic reference to using the fly agaric toadstool to achieve a trance state and contact with the Otherworld.

A ritual potion was then drunk from the sacred cup made from a horse's skull. The horse was one of the animal totems of the Goddess, especially in her dark aspect as the 'night mare'. The new witch was then presented with a jar of lifting balm or flying ointment. This, combined with the wearing of a snake-skin garter, allegedly gave the witch the power to 'Make a broomstick do duty as a horse.' [4]

The above two accounts, of course, merely describe the practical and physical mechanics of the initiation ceremony. They do not deal with what happens on an inner level. Unless the candidate can establish his or her own psychic link with the Old Ones and the 'guardians' of the coven, tradition or family, then the ritual will be meaningless. The old tales about witches not being able to die until they have passed on their powers to a suitable candidate illustrate this point. Until the initiate has forged contact with his or her spirit guides and helpers from the Other Side then it could be said that no real initiation into the Craft has taken place. This 'passing of the power' has been described quite accurately as 'the magical act whereby the entire power of the Tradition is transmitted directly from an Initiator to his/her pupil, as from Master to apprentice.' Within this rite of 'passing-on the entire knowledge of the Tradition flows into the candidate in a state of gnostic transmission' [5]

Alternative methods of 'passing the power' can be made outside of a ritual of initiation performed in a circle. These possibly date from a time when the group was unable to convene or when initiation was from solitary witch or wizard to apprentice. These alternative methods include the transmission from one person to another of written texts or rituals. Usually, but not always, this is by 'mouth to ear' as are most teachings in the Craft.

Another method is the handing on or inheriting of magical artifacts and this is described as follows: 'For instance, the passing on of the wand or stave from Master to apprentice is a form of custom active in the Essex Craft. This establishes a link between initiates over successive generations and endows such objects with a distinctive numen or spiritual aura approximating personality. Such objects often bear names which testify to the belief that they have become the dwelling place of a spirit.' [5]

This brings us, finally, to the subject of the 'passing of power' by sexual induction. This is a controversial area and only recently one traditional group who went public in recent years have been accused of 'sexual abuse' in this context. It has been boldly stated that 'sexual induction is a hallmark of the Hereditary Craft'. The 'witch alone' will insist on sexual induction when lawfully passing the power' to a person of the opposite sex. The lone witch's 'power', abilities, psychic gifts, spirit guides and elementals are actually transferred to his or her spiritual heir during the sex act.' [6]. It has been suggested this practice was regarded as a 'barbarous anachronism' by the 17th century intellectuals who were attracted to the Craft and they abandoned it at that time [7].

In Romany witchcraft some young female witches receive their psychic powers from astral sexual congress with water and earth spirits. The astral sex takes place while they are sleeping and often without their consent. It is only when they wake that the new witch realises something has changed and she now possesses remarkable powers of clairvoyance and seership. This connects with the arcane lore about faery lovers, the myth of the fallen angels who mated with human women and taught them magick, and the medieval belief in the sexual demons known as incubi and succubi.

In modern Wicca the neophyte is expected to pass through three degrees of initiation. It has been suggested that this system was borrowed from Freemasonry with its three degrees of Entered Apprentice, Journeyman and Master Mason. Whether this took place in the Middle Ages, the 18th century or the 1930s of this century is a matter for hot debate in both Craft and academic circles. It is known that Gerald Gardner and the members of the New Forest coven were Co-Masons, but Traditional and Hereditary sources point out the similarities between witchcraft and Masonic symbolism and suggest, however speculatively, a common origin in the ancient past.

A tristructural initiation system was also observed by the Celtic druids and, more importantly, by those who revived druidism in the 18th century. Three stages of initiation are also mentioned in some of the witch trials.

One source describes three levels of admission into the witch cult. In the first the female candidate is accepted as a novice. In the second she takes an oath of allegiance to the Devil (Magister), and in the third she gives herself to him 'Body and soul', which sounds like a sexual induction. [8]

In some branches of the Hereditary Craft it is said that two grades were recognized known as the First and Second Rite. The First Rite was the sexual induction of the candidate by either a solitary witch or the Master or Mistress of a coven to 'pass the power'. This did not give the initiate the power to initiate anyone else. Only the Second Rite, sometimes known as the Rite of Admission, granted full Craft membership and the authority to initiate others.

It is further claimed that the French Craft, variations of which were allegedly introduced into East Anglia and Scotland during the Hundred Years War in the 15th century, had Three Rites. These, it is claimed, influenced the three degree system of modern Wicca through George Pickingill and his Nine Covens. The Third Rite was designed to give authority to initiates to found their own covens and take the title of Magister or Lady [9]. In some cases in the Hereditary Craft, where there is the danger of the bloodline running out, cowans can be adopted into the family tradition This sometimes happens if a member of the family marries outside of the Craft.

Today there is a great debate in Craft circles about the rights and wrongs of self-initiation, or more accurately self-dedication, and the idea has arisen that one can only become a witch by being initiated into a coven or by a practising witch. There are many who dogmatically cling to the belief that a person cannot be a witch unless they have been initiated. Such a rigid view takes no account of those who are 'natural born witches' and who are truly of the 'witch blood' by either birthright or soul incarnation. This is summed up in the old saying 'A witch is born - not made'.

In the old days the solitary witch was the norm and she often worked alone. Despite the modern revival many seekers still find it difficult to find a suitable coven to initiate them. This is specially true if they are seeking traditional forms of witchcraft. Others may not be interested in ;joining a group and prefer to be solitaries. There is no valid reason why those who are genuinely attracted to the Craft for the right reasons should not make direct contact with the Old Ones, the Lord and Lady, and receive the 'passing of the power' direct. After all, at best, the Master and Lady of any group can only be pale reflections of the Bright Powers in their role as human representatives of the God and Goddess.

As one modern traditional witch says: ' You stand a far better chance of gaining true initiation and the touch of power that will bring it, quite alone in a wild place when, with your knees knocking and your hand clutching the lantern shaking like an aspen, you actually encounter the High Ones face to face' [10].

More and more modern witches are finding the truth in those words and they are actively seeking the solitary path of the wise woman, wizard and hedgewitch. In this respect they should not be condemned or criticised, for they are simply reviving the practices of the past when the majority of the Craft were solo practitioners of the Art.

Chapter Six
The Wheel of the Year

As was noted in Chapter One, the arrival of the pagan Saxons, Jutes and Angles in southern England in the 5th century CE brought with it an influx of pagan beliefs and practices which survived almost intact for the next two hundred years. Historians argue about the cultural impact of the German tribes on the Romano-British population and whether it was a bloody invasion or a peaceful colonisation, but there can be no doubts about the impact of their native paganism.

The newcomers and their pagan deities are reflected in English and Welsh placenames dating back to this period. The most obvious of these are local references to sacred sites where Woden, Thor, Tiw, Frey and Freyja were worshipped, or with which they became associated by folk tradition and legends. Some notable examples are Wansdyke or Woden's Dyke (ditch or causeway) in the Vale of Pewsey in southern England, while in the modern West Midlands, known as Mercia in Anglo-Saxon times, can be found Wednesbury or Woden's Fort, and Wednesfield, or Woden's Field. In Derbyshire, where Woden is still remembered as the leader of the Wild Hunt, there is Wensley, or Woden's Grove, and in Kent the village of Woodnesborough was still known as Wodensbeorge as late as the 12th century. Several earthworks of prehistoric origin in southern England are called Grimsdyke, from Woden's nickname of Grim or Grimnr, meaning 'the Masked One'.

Thundersley and its variants, such as Thundersfield, appear in Essex, Hertfordshire, Surrey, Sussex and Hampshire and all indicate a place were the weather god Thor was venerated. In Old English ley or leigh means a woodland clearing and is a reference to the sacred groves where the Saxons worshipped. The war god Tiw or Tyr is remembered in Tuesley in Surrey, Tislea in Hampshire, and Tyesmore and Tysoe in Warwickshire.

Frigga, wife of Odin and Mother of the Gods, and Freyja turn up in Freefolk in Hampshire, which was called Frigefolk or Frigg's Folk in the 11th century. In the same county the villages of Froye and Frobury were originally called Freohyll, or 'the hill of Freyja'. The oddly named Fryup and Fridaythorpe in Yorkshire are also folk memories of the goddess. In Pembrokeshire in south-west Wales the colonisation of the area by Danish Vikings left its traces in Freythorp. Finally, Weyland's Smithy is a prehistoric burial mound with chamber named after the smith god in Saxon times. It is located near to the Bronze Age White Horse of Uffington hill figure.

Other English place names signify sites of heathen worship or pagan temples established by the Angle-Saxons, possibly on sites already sanctified to Celtic gods. The Saxons certainly buried their dead on former sites including prehistoric ones. Three English words alert us to Saxon sacred sites and they are *ealh*, or temple; *heath* or *eharg*, sanctuary; and *weoh*, a shrine or sacred place. *Ealh* is found in Kent and variations of *weolh* all across southern England and as far north as the Midlands. *Hearg* has been Anglicized as Harrow and one classic example is Harrow-on-the-Hill, site of the famous public school, in Middlesex. Quite literally its name means 'sanctuary on the hill' [1]. Its highest point now has a church built on it and today it is a place of pilgrimage by modern Odinists.

As was also discussed in Chapter One, the attempted conversion of the pagan English tribes in the early 7th century was not an easy task for the Roman Catholic missionaries. Pope Gregory had sent his mission to England because he had heard that the Jutish king of Kent, Ethelbert, was already sympathetic to the new religion. The king's wife Berctha or Bertha (a pagan name and possibly a derivative of Holda) was of Merovingian descent and had already been baptised. Ethelbert however was still a pagan at heart and his reasons for wishing to become a Christian were political and commercial. He wanted to forge economic links with the already Christianised Merovingians and he also believed that the Christian god had given his European converts victory in battle. If this was true then the king was ready to embrace the Christian faith.

Ethelbert's subjects were still committed pagans and they had little interest in the new faith from the Middle East. It has been established that there were twelve major centres of pagan worship in a twelve mile radius of the church Augustine eventually built in Canterbury. When Ethelbert did agree to meet the foreign missionaries he insisted that it should be out doors and under a sacred oak to protect from their malefic magick. Although the king was baptised by Augustine his son Eadbald refused to accept it, After his father's death it was some time before he finally renounced his pagan beliefs and became a practising Christian. In Essex when Sabert, king of the East Saxons died in 617 as a Christian convert, his three sons reverted to the Old Ways. King Redwald of the East Angles, who some historians believe was buried at Sutton Hoo, was converted during a visit to Eadbald, but when he returned home his pagan wife persuaded him not to completely give up his allegiance to the pagan gods. Like many 'rice Christians', Redwald followed both religions. It is said that he had an altar dedicated to Christ and another for the worship of 'demons'.

The reversion of the sons of Sabert was a bitter blow to the papal mission. Following the death of Augustine in 604, it was being led by Bishop Meelitus and he decided it would be safer if the mission temporarily withdrew from England. It therefore decamped to Gaul (France) in 616 and only returned when a missionary who remained behind had persuaded the Saxons to accept the Christian faith. Even then the citizens of London refused to accept the bishop's spiritual authority as they preferred their own pagan priests.

In 669 another mission was sent from Rome to prevent the complete collapse of the new English Church. When the Archbishop of Canterbury died in 664 his replacement did not arrive for five years. Eventually Bishop Theodore, a Greek, was sent from Rome accompanied by a black African bishop. He quickly moved to re-establish the Church with laws to outlaw pagan practices. However the kingdom of the south Saxons, Sussex, was not fully converted until 680. Before Theodore had arrived several Saxon kings had reverted to paganism when plague swept the country. They believed that only by offering blot (sacrifice) to the Gods could they be saved.

By the beginning of the 8th century the Roman Church was busy converting pagans and it had also successfully weakened the position of the Celtic Church in Wales and the North. However there was more trouble on the pagan horizon when the Vikings began to raid the coasts of Wales, Scotland and Ireland. In the middle of the 9th century many churches in Ireland were looted and burned. Others were closed for Christian worship and converted into temples to Odin and Thor.

During the 8th and early 9th centuries the Vikings frequently raided Iona, Lindisfarne, Northumbria, the South and West of Wales and the Isle of Man. Colonies of Norsemen were established in south-west Wales and in northern Scotland. In 878 the situation was so desperate that King Alfred sued for peace and as a result England was effectively cut in half. The area under so called Danelaw extended from Yorkshire to the River Thames. King Edward defeated the Danes in 927 and united with them against the Norwegians. In 1002 a massacre of Danes by Ethelred led to a Viking invasion, the defeat of the Angle-Saxons and the rule of England by the Danish king Canute from 1016 to 1035. This was only thirty years before the Norman Conquest.

The Vikings - a generic name for the Swedes, Norwegians and Danes - were initially pagans and they were only converted when they had settled o the lands they had colonised. For instance, in 918 a band of Viking pirates led by a warlord called Rollo or Rolf settled in the lower valley of the Seine in France by agreement with Charles, the king of the Franks. As part of the agreement Rollo, a pagan, agreed to be baptised. Eventually Rollo's men extended their lands into the duchy of Normandy and Rollo became the great-great grandfather of William the Conqueror. On his death-bed Rollo recanted his Christian beliefs and had a hundred captives sacrificed to the Old Gods. Afterwards, filled with Christian remorse and guilt, he donated a pound of gold for each captive to the local churches [2]

Canute's father, Sweyn, was described as a 'Christian of sorts' [3] and one chronicler suggested he reverted to paganism after his own father's death. His son, as we have seen, passed laws prohibiting the practice of witchcraft and paganism. However when he minted some coins marked with the cross and sent one as a present to the bishop of Chartres, the cleric reacted with surprise as he believed the king was still a pagan [4] Canute married the widow of his Saxon predecessor King Aethelred. She was older than him and it is possible this arranged marriage was the remnant of a pagan custom. In pagan Scandinavia the king was often regarded as the husband and consort of Freyja so the new king must possess the old queen who came to represent the deity' [5]. The pagan king Eadbald married his stepmother when his Christian father died and thereby gained the crown, although he was condemned by the Church. Queen Judith of Wessex married her stepson when the old king died so he became the new ruler. The widow is an important aspect of the Goddess who mourns her sacrificed lover/son. This also relates to sovereignty, or the goddess of the land, who grants sacred kingship on the successor to the old king.

Despite the edicts of the rulers of England against paganism the old customs carried on regardless of Christian sanction and censure. In the IIth century the Bishop of Worms was forced to ask his parishioners: "Hast thou done anything like what the pagans did, and still do, on the Ist of January in (the guise of) a stag or calf" Pagan beliefs also survived in Ireland where in 1096 the Church denounced 'heathenism', including wizardry, divination using wooden staves, charms, philtres and enchantment. As late as the 12th century an English herbalist was still directing a pagan prayer to the Goddess as 'Earth, divine goddess, Mother Earth, who doest generate all things and bringest forth anew, the sun which thou hast given to the nations; guardian of sky and sea, and of all the Gods and powers...' [6]

Today historians and folklorists debate endlessly about which of the many folk customs and festivals survived from pagan times or are historical inventions. Certainly when the papal mission arrived here in 597 CE the Pope was to issue it strict instructions to take over the old sites of worship and re-dedicate the pagan festivals to the celebration of the Christian God and saints. Many of the Christian saints and their festivals took on pagan elements, and new saints were created who were thinly disguised pagan gods.

In Northern Europe the important seasonal festivals for marking the turning of the Wheel of the Year were based on the equinoxes and solstices. At midwinter there was the winter solstice on December 21/22 when sacrifices were made for good crops at next year s harvest. A spring festival coincided with the vernal equinox around March 21/22 and had a fertility theme. In the Viking period it was the time when *blot* was offered for the success of the summer raiding parties. The midsummer solstice, around June 21/22, celebrated the power of the sun at its highest point in the sky. At the end of August or in September, near the autumn equinox on the 21/23, there was a harvest festival dedicated to the phallic fertility god Frey, twin brother of Freyja. Finally, in early November, came the festival of Winter's Night celebrating or marking the beginning of the dark season.

The midwinter ritual for a good harvest still survives in the Christian folk custom of Blessing the Plough on the first Monday in January after Twelfth Night. In the days of the old calender before the 18th century change this festival would have been closer to the winter solstice. Sometimes a decorated plough was carried around the fields by young men dressed up as witches and goblins. The plough was then taken around the parish and the villagers touched it 'for good luck' and made offerings of money to the ploughboys. Before the Reformation the money was used to buy a large candle for the church called the Plough Light. The superstitious said that burning this candle on the altar ensured good weather for ploughing, a bumper harvest and protection to the farm workers from sickness, injury and evil forces. [7]

The ploughboys who carried around the plough wore cloth patches on their clothing in the shape of agricultural tools or farm animals. They were led by a 'captain' who wore a costume made from tattered rags or animal skins and sometimes a bullock's tail. The group was often accompanied by a hunchbacked Fool or trickster figure and a 'she-male', or man dressed in female clothes, who represented the spirit of winter.

This ritualised act marking the first ploughing and the honouring of the plough as a sacred object has a long history. In Jutland there is a Bronze Age rock carving depicting a man with an erect penis with an ox-drawn plough. It is 'obvious that he is engaged in the first ploughing of the year to awaken the earth's fruitfulness after the sleep of winter with the phallus of the plough...' [8] That he is ithyphallic underlines the ancient connection between the fertility of the earth and human sexuality which is found, often heavily sublimated, in folk ritual and seasonal customs.

The spring festivals for fertility survived in the Christian calendar as Easter and Whitsun. Midsummer's Day is the festival of St John the Baptist on June 24th, shortly after the summer solstice. Michaelmas, on September 29, All Souls on November 1st and Martinmas on November 11th are Christian versions of the old autumn festivals of the pagan year. The Church of England's modern Harvest Festival is a 19th century invention but it replaced the old Harvest Home rituals which had become too rowdy and riotous for the Victorians.

Whatever some historians claim to the contrary, pagan rituals in the form of folkloric customs survived into historical times. In 17th century Scotland and Wales there are reports of the sacrifice of bulls to saints at the end of August, rituals carried out at holy wells and sacred oak trees and the pouring of libations of milk on hills. In 1668 a group of women were found at a holy well in Scotland dancing in a circle with their skirts held up above the waist. A crone sat in their midst, dipping a small vessel in the water and sprinkling the dancers. This was supposed to be a fertility rite for childless women. [9]

As late as 1801 peasants in Cumbria assembled at midsummer at a local standing stone. A phallic figure was dressed in coloured rags, presumably to represent the sun god. It was then smeared with sheep salve, tar and butter and crowned with flowers [10]. In Pembrokeshire at the same period offerings were still made to stones in divination rites. Young women baked a special cinnamon and honey cake and took it to a local cromlech at midnight on the full moon. They laid the cake on the capstone of the burial chamber and then walked around the monument three times widdershins. At the end of the third circuit it was said the fetch or spirit form of their future lover or husband would appear.

In the 1820s the Beltane fires were still being lit in country areas of Ireland. Cows were being forced through these fires to prevent their milk being stolen by the Good People or the faeries who were said to be active between May Day and Midsummer's Day. Men about to undertake a long journey, especially emigrants to the Americas, leapt the fire for luck and safe journey, as did pregnant women wanting healthy babies and young women looking for a husband.

An article in the Saturday magazine of 1837 described a survival of 'druidic rites' in rural Ireland. These involved people visiting holy wells at special times of the year. Often these wells had an old oak tree or a standing stone in their vicinity. The worshippers would crawl around the well on their knees in a deosil direction praying to the Virgin Mary or the saints.

As late as the end of the 19th century in Perthshire, Scotland the locals gathered in a stone stone circle on Beltane (May 1) A fire was lit in the centre of the circle and each of the assembly placed a piece of oatcake in a shepherd's cap. Everyone was then blind-folded and took turns to select a piece of the cake from the hat.

The one who selected the blackest burnt portion was named 'the beloved (of the Gods)'. They had to either to pay a forfeit or jump the bonfire. [11] All of which sounds suspiciously like the folk memory of a game of fate to choose a human sacrifice in ancient times.

In Wales in the springtime as late as the 1960s old farmers drew a special symbol in a field before planting their crops. It was a circle with rays coming from it to represent the power of the sun. This was drawn inside a triangle with the point upwards, known as 'the trine of the moon'. These two sigils were symbolic of the mating between the sky god and the earth goddess, although it is doubtful the farmers realised the symbolism. They also drew an oblong shape bisected with a line. This was said to be the symbol of the 'angel of the land' who brought a good harvest.

The tradition of the Beltane fires was exported to America with European immigrants. In 1971 it was reported that some of the old families in the Appalachian Mountains still gather on hilltops on May Eve to light a bonfire. They sing songs, drink moonshine or homemade whisky, and dance till dawn. By doing this they believe they are 'calling down the sun' to bless their crops and animals. They claim that the custom is very old and was brought over by their Scottish ancestors.

In the 1970s, when the BBC's *Chronicle* programme was making a documentary about the family tradition known as the Guardians in Derbyshire, the film crew were told that wells and springs in the area were still decorated with floral offerings at 'important' times of the year. Balefires were still lit at Beltane, 'Celtic' heads were still being carved and placed above farm doorways to ward off evil, and there was a strong local belief in the Wild Hunt, a Mother Goddess and the Horned God [12].

Even where commercialisation has taken over folk customs based on old pagan themes are still being revived in our materialistic society. At a willow growers farm in Suffolk a new custom has been introduced with serious intent. At the full moon in May a Green Man type figure is made from willow strippings. At the end of an evening of food and drink, he is 'danced' to a nearby pond and thrown in as a 'ritual sacrifice'. This modern custom is said to be done for 'good luck' and to improve the willow harvest for the benefit of the farm owner.

A well-known cider company in Herefordshire has revived the old custom of wassailing their apple orchards on Twelfth Night. This is the folk survival of the pagan ritual of making offerings to the spirits of the apple trees for a good harvest. A sample of last year's cider is poured over the roots as a libation, horns are blown and shotguns fired in the air to 'scare off evil spirits' who might bring disease. The managing director of the company 'resplendent in a top hat decorated with holly and ivy, told a television interviewer that the ceremony was 'essential if a commercial crop was to be produced each year.' (13)

It should be noted that such folk revivals and old customs in the countryside are carried out with some seriousness by their participants. There is a firm belief that good or bad luck will follow depending on how well the ceremony is carried out. They are always performed by local people who have lived in the area for generations and regard themselves as 'guardians' protecting and preserving these customs and traditions. Although they attract the attention of tourists they are not performed for their benefit, but for the benefit of the local community and its luck.

This brings us neatly to the practice of the rituals of the Wheel of the Year by modern witches and their connection with the folk calendar. Today's pagans and witch are lucky in having a festival to celebrate about every six weeks. However, in the nature of our beliefs, few seem to agree on how many of these festivals should be celebrated or when they should be held. This uncertainty has also influenced the Traditional Craft. Some groups only acknowledge the four fire festivals which are basically of Celtic origin and follow the agricultural cycle. These are Imbolc or Candlemas (February 1), Beltane or May Day (May 1), Lughnasadh or Lammas (August 1), and Samhain or Hallowe'en (November 1). Other groups and traditions also celebrate the summer and winter solstices and the spring and autumn equinoxes. A few traditionalists add Twelfth Night, giving nine festivals, or Michaelmas (September 29).

Traditionally the festivals are celebrated on the evening of the day before - hence we have February Eve, May Eve, Lammas Eve and Hallows Eve. Some traditionalist follow the Old Calendar observed before 1752, which is approximately eleven days adrift of our modern one. Therefore, for instance, January 6th is Old Christmas Day, still celebrated by the Russian Orthodox Church.

Because of the calendar changeover the festivals often extend between the old and new dates e.g. the rites to welcome summer and move livestock to their new pastures went on in the folk calendar from May Eve (April 30) to Old May Day (May 12).

Some groups celebrate the festivals on the nearest full moon and there is a school of thought that says the festivals should not be held on fixed dates at all, but when the seasonal changes dictate. With the unpredictable British weather, and climate change in the future, this could produce plenty of problems.

How did witches, or those called witches, practice the festivals in the past? Traditionally it is said they met at the ancient sacred sites to worship the Powers and to make offerings to the lesser gods, the nature spirits and faeries etc. According to their Christian persecutors, the witches mocked Christianity by holding their meetings on or near the dates of the Church's festivals. In fact they were just following the pattern of pre-Christian rituals which had been taken over by the early Church when it tried to suppress paganism.

One of the Berwick witches in 17th century Scotland was accused of attending 'the convention' at Lammas Eve and All Hallows, when she danced in the churchyard. The latter is not a 'Satanic' practice as many pre-Reformation churches in the British isles were built on sites of former pagan worship. Modern witches are still known to meet at ruined churches on former pagan sites. Some years ago a traditional group using a ruined church near Henley-on-Thames in Berkshire caused allegations of 'black magic rites' in the local newspapers after one of their meets was disturbed.

The Aberdeen witches also met on All Hallows Eve (October 31) and the famous Pendle coven in Lancashire was supposed to have met on Samhain (November 1). In 1662 Isobel Gowdie confessed that a 'Grand Meeting was held about the end of each quarter'. There is also evidence that medieval witches met at the equinoxes and the solstices. In France covens gathered on St John's Eve (June 23). The 17th century, Devon witches gathered on St Andrew's Day at the end of November, which may have been an early midwinter festival. (14)

Where did the old-time, and modern traditional, witches meet? Their meeting places included near running water, where two or three streams met, near a waterfall, at an old tree or at the crossroads. In Greek folk tradition crossroads were sacred to the goddess Hecate and they are liminal places where contact can be made with the spirit world. They are also sacred to the Greek god of wisdom Hermes and to his Norse counterpart, Woden or Odin. Originally Hermes was a god of the herds and fertility. His cult symbol was a block of stone or a standing stone carved with his face and an erect phallus. He later became the messenger of the gods, the guide to the dead and the deity of boundaries, between land and between Middle Earth and the spirit realm.

The uncultivated plots of land found near crossroads were some-times called No Man's Land, the Devil's Plot or the Devil's Acre. This signified that the area was a crossing point between the worlds. The crossroad was also often the place where the boundaries of several parishes met. In the olden days they were the sites of gallow trees and gibbets linking them with Odin as the Hanging Man and his sacrificial victims.

Crossroads were also places for practising dark magick, hence the old saying 'dirty work at the crossroads'. It is recorded that a 19th century witch from Sancreed, Cornwall tried to buy some cows from a local farmer. She offered him a fair price but he refused to sell them so she ill-wished him. In her own words: "I

95

went on my knees under a whitethorn tree by the crossroads and there, for the best part of the night, I called on the Powers till they helped me cast the spell that gave Old Jenny and his family plenty of junket and sour milk for a time" [15].

Sometimes witches met at the ancient sites dating from prehistoric times.. In 1667 a Bedfordshire woman called Elizabeth Pratt was accused of bewitching two children. She was said to have met with other witches at the Five Knells barrow on Dunstable Downs. The 17th century Scottish witch Isobel Gowdie met with her coven at the Auldearn standing stones in Nairn. Three witches living at Bluebell Hill in Kent gathered at the nearby burial chamber of Kit's Coty. The witches of Somerset convened at the Celtic hillfort of Cadbury Camp believed by some archaeologists who excavated it in the 1960s to be the site of the Arthurian Camelot.

In Snowdonia, North Wales the Penmaenwr stone circle was said to be a frequent haunt of witches. In Cornwall it was the Witch's Rock at Zennor, near Penzance, while in Cumbria it was the stone circle of Long Meg and her Daughters. This circle of standing stones was said to be the petrified remains of a witches coven and their female leader who were turned to stone by God for their wickedness. Such legends are obvious folk memories of the use of these ancient sites for the practice of the Craft.

The most famous prehistoric site associated with traditional witchcraft is the Rollright Stones on the Oxfordshire-Warwickshire border and not far from Stratford-on-Avon. The popular legend associated with the stones say that in ancient times a king, possibly Danish, was ambushed by a local witch as he and his army neared the stones. She said: "Seven strides shalt thou take, and if Long Compton thou can see, King of England thou shalt be". The king took the steps but as he reached a rise in the ground a large hillock suddenly rose up from the ground and obscured his view. The witch then turned the king and his men into stones, while she became an elder tree.

In the 19th century an Arthurian-type legend grew up in the area that there was a cave under the stone circle. Inside lay the king and his men and it was said they were only sleeping and would awake when they were needed. There are several interesting esoteric elements to this myth and the others surrounding the site. They include the sacredness of the land, its guardianship by a wise woman or priestess and her use of magickal earth energy to protect it, a landscape alignment which offers kingship, the witch's role as kingmaker, her transformation into an elder tree sacred to the Dark Goddess of the underworld, and the death and possible rebirth of the king and his warriors, sleeping in their tomb-womb of the Earth Mother under a sacred ring of ancient stones.

Reports of witch meetings at the Rollrights were compiled by the witch-hunters commission at nearby Oxford in Tudor times. A hundred years later in the reign of Charles I a 'Rollrighte wytch' was hanged after confessing to attending rites at the stone circle. In the 18th century it was reported that young people gathered on Midsummer's Day at the stones to make merry with cakes and ale'.

Witches sabbats were allegedly held at the site in the 1890s and 1900s. Before the last war there were rumours of a witchcraft revival in the area and in 1949 concealed observers watched five cloaked figures dancing around a goat-masked leader on Old May Day. They were dancing widdershins around the standing stone opposite the circle known as the King Stone.

The witch at the Rollrights was the guardian of the sacred site and this is a role well known in the Traditional Craft. At the Madron holy well in Cornwall, for instance, an 'elderly dame' attended the site in the 1870s. She was well-known locally as a charmer who used the healing waters of the well to cure skin diseases. At Fynnon Chwerthin holy well in Gwynedd, North Wales the place was haunted by the elemental servants of the local witch brood. These spirits were known locally as 'the little old men in black' from their appearance. In the 19th century an old witch lived in Hell's Wood, Monmouthshire. There was a local

97

tradition that a convent once stood in the wood, but this could be an older folk memory of a community of pagan priestesses who guarded the well in pre-Christian times.

In 1984 at Mouselow Hill, near Old Glossop in Derbyshire, an archaeological dig incurred the wrath of the local human guardians of a sacred site. The hill is crowned by a grove of oak trees and as soon as the team began their work they began to receive anonymous telephone calls. These calls warned them off and mentioned 'the Old Ways' and 'Horned figures'. When the dig was resumed in the summer of 1985 every member of the team had an accident on the site. The team leader became convinced that they were digging on a sacred site still being used for secret worship by an old tradition in the area. [16]

As the human guardians of ancient sites, traditional witches are in close contact with the 'psychic guardians' of the sacred landscape, who are sometimes called the *genii loci* or spirits of place. They can appear in many different forms including White Ladies, Black Dogs, ghostly horses, creatures which are half-human and half-animal, giant slugs, and perhaps today as the mysterious 'black pumas' of urban folk tale. Although we regard the sightings of out-of-place big black cats as a modern phenomena, they were reported as early as 1904 in the North Country, Southern England and South Wales. There were those at the time who fervently believed they could only be killed by a silver bullet rubbed with garlic and blessed by a priest.

Like the black panthers or pumas, not all place guardians are friendly to humans, especially if a sacred site has been vandalized or is under threat. Anyone who visits Stonehenge at present should ensure they are well psychically protected. There are also places in the sacred landscape (and in towns and cities) were malefic elemental forces are concentrated and can be felt by even the most non-sensitive. Witches says these are where the so-called 'black leys' or 'black streams' cross. Such dark places are often recognizable because they are accident 'black spots', badly haunted houses, 'cancer clusters' or sites (sights?) of manifestations of a demonic nature. The recent New Age craze for feng shui by the middle-classes may be an unconscious recognition of such places and the dangers they can represent on both a physical and psychic level.

The rituals used by traditionalist witches at the festivals are often simple and improvised. They do not 'use scripts and so to the outsider little seems to happen'. (17) At least not on the outer level. An example of the atmosphere and ambience of a traditional ritual is given in the following account: 'In a wooded island of oak, holly and hazel in the Greater London area a solemn ritual is taking place. One by one the attendees step forward, kneel to the Deities and pour their libations. each may say as little or as much as they wish in prayer; the dignity of the great oaks, the awesome presence of the God and Goddess, the quietness of the moment is often prayer enough. The libations poured, each person resumes his or her place in the circle. An owl hoots as the last libation is poured and the God and Goddess step forward to place the spiced cake and red wine in the mouths of the worshipper'. (18)

In traditional types of ritual what happens on the inner level is often more important then theatrical outer actions. This is why trance and deep meditation are regarded highly as methods for contacting the spirit world. The goals of this type of ritual have been described by a modern traditional witch as poetic vision in which the practitioner sees dreams, images and symbols; the vision of memory in which past lives are recalled; magical vision whereby the inner levels of being are contacted; religious vision by which the worshipper achieves a brief contact with Godhead; and, finally, the mystical vision when the devotee enters into union with the Godhead (19). It is the latter condition which is the ultimate quest in all genuine religions.

In contrast to trance and meditation, dancing can also be a very important aspect of traditional ritual, both for raising power and to celebrate the seasons. The following is a description for suitable dances for the seasonal cycle with their symbolism: 'At Yule there is the dance of the flaming wheel, while at Candlemas, the great festival of purification, there is the broom dance which sweeps out the old. With the return of life to the world from the underworld, spring sees the snake dance. The snake being a symbol of the fertile earth energy. For Beltane there is the spiral meeting dance, where the men and women all kiss on the outward spiral movement, and there is the Maypole dance for fertility. At Midsummer the dual aspects of the Sacred King are shown in the hobby horse dance, the head showing death and the pole the fertility stemming from it. A stag or ram's head would be equally appropriate at the end of the pole. Moving on to Lammas, the harvest and the cutting down of the grain, there is the sword dance, though sickles and reaping hooks are better used. And this leads us to autumn with the Lord of the Wild Hunt. Here the chain dance, fast, furious: and widdershins, is appropriate, sweeping all down into the dark depths. Lastly, Samhain has the maze dance for the journey to the Spiral Castle. The maze can be marked with leaves and alder, and its centre is often the cauldron'. [20]

The Chain Dance at the autumn equinox is based on the shapeshifting/ initiation legend of Ceridwen and Gwion. This, as we have seen, represents the underworld initiation of the God/hero by the Dark Lady. Alternatively it 'celebrates the transformation of the seasons and its dance is that of the pursuit of an animal by a predator' [21]. Traditionally the Chain dance is led by the Lady, with the Magister bringing up the rear. Hence the old saying: 'May the Devil take the hindmost'. Indoors lighted candles or tapers are held by the animal masked dancers, but outdoors torches or lanterns are carried in the processional dance.

The dancers go around the circle deosil, or sunways, and, if it is out of doors, they leave by the northern gate of the circle and process around the surrounding area before returning again in the north. During the dance a special song or rhyme is recited and the coven imitate the animals they are representing in each of the verses. In one version the animals are a wren, falcon or hawk, mouse, cat, hare, hound, fish and an otter. [22]

These ceremonial dances illustrate the Mythic Theme of the Wheel of the Year which is also contained within the mytho-poetic vision of the Journey of the God previously described. This theme in the form of traditional Craft described in this book, traces the progress of the God through the seasonal cycle from birth, to death, to rebirth. At first he is the Star Child born at Yule, then at Eostre he is bethrothed to the Goddess who is the Maiden, at Beltane they marry in the greenwood and consummate the sacred marriage, at midsummer he is the king stag at the height of his power ruling the land. Lammas brings with it death among the blood red poppies of the cornfield. At the autumn equinox the God returns to the underworld to rule from Hallows as the Lord of the Wildwood and the Wild Hunt. At Yule, when the Wheel turns anew, the Lord of Light is reborn from the Cauldron of Creation.

The Goddess is also transformed through her journey as the seasons change. She is the Old Crone or Dark Hag of Winter's Night, the Great Mother who gives birth to the sun child at Yule, the spring Maiden at Candlemas and the Flower Bride of Beltane. She is the Queen of Faery at Midsummer, but at Lammas she becomes the Destroyer who cuts the silver cord of the God.

As the witch god and goddess are shapeshifting, cthonic deities of the twilight, their dark and bright aspects change through the shifting pattern of the seasons. Behind the grinning foliate mask of Green Jack lurks the grim stag skull of the Wild Hunter. The Lady can be a hideous old hag or a beautiful faery woman. This is the key to understanding: the Wheel of the year and its turning.

Chapter Seven

Yuletíde & the Festíval of Lights

In the account of the Wheel for the year from Yule to Hallows that follows in the next few chapters, we will journey the path of the solar year and observe the changing pattern of the agricultural cycle. This journey will explore our Celtic, Germanic and Norse ancestral heritage along the way.

The four so-called 'fire festivals' are markers in the agricultural cycle and, in their present form, are basically Celtic in nature - although archaeologists have speculated that some festivals like Hallowe'en may date back to Neolithic times. The 'fire festivals' are Imbolc or Candlemas, Beltane or May Day, Lughnasadh or Lammas, and Samhain or Hallows. The spring and autumn equinoxes and the winter and summer solstices are markers or stations in the solar year and have a more Northern European flavour.

In the British folk calendar, influenced by incomers over the centuries, the Celtic and Nordic/Germanic festivals have been combined. This also reflects the Mythic Theme of the Wheel of the Year described in the version of the traditional Craft in this book. In exploring the esoteric symbolism of these festivals, the way they were and are celebrated and the theme that binds them together, we will be looking at examples in those folk customs and rural superstitions which can be identified as survivals of the old pagan ways [1] As we shall see, many of the superstitions regarding evil plants and trees, such as elder and hawthorn, and protective rites or charms against witches, faeries and evil spirits were a reaction by God-fearing country folk to the survival of pagan beliefs. In our journey around the Wheel we shall also be delving deeper into the nature of the witch god and goddess and how their story changes with the seasons.

The Saxons introduced the word 'Yule' to describe the midwinter festival around the winter solstice or the full moon in December and this is where the Wheel of the Year has its natural beginning. The word comes from the Old Norse *joi* or *jol*, which in turn relates to the Gothic *heul* and Anglo-Saxon *hweal*, meaning a wheel. The Saxons celebrated the midwinter solstice with a festival called Mother Night on December 24. This was dedicated to the goddesses Holda and Freyja and the female spirits in their retinue called the disir. It marked their New Year.

The Angle-Saxons, of course, were not the first Europeans to celebrate the winter solstice. At Newgrange in Ireland the famous prehistoric passage grave was built so that on the winter solstice a ray of sunlight penetrates the inner sanctum of the chamber. Therein it illuminates three spirals carved on a stone slab. This may have signified '...the sun fertilizing the 'body' of the Earth and so awakening her after her winter sleep to the renewed cycle of life' [2] It may also represent the (re) birth of the sun child in the womb of the Great Mother Goddess.

A similar event occurs at Maes Howe burial chamber on Orkney and several megalithic circles have alignments to the midwinter sunrise or sunset. At Stonehenge archaeologists and historians have recently speculated that at the winter solstice sunset the ancient people regarded the henge as a 'place between the worlds' or 'a gateway to the Otherworld' where the dead could be contacted and the living pass between the worlds. It is suggested that dancing, drumming and hallucinogenic plants may have been used to achieve trance states in such rituals.

In Irish mythology Newgrange is the home of the mysterious Tuatha de Danaan, or People of the goddess Danu. They were a mythical race of magicians with supernatural powers known as the Lords of Light. Myth says they descended from the sky on to the holy hill of Tara one Beltane. They have been compared with

103

the Watchers in the Biblical legend and identified as the pre-Celtic gods of ancient Ireland. In Celtic myth Newgrange is an '...Otherworld palace or festive hall, existing in an eternal timeless realm of the supernatural..It is the domain of the Gods, a place of perpetual festivities and a land where no one ever dies' [3]. It corresponds to the Summerland and Hollow Hill of the Traditional Craft and this description of it as an Otherworldly place probably dates back to pre-Celtic times.

In the 4th century the Church took over the winter solstice, when 'pagans celebrated the birth of the sun' [4] as the time of the Nativity once they realised newly converted Christians were also attending the pagan midwinter rites. The Romans celebrated the solstice as the birthday of Sol Invictus or 'the unconquered sun'. December 25 was also the birth date of the Persian god of light, Mithras, whose cult was popular among the Roman legions and was a rival to early Christianity. Although Jesus was probably born in the autumn, the Church made the period of the winter solstice his official birthtime. By the 10th century both the pagan and the Christian terms 'Yule' and 'Christmas' were in common use to describe the midwinter festivities.

The winter solstice is the shortest day of the year with the longest night. It has been called the time 'when the sun, the true country god of life, begins to climb the sky and turn the year towards summer and green leaves.' [5] In fact this is not strictly true as solstice actually means 'sun still'. It indicates a short period of time in the year when the sun appears to stand still in the sky, before it begins its gradual ascent towards the vernal equinox in March. It is several weeks into January before any real difference is seen in the length of the daylight hours.

Esoterically the midwinter and solstice period of Yule and the Twelve Days is known as 'the inbetween time' or 'the time between time'. As the sun appears to stand still in the sky the Old Year is dying and the New Year waits to be born. It is a strange and special period and this is still acknowledged in secular society by tales of 'Christmas magic' and miracles or ghost stories told around the fire, or today on the wireless or television. These are folk memories of the ancient past when the darkest period of the year was a magickal and unearthly time.

Various folk rituals were performed at Yule to welcome the rebirth of the sun or encourage its return by sympathetic magick and banish the evil spirits of winter. These often involved the lighting of special fires and one folk custom of this type, which has been successfully adopted by modern traditional witches, is the Yule Log. Traditionally of ash or oak, the 'male' trees of the God, it was a large branch collected from the woods on Christmas Eve. Anyone who passed the Log on its journey to the house was obliged to bow and raise their hat. If they refused then bad luck would follow in the New Year. Once in the house the Log was libated with cider or beer and placed in the hearth. It was then lit from a piece of the previous year's Log. It was either burnt on Christmas Eve or, if large enough, re-lit during the festive Twelve Days each evening. It was symbolic of the sun shining through the twelve months of the year. [6]

In Scotland the Yule Log was significantly called the 'Christmas Old Wife' and it represented the ritual burning of the Cailleach or winter hag goddess. The head of the household brought in a withered tree stump or a twisted branch and this was then carved to represent an old woman. It was thrown on the fire to loud cheers, toasts of whisky and then the telling of ghost stories into the night. [7] In Cornwall it was a male figure (the God) who was chalked on to the log before it was consumed by the flames.

The symbolism of the God and Goddess come together in the old Somerset custom where the traditional Yule Log is replaced by an ash faggot tied together with willow withies. It was lit with charred twigs saved from the previous year's fire. The ashes of the Yule Log or the faggot were either kept as a lucky charm or were scattered on the fields to bring fertility to the land.

In some urban areas of the country the Yule Log was replaced by a Yule Candle. This was and is a useful substitute in homes with central heating and no open fire. It was a large red or white candle decorated with glitter and holly sprigs. Traditionally it was lit at bedtime or midnight on Christmas Eve and allowed to burn all night. Alternatively, it was lit every evening after dusk for a short period during the Twelve Days. In the modern Traditional Craft the Yule Candle stands on the altar and each member of the coven lights a candle from it.

Strange to relate, but the blazing round Christmas Pudding is a folk memory of the rising sun at midwinter. This is indicated by the curious folk tradition surrounding its making in Sussex in bygone times. The mixture was stirred sunwise 'three times three' using only a wooden spoon. No metal was allowed near the pudding. Three wishes were made as it was mixed using thirteen ingredients. A silver coin was placed inside and whoever found it was said to have good luck throughout the year. Thirteen puddings were made in each batch, but only twelve were eaten. The 'unlucky' thirteenth had to be given away during the Twelve Days to a passing stranger, usually a gypsy or tramp. This all connects with the the solar and lunar year, with its thirteen moons, and to top it off the holly spring on top of the blazing pudding is symbolic of the solar god.

The God at midwinter is represented as the sun child and in folk mythology by the magickal figure of Father Christmas. In the 17th century he was known as Lord Christmas or Old Father Christmas and he was an old gentleman in a furry hooded gown. He carried a knobbly stick or club and wore a crown of holly leaves. As such he was the symbolic representation or spirit of midwinter. In 1809 the American writer Washington Irving seems to have 'invented' the modern version of Father Christmas. He depicted him as a jolly, fat figure with a long white beard, dressed in fur, riding through the sky in his sleigh pulled by reindeer and distributing gifts to children. This was a combination of the Olde English Father Christmas and the European saint St Nicholas.

In his archetypal form this midwinter folk figure has connections with Odin or Woden, who rides through the night sky on his eight-legged horse Sleipnir at midwinter. He brings gifts to his loyal followers and he is also the male leader of the Wild Hunt that rides the skies collect ing the souls of the dead. As we have seen, the female leader of the Hunt was Dame Holda or Frau Holle. She also rode at midwinter with a company of female spirits known as 'Good Women' (another name for the witches in Middle Ages) and distributed gifts.

The winter goddess was also represented at this time of the year by the folk character known as the 'Queen of Light'. Her festival was widely celebrated in Northern Europe on December 13, St Lucy's Day. Lucy or Lucia, whose name means light, was an early Christian saint martyred for her beliefs. She was to be burnt at the stake but the flames refused to harm her. Instead she was stabbed to death. It has been suggested that St Lucy was a version of Freyja in her solar aspect [8].

In Scandinavia Lucy Day was often called Little Yule. On that day bonfires were lit and a young woman was crowned as the Lucy Queen or Bride. She wore a white dress and was crowned with a wreath of twigs holding nine burning candles. Children attended her wearing grotesque masks as trolls and the spirits of winter. She visited all the houses and farms in the area bestowing her blessings and good luck. In Austria it was believed that the witches flew on St Lucy's Day [9]. All this links her to the Maiden aspect of the Goddess who is preparing to take over from the Hag at Candlemas.

Another aspect of the winter goddess who is acknowledged around the solstice is the third Norn known as Skadi. She has been described as the winter and destroyer aspect of the earth goddess Nerthus, mother of Freyja, and she was popularly known as The Shadow or the Veiled One. Skadi was associated with the North or Pole Star and was the 'Dark Hag Goddess of the frozen North with its high mountains and icy wastes' [10] She was and is an archetypal Snow Queen in silver furs and 'the huntress with bow and arrows, travelling on skis, or behind a sledge of ice crystals (drawn by wolves?), dressed in snow-white furs...' [11]

Another version of the God appears in popular folk tradition as the ghostly stranger who appeared at midnight on Christmas Eve. He came as a tall, dark man known as 'the lucky bird' with a sprig of greenery in his hat to 'let Christmas in'. In Lancashire a silver coin was left out for him by the hearth. He was not the only pagan person out and about for, imitating the Wild Hunt, the Holly Riders visited homes in northern Somerset after dark. They rode on Exmoor ponies, with holly in their hats and sang carols in exchange for cake, cider and pennies [12].

The 'lucky bird' sounds like a version of the Holly King and some traditional witches today recognize a ritual combat between him and the Oak King at midwinter. This was symbolized in the folk calendar by the hunting of the wren which took place at this time. In the old nursery rhyme it is the wren who kills Cock Robin or Robin Redbreast, who is the God in his summer aspect as the Green Man and Robin Hood.

The medieval practice of placing evergreens in churches, and later in private homes, dates from paganism. The most popular were holly, ivy, mistletoe, rosemary and box. The holly and the ivy are seen by country folk as 'male' and 'female' trees. They are known at Christmas as the Holly Boy (the God) and the Ivy Girl (the Goddess).

As the sun child born at the darkest time of the year, the God is seen at Yule as the stag with a sun wheel between his antlers. This is a very ancient image and its association with the Horned God is connected to the '.....virility of the beast, coupled with the autumn-shedding and spring-growth of the antlers which imitates the cyclical, seasonal image of winter and summer, and indeed also the winter and summer loss and regrowth of leaves on deciduous trees, and the waxing and waning of the strength according to the season' [13]. This image of the solar stag dates back at least to the Bronze Age and is also found in the Celtic period and Iron Age Scandinavia.

The God at midwinter was also the trickster, anarchic, jester figure from folklore known as the Lord of Misrule who was associated with Twelfth Night and the end of the Twelve Days of festivities and merrymaking. He is a folk character who appears in the Middle Ages and may have been inspired by the Roman saturnalia. That was the festival when masters and slaves swopped places during the midwinter festival dedicated to the god of agriculture Saturn. The Church already had its Feast of Fools when a boy Bishop or Abbot of Misrule was elected to preside over almost blasphemous church services, and the idea of a secular Lord of Misrule was eagerly adopted by the royal court in the late medieval period.

The Lord of Misrule was selected by a form of divination dating back to the dark days of human sacrifice. He was called the King of the Bean and was selected by choosing a cake containing a bean from a plate of many others. The Lord of Misrule represents the powers of darkness and chaos who rule the 'inbetween time' and have to be propitiated unless they do humans harm. Yuletide is a time of role reversal, anarchy, rebellion, the challenging of social norms and the defying of convention. As the Old Year died and the New Year began it was a time when the trickster spirits of winter had their last fling and the 'gates between the world', ruled over by the two-faced Janus, opened and closed.

As late as the 12th century the Bishop of Exeter had ordered penances for those who still celebrated the New Year with 'heathen practices'. This included, as we have seen, dressing up in animal costumes and as an 'old woman' (the hag goddess of winter). One survival of these 'heathen practices' was the Christmas Bull who appeared at Yule or New Year. He was a farm worker dressed up in the hide of a bull, complete with horns, tail and hooves. This creature processed around the farms while its attendants beat it with sticks. Sometimes the tail of the bull was lit and in a bizarre ceremony the smoke was inhaled. This was said to protect the household from bad luck in the coming year [14]. Midnight on New Year's Eve was commonly known as Bull's Noon, suggesting a reversal of the normal idea of time.

In the West Country the Christmas Bull was a man wearing or holding a bull's head on a pole and concealed beneath a sheet. The most famous version was the Dorset Ooser or Wooser, the mask of a bull passed down through the generations and in use until about 1900. In Warwickshire the Bull was known as 'Old Brazen Face'. This was a popular name for the sun and indicates he was a version of Old Hornie in his solar aspect.

On New Year's Eve ashes were cleaned from the hearth so a new fire could be lit after midnight. When the tall dark stranger (the God again) came first-footing the acceptable gifts were salt, bread and coal representing the essentials of life - food and warmth. In Hertfordshire the Goddess was not forgotten as cakes in female shape were traditionally baked on the morning of New Year's Day. A special cake in Derbyshire was made from the eggs of the winter goddess' sacred bird, the goose. The first new moon of the year had to be bowed to nine times when it was seen in the sky for the first time. This ensured good luck for the next twelve moons.

Twelfth Night, as we saw in the previous chapter, was when the apple orchards were wassailed for a good summer and autumn crop. This was also a time when torches were carried around the fields to purify them with fire ready for the ploughing and sowing in the spring. In village halls the mumming plays were performed, featuring the Old Woman, the spirit of winter who paradoxically gives birth, Green George and the Fool who dies and is reborn. The plough was blessed and taken out into the fields to symbolically cut the first furrow. Into this was placed the corn dolly from last year's harvest - a substitute for the *blot* or blood sacrifices performed in pagan times when the new year dawned.

Imbolc is celebrated on February 1 and it was Christianised as the Purification of the Virgin Mary in the temple after childbirth. It was also known as Candlemas and this derives from the old pagan custom of lighting torches in honour of the winter goddess at this time. The Church transformed this into the ceremony of lighting a candle for the Virgin Mary and having a special Mass to bless the candles that will be used during the year. Imbolc derives its Gaelic name from the first milking of the ewes which was regarded as a sign that the spring was on its way. Traditional witches call it the Festival of Lights or The Quickening.

The festival is sacred to the Celtic solar and fire goddess Brigid, or 'Great One', 'Fiery Arrow' or 'Bright One'. She was Christianized as St Bridget or St Bride (pronounced Breed) and was said to be the midwife and foster-mother of Jesus. In the legend of St Bridget it was said she was born 'neither within the house or without it' In fact her mother had one foot over the threshold of a house and one outside when she gave birth. This indicates Brigid's pagan origins as a deity of the liminal 'inbetween time'. In her case it is the transition between winter and spring.

Brigid was a goddess with many attributes. She ruled sacred fire, healing prophecy, poetry, childbirth and smithcraft. Some writers have linked her with the Celtic goddess Brigantia, 'Mighty Queen', who was worshipped in Northern Britain, and with the Morrigan, the triple battle goddess of death and sexuality. Brigid has also been linked with the Greek goddess Minerva who was worshipped here in the Romano-British period. As a smith she is responsible for casting the Cauldron of Inspiration and Regeneration and her role is very much as a cultural exemplar.

In some versions of the Hereditary Craft, Brigid has an important role as the Bright Goddess. As such she allegedly personifies the right hand spiral. 'She is the female polarity of that creative energy which interpolates the Earth and is focused at specific sites on its surface. Holy wells and sacred springs were dedicated to Bride once it was determined they could not be contaminated by the cyclic evil which is regularly released from Mother Earth...the Old People of our Isles understood that the pure and chaste goddess was the mother of both inspiration and destruction. Love, poetry, prophecy and inspiration were actively fostered and heightened by 'tapping' the 'leys' at propitious times'. [15]

The primary symbol of Brigid is the sun-wheel or fire-wheel and it is a version of the ancient swastika that represents the cosmic life force. Brigid's sun-wheel flows left to right in the deosil movement of the sun, unlike the reversed Nazi version. This sun-wheel appears in the celebrations of Imbolc and is known as St Bridget's Cross. It is made from intertwined rushes and is hung above doors, windows and the cradles of babies to ward off evil.

In rural areas Candlemas was known as 'the quickening of the year' or 'the budding' when the first flowering of the snowdrops heralded the coming of the spring. Although the snowdrop was only first recorded in this country at the end of the 16th century, it has since become widely associated with Candlemas and Brigid as the spring maiden. This is reflected in its folk names of Candlemas Bells and February's Fair Maid.

In the Western Isles of Scotland, Brigid was regarded as a fertility goddess with an influence over the outcome of the harvest. She is comparable to the aspect of the corn goddess we shall encounter later at Lammas. In the 17th century the Scottish custom was to take a sheaf of oats and dress it in female clothing like a doll. They put this in a basket and laid a club beside it. This was 'Bride's Bed' and next morning they looked in the ashes of the fire to see if there was an impression of Bride's club. If it was there then a good harvest would be gathered in that year. If there was no sign then it was taken as a bad omen and a poor harvest.

Country folklore said that our native snake, the adder, first stirs from its hibernation on Candlemas Day. In Scotland the chant was:

"Today is the day of Bride,

The serpent shall come from the hole,

The Queen will come from the mound,

I will not molest the serpent,

The serpent will no t molest me."

This symbolises the emergence of the spring goddess from the Hollow Hill of the underworld [16]. The serpent is a symbol of the earth energy that once more starts to flow through the land fertilizing and revitalising it with new life.

In Celtic mythology the dark season from Hallows to Candlemas was ruled over by the Cailleach or Old Woman. She is said to live on Ben Nevis and on Winter's Night she washes her plaid until it is white and this act brings the first snow to the mountains. She is also the owner of a black wand which she uses to blast the vegetation, bring the leaves tumbling down from the trees and raise the winter storms. She and Brigid are the two aspects of the Goddess as 'She Who Dwells Below, the Goddess of the Underworld, the Dark Mother, and She Who Dwells Above, the Universal Goddess of the Stars' [17].

In Scottish legend, the Cailleach imprisons Brigid during the long winter inside her cave on Ben Nevis. As in fairy tales, Brigid is rescued by a knight on a shining steed. He is Aengus of the White Steed and he lives in Tir-na-nog, the Land-of-the-Ever-Young in the Western ocean. He sees Brigid in a dream and rides to her aid so they are united on Brigid's Day.

An alternative legend. sees Brigid and Cailleach as one entity. On Imbolc Eve the hag goddess of winter travels to the Land-of-the-ever-Young. There she finds the Well of Youth and drinks deeply from it. Immediately she is transformed into a beautiful maiden and her black blasting rod turns into a white healing wand. At a touch of this wand the grass turns green and the snowdrops begin to blossom [18].

In the Traditional Craft the Festival of Lights is a time of birth, purification and initiation. It is a time for spring cleaning, both physically and spiritually, and for driving out the spirit of the Old Year. This is done by performing a banishing ritual and cleansing the circle or meeting ground with salt afterwards. This is also traditionally the last outing for the Wild Hunt. If the festival is performed out of doors, then after the ritual the coven will leave the site to the sound of a horn and making wild noises to imitate the Hunt in full cry [19] After Candlemas, as the days lengthen and the light increases, it is soon time to think about the rites of spring and the coming of summer.

Chapter Eight
The Rites of Spring

The vernal or spring equinox falls between March 20 and 22 and is regarded by most people as the first day of the spring season. The weather centre however date this event from March 1 to divide the year neatly into three month seasons. Country people saw February as a spring month with the appearance of the early flowers as a herald of spring arriving. In fact dividing the year into equal three month seasons based on the equinoxes and solstices dates back to a 1st century BCE Roman astronomer.

The equinoxes in spring and autumn are the two dates in the year when the sun is precisely positioned over the equator at noon. In theory on those date day and night are of equal length i.e. 12 hours each. In reality, due to the refraction or bending of the sun's rays as they pass through the Earth's atmosphere, this magickal event never actually occurs exactly. There is always a few minutes difference in the sun rising and setting above the horizon as we see it.

In the spring the days are beginning to get longer and the sun rises in the sky. With this increase in daylight hours there comes the natural urge to 'spring clean', to throw out all the unwanted physical objects collected during the dark season, and also to clear out bad habits built up in the preceding twelve months. This process often involves symbolically cleaning the house from top to bottom for the 'new season', changing the furniture around and buying new clothes and household goods for the summer.

Spring proper is when nature slowly awakes from its winter's sleep and the first green buds begin to appear representing new life and beginnings. Animals emerge from their hibernation, birds begin to build nests and the dawn chorus gets louder as the male birds stake out their territory. Generally people begin to feel more refreshed and energetic as the nights draw out and gradually the weather begins to get warmer.

The spring full moon in March is known as the Hare Moon or the Awakening Moon. It is during this period that the cosmic tides change. We move from the cleansing or destructive tide that has ruled since the winter solstice to the sowing tide. This is a time for new beginnings on a personal, magickal and spiritual level as we sow the seeds that will be harvested later in the year. It is the time when 'the young ram-headed god is complimented by the willow) enchanting moon maiden' [1]. It is at the spring equinox that the sun enters the Zodiac sign of Aries the. Ram, the symbol of the virile young Horned God lusting for life and experiences.

The vernal equinox was Christianized as Easter which is the festival mourning and celebrating the death and resurrection of Jesus. The early Celtic Church originally celebrated Easter at the same time as the Jewish Passover. This reflected the fact that the first Christian Church in Jerusalem founded after the crucifixion followed many Judaic customs. The Roman Church fixed the date of Easter as the first Sunday after the full moon that followed the spring equinox. This dating was eventually accepted by the British Church in the 7th century after many years of debate and controversy. The old method of dating Easter based on the Passover was kept by the Eastern Orthodox Church, but recently they have agreed to accept the Roman practice.

Many pagan beliefs and symbols survived in the Christian celebration of Easter. The most obvious is the name itself which comes from a Germanic goddess Oestara or Eostre of the spring and dawn. In modern German Easter is Ostern. In Greek myth she was Aurora, the daughter of a Titan (the primordial gods of chaos) and the mother of the four winds. She was the daughter of Jord, or Mother Earth, in Germanic mythology. In the 19th century young people were still setting up altars to her covered with flowers on Easter Day [2].

116

Other Easter symbols, such as the Easter Bunny or Easter Hare, the Easter Egg and hot-cross buns are also pre-Christian. The hare was the sacred animal of Nerthus, Freyja and Eostre and so it is not surprising that it was also one of the shapeshifting forms taken by witches. Today it is still an important totem in the Traditional Craft. In the past at Easter the traditional dish was hare. Some people however refused to touch it as there was a taboo dating back to pagan times that it was unlucky to kill or eat hares.

Ancient rituals of hunting the hare at Eastertime have survived in the traditional spring hare hunts across the country. The taboo about hunting hares meant that often the quarry was a dead cat's skin soaked in aniseed water and dragged behind a horse for the hounds to follow [3]. Other events that still continue to this day, like the famous Waterloo Cup, use live wild hares.

The Easter Bunny may be a modern form of the hare and it is an obvious symbol of fertility and increase in springtime. It may also be connected with the Tinner's Rabbit symbol found in parts of Cornwall and linked by some folklorists with the survival of the Old Religion. This symbol can be found carved in several churches on Dartmoor which were either restored or built by the owners of the local tin mines. This curious symbol consists of three rabbits chasing each other to form a triangle with only three ears between them. It is claimed this is an old alchemical sigil for tin or a pagan symbol of the moon goddess. It has also been linked to the Easter Bunny and witchcraft [4].

Tinsmiths, who gave their name to the tribe of tinkers, as gypsies were excellent smiths, probably also worked magick as well as metal like their cousins the blacksmiths. It has been claimed that the tinsmith was commonly known as a whitesmith and this linked him with the bright elves of Nordic mythology who teach humans ancient wisdom and knowledge. The black elves are said to be associated with the blacksmiths and are 'forgers of shapes that will manifest in the material world' [5]. This duality of black and white fits in neatly with the equality of hours of darkness and light at the vernal equinox.

The Easter Egg is another potent symbol of birth, fertility and new life which are all celebrated in the rites of spring. Many ancient creation myths feature the birth of the universe or its life forms from an egg. The Neolithic sun bird goddess survives in the fairy tale about the goose who laid the golden eggs. The egg was also closely associated to witchery, as a rather unlikely magical vehicle for getting to the witches' sabbat. Less fantastically, they have been used for divination from the yolk, as a sacrificial substitute and in spell casting [6].

The traditional hot-cross bun consumed in their millions on Good Friday has its origins in the sacred cakes made by Roman bakers as offerings to the moon goddess Diana. The equal-armed cross design represented the four phases of the moon. Offerings of these cakes were made to Hecate and buried at crossroads. Although many modern Wiccans wear pentagrams, traditional witches have the equal-armed cross in a circle. It is a multi-faceted symbol and can represent the sun, the moon, or the four elements and all contained in a circle symbolising spirit.

Towards the end of April, and just a week or so before Beltane or May 1st, is St George's Day. George was Greek and it is believed his cult was introduced into England by crusaders returning from the Holy Land. In the 13th century he replaced St Edward as the English patron saint by popular demand. In the legend of St George he is a brave knight who rescues a fair virgin or maiden from a dragon who is holding her prison in a cave.

The symbolism of this legend is connected with the coming of spring; the knight is the young God fully armed in his warrior aspect, the 'virgin' is the spring goddess and the dragon is the life force stirring within the cave, or the womb of Mother Earth. This symbolism is underlined by the story that George is martyred and then, Christ-like, rises from the dead.

The medieval Christian legend of George and the Dragon goes back to the myth of the Middle Eastern god Bel who slew the sea-beast Tiamat [7]. In the Canaanite myth it is Baal who killed the serpent, died, went to the underworld and was rescued by his sister- consort Anat. In Greek myth it is Zeus, the father of the Gods, who slays the 'great serpent' Typhon

The Christians associated the serpent or dragon with Satan. In the Biblical myth of the War in Heaven St Michael battles Lucifer and his rebel angels. The archangel of light, first-born of God, is cast down to Earth and becomes the Lord of the World. An emerald falls from his crown as he falls and is eventually carved into the cup used by Jesus at the Last Supper. Lucifer, often wrongly equated with Satan, is described as 'the great dragon' or the 'old serpent'

This eternal struggle between a male god and a serpent has been interpreted by some modern feminists in terms of the suppression of ancient Goddess worship by the patriarchal Aryan culture. In many cultures the serpent was feminine and 'the coiling path of the serpent, like the great rivers of the Earth, winding from mountain to sea, traces the spiralling of the life force as it travels from one dimension to another' [8].

However, like many feminist ideas and concepts, it is a simplistic explanation for the demonisation of the serpent by patriarchy. The truth is, as always, slightly more complex. In the legend of St George, for instance, he is 'closely associated with the eternal motif of death and rebirth and the battle between good and evil, light and darkness, summer and winter, which lies at the heart of the mythic Wheel of the Year and the pagan drama of divine kingship and the sacrificed god' [9].

St George also appears as a folk character in the Yule and Twelfth Night mummers' plays with their mythic theme of death and rebirth. Brigid, as we have seen, is the spring goddess who conjures the serpent from its winter hibernation in the mound or Hollow Hill. By the old calendar, St George's Day used to be on May 4 and was therefore part and parcel of the Beltane festival.

Some folklorists have linked George with the Green Man, the Jack- in-the-Green of the late 18th century sweep processions. It has even been suggested that, as the patron of the royal Order of the Garter, St George was linked in some way with the 'divine right' of the sacred king and a breeding programme at Beltane to bring old souls into incarnation. In this interesting, if highly speculative, scenario George guarded and inspired members of a chosen order of sacred kings or sacrificial victims, whose blood-line was probably inherited from the female side' [10]. This theory links to the legend of the Holy Grail as the pagan Cauldron of Inspiration and Regeneration, to the inner mysteries of the Arthurian mythos or Matter of Britain, to the mystical concept of 'sacred blood and sacred land', and to the Mythic Theme in traditional witchcraft as described in this book.

The rites of spring in Bronze and Iron Age Northern Europe were carried out to stimulate vegetation growth, to bring rain for the

The Green Man (13th century France)

seeds to sprout and encourage a good crop in the coming harvest. These rites are represented on Bronze Age rock carvings found in Jutland and Denmark. They show an ithyphallic naked man ploughing with oxen and carrying a small tree or bush, a man and woman having sex in a 'spring wedding', a man fornicating with a cow and carvings of a tree, stag and serpent. A Bronze Age stone disc from Denmark also show a man and woman reaching out to embrace each other. The man has an erection and the woman stands in front of a Tree of Life. The stone has a hole in its centre and the two figures are surrounded by a circle or hedge of foliage. All these carvings have been identified by archaeologists as symbols of spring and the life force, possibly associated with the cult of a Northern European horned god in the form of a stag [11].

The Goddess, of course, was not far away. The solar or sky god of ancient Scandinavia, with his horns, sacred axe and twin brother, is depicted with an earth goddess wearing her distinctive corded skirt, large hooped earrings and long hair. It has been suggested that this earth goddess was imported into Northern Europe from the south in the Neolithic Age by early migrating farmers. One rock carving of a woman and a sexually aroused man, with a body in the form of a cross in a circle, may be an image of the 'sacred marriage' between the sky god and the earth goddess. This sympathetic act of fertility magick took place in the spring to awaken the life-force in nature.

The end of April and most of May in the northern hemisphere is ruled over by the Zodiac sign of Taurus the Bull. The bull is a neglected form of the horned witch god, but one that dates back to the Bronze Age at least. In Cretan and Greek mythology the bull is associated with the maze or labyrinth and the Minotaur - the half-bull, half-human creature that receives the sacrifice of young virgins. The hero Theseus descended into the underground labyrinth to hunt down and kill the bull-beast. He was helped to find his way back to the upper world by a thread or ball of wood given to him by the king of Crete's daughter, Ariadne.

Ariadne

Ariadne in fact is a humanised version of the spring goddess. She is also the goddess of Fate or the Spider Goddess and in the Cretan legend she assists the hero in his guest to achieve his wyrd. As the Spider Goddess or Black Widow she can also sacrifice the hero using her noose made of twisted cobwebs, so he becomes the Hanged Man on the World Tree. As in the Cretan legend, she can give life, but she can also take it away for she is both the Bright and Dark Goddess, the creator and the destroyer.

As the Spider Goddess she controls the Web of Wyrd and is the ruler of the thirteen moon calendar. She is the ruler of the so-called thirteenth sign of the Zodiac, Arachne, from May 16 to June 13 [12]. In the Celtic myths Ariadne is Arianrhod the Lady of the Silver Wheel, who rules Caer Sidi, the turning or spinning castle, which is the Castle of the Roses in some Craft traditions. We will be meeting her later in the book.

Mazes, spiral and labyrinths are feminine symbols of the Goddess and can be found carved in prehistoric burial mounds. In springtime the young God and the spring Goddess meet in the centre of the mystic maze for a lovers' tryst. 'We can imagine the young Goddess taking off her white cloak and revealing herself in scarlet splendour, copper discs twinkling around her hem and ankles' [13].

In Scandinavian folk tradition this meeting survives in a game played by young couples. The boy walks the maze and finds a girl standing at its centre who plays the role of a princess. This game 'may be a survival of a pagan ritual which involved a human hero fighting a god of darkness who is holding captive the sun goddess at the centre of the labyrinth' [14].

German mazes were associated with the election of a May King organised by a guild of cobblers and shoemakers. The May King danced into the maze using what is described as the 'lapwing step' along a path strewn with flowers. This dance, involving a skipping motion, has been identified with the 'crane dance' of Theseus and his warriors danced in ancient Crete. This in turn links with the Heron King and Hawthorn Queen, the sun god and moon goddess, who dance the maze in spring to reactivate nature and the earth energies.

Maypoles were sometimes erected in the centre of the old turf mazes combing the image of the phallic World Tree with the spiral of the Goddess. In England some mazes had standing stones or trees in their centres. The famous Saffron Walden maze in Essex had an ash tree in its centre representing the Yggdrasil in Norse mythology. At Louth in Lincolnshire there was a large stone which was later replaced by a Christian cross. When the Church took over the maze it became a representation of the journey of the pilgrim to Jerusalem, or the route taken by the soul to heaven.

Some of the Scandinavian mazes are found in sacred groves formerly used for the worship of Nerthus. In these groves in the spring the marriage between the God and Goddess was re-enacted by a priest and priestess. Mazes are also to be found in burial grounds in Northern Europe. As we have seen spirals and mazes are also a feature of the interiors of prehistoric burial chambers like Newgrange in Ireland and Bryn Celli Ddu in North Wales.

The maze can be a symbolic entrance to the underworld and in ancient times it is believed by archaeologists that burial chambers were used for religious rites, including initiations, as well as for the safe storage of the remains of the dead. The hero who travels through the maze or labyrinth is therefore undergoing the underworld initiation at the hands of the Dark Goddess. The maze dance is repeated at Hallowe'en, the opposite period of the year to Beltane, when the God rules the underworld. At the dark time of the year it is the dance of the Lame God who limps or drags his left leg. The hero emerging from the maze in spring is the return of the Son of Light, while at Hallows he is the dying sun whose path takes it down into the underworld.

The 'sacred marriage' of the human representatives of the Lord and Lady at the spring equinox or at Beltane is linked with the cult of divine kingship and the concept of the *sang rael* or 'sacred blood' sometimes symbolised by the Cauldron or Grail. In the fateful meeting in the maze between the young Horn God and his Spring Maiden or Flower Bride, the relationship between the young lovers is stronger and deeper then the mere primal urges of physical desire, sexuality and reproduction. By the old custom the priest and priestess are twin souls, brother and sister, in spirit if not in reality. In our modern age incest is outlawed as both a social taboo and a crime. It is therefore difficult for us to understand, or condone, ancient cultures where brother and sister marriages and unions passed on the royal blood or the priestly caste. These were earthly reflections of the relationships between Isis and Osiris in Egypt and Freyr and Freyja in Northern Europe for instance.

On an esoteric level, as we have evolved beyond these atavistic practices in a physical context, this custom represents the passing on of the 'witch blood' or 'faery blood' along hereditary and spirit lines from the Divine First Parents. As a traditional Cheshire witch explains it in the context of the Craft: 'Many would scoff at the suggestions of 'elven blood', but it is the bearers of such who make the traditional witches...These people have that special spark of consciousness and perception about them; it sets them apart from others...' [15].

This continuity of the bloodline is more important in the mysteries of Beltane and Midsummer when the marriage of the divine lovers has taken place and been consummated. Then, by the power and will of the Goddess, the young Horn God is mated to the land and takes on the fated role of the Sacred King. The meeting in the springtime maze foreshadows the events of summer and the autumn.

The Spider Goddess or Black Widow is sometimes connected in a mythic sense with the Queen Bee ruling over the hive and its drones. Bees have always been regarded as important because of their almost magickal power to create honey from the nectar of flowers. Honey was and is regarded as an 'elixir of life' per-meated as with the essence of the life force. This accounts for the large sales of products such as Royal Jelly. In ancient times bees were a symbol of regeneration because they were said to be born in the carcasses of bulls. Mead, made from honey and the fruit of immortality, apples, was always a sacred drink for ritual use in Northern Europe among both the Celts and Nordics.

The bee however has a sting and the male dies after mating with the Queen Bee, as does the Horned God when summer reaches its end. His last drink is a ritual draught of mead. In reality the bee mysteries are connected with 'fertility and death encompassing the Maid, the Queen and the Crone, who lays out the slain king in the beehive shaped tomb' [16].

In the folklore calendar Beltane was not only the time for orgiastic revels to mark the coming of summer, but also for more serious rituals to protect the land and the livestock. Beltane was when the castle and sheep were turned out into their summer pastures or taken up into the hills. In post-Christian times protective methods used to guard the animals from harm were extended to humans who were believed to face danger from the activities of witches and faeries.

One of the earliest Christian references to the 'fires of Baal' comes from an Irish monk in the 10th century who said they were kindled at the beginning of the summer season by the druids. Two fires were lit a few yards apart and cattle were driven through the gap to protect them from disease before they were let out to pasture. Bel in fact means 'bright', hence Beltane is 'bright fire', but it is possible the monk was referring to the Canaanite god of fertility Baal who was often used in describing pagan rites by clerics who regarded the gods in the Old Testament as demons.

The underlying pagan nature of the Bel fires is emphasised by the taboos surrounding them. They had to be prepared using nine woods, for instance, and in Wales a team of men were specially chosen to light the May Day balefire. Before starting work they had to remove all metal items from their clothing. They then went into the woods to collect the nine types of wood and the fire had to be lit by natural means. Again the use of metal was prohibited [17]. A trench or ditch was dug around the fire to make a protective circle or barrier.

In the 1900s there were still reports of 'incidents' at the Beltane fires. For instance, if there were an outbreak of disease among the herd farmers would throw a live calf into the flames. In the Scottish Highlands the women prepared a male lamb 'without blemish' for the May Day feast which was shared with friends, neighbours and relatives 'for the increase of the flock'. Less subtly, offerings of milk, honey, butter and eggs were left at the Beltane fire sites 'for the faeries'. As we saw in Chapter Six, there were also atavistic echoes of human sacrifice at the fires.

Young people often spent the night in vigil at the Beltane fire so they could greet the rising sun at dawn. Torches were lit from the balefire and carried around the fields by young men. They circled three times deosil to imitate the movement of the sun. The torches were then carried home to light the first fire of the summer.

In Roman Catholic countries, May was the special month of the Virgin Mary hence the 'merry month of May'. In Spain her image is carried through the streets decked with flowers as if she was the May Queen herself. However, in England, in the late medieval masques and folk rites to celebrate May Day the May King and Queen were Robin Hood and Maid Marian. It has been proposed that Robin Hood and his Merry Men were a 'Grand Master and his coven' [18], but this seems unlikely. The 19th century theory that he was a woodland spirit or god of the woods has however been accepted by many traditional witches. To them Robin is '..on a mythical level the summer aspect of the witch god and as such is linked with divine figures such as Woden, Herne, Puck and Robin Goodfellow. He is also the Green Man or Jack-in-the-Green, who appears in the Beltane revels as the May King' [19].

One of the central symbols of Beltane was and is still the Maypole. Various theories have been put forward to explain the origin of this blatantly phallic object. At one level it is the Tree of Life as depicted in the Bronze Age rock carvings and associated with the sexual rites of spring . In Roman times March 25 (Lady Day in the modern Christian calendar) was the festival of the vegetation god Attis, the son and love of the Syrian goddess Cybele. At the vernal equinox a pine tree sacred to Attis was cut down and decorated with flowers and ribbons in his honour. This festival commemorated his rebirth from the underworld and in 46 CE was moved from March to May Ist. The Saxons also worshipped a sacred oak tree in the spring as a symbol of the Irminsul or World Pillar (*axis mundi*) that they believed held up the heavens.

May Eve was the time when the young men 'hurled up maiden's coats' and went off to the woods to consummate their passion. From this came the idea of the so-called 'greenwood marriage' which lasted just for the summer or for a year and a day. After the ceremony the couple leapt the balefire or jumped over the broomstick for 'good luck' and many children.

A woman who was made pregnant on May Eve was said to be 'wearing the green gown' (of the Goddess as Flower Bride). The so-called 'merrybegots' - the children born of these woodland liasons or the Great Rite in the witches' circle - often took names which denoted their origin. Common English surnames such as Jackson, Johnson, Robson, Robinson, Hobson, Dobson, Green-wood, Jenkinson and Hood are all said to indicate the offspring conceived in this manner

On Walpurgis Night or May Eve the witches from all over Europe were said to gather for the Grand Sabbat of the year on the Brocken mountain in Germany. There, it was commonly believed, wild orgies were held ruled over by the Devil. This scene has been conjured up in an artistic form in both classical works of music and in a Walt Disney cartoon. In the 1930s the English psychic investigator Harry Price staged a publicity stunt on the Brocken with a goat in the hope of summoning up the Devil. In the real world Brocken is the sacred mountain of Freyja and Holda. Near its summit is a holy well, an ancient stone altar and a dancing ground. It was probably sacred to the old-time witches and it can be compared with the Venusberg ruled by Dame Venus or Holda and the Hollow Hill of Craft mythology.

In folk tradition therefore Beltane was heavily connected with witchcraft and witches. The fact that it is one of their major festivals is illustrated by the custom in country areas of placing birch and rowan over the door on May Eve 'to keep the witches away'. In Somerset crosses were woven from hazel twigs and placed over the hearth. Primroses were used to decorate the door lintels of the house and cowsheds [21]. The rowan had to be tied with red thread and this in fact made it a symbol of the witch goddess. Spinning wheels and spindles were also made from rowan and birch was the sacred tree of the spring goddess as it symbolised birth and fertility.

Hawthorn was the very special flower of the Goddess in her spring maiden aspect. Because of this it was greatly feared and hated by good Christians. An old country saying was 'Hawthorn bloom and elderflowers fill the house with evil powers.' Elder is the tree of the Dark Goddess and the reference to 'evil powers' is her role as the alter-ego of the Bright Goddess of spring. Where oak, ash and thorn grew together was where there is a gateway to the Otherworld used by hedgewitches. In fairy tales and folk legends the entrance to Faeryland was often found through an old oak door concealed in the roots of a tree.

It was considered very unlucky to bring hawthorn into the house because it was a pagan tree. This is one superstition ignored by witches and oddly even church altars were decorated with hawthorn sprays as it was the flower of the Virgin Mary. This is logical as she took over many symbols of the ancient goddesses. Witches used the hawthorn to protect their homes from evil forces and also to acknowledge the time of the year in a ritual sense. Hawthorn was placed at the eastern window of the house to welcome the sun god. A sprig was placed at any northern door or window to acknowledge the moon goddess as well. On the western side of the house the hawthorn represented the gateway to death and the dark quarter of the moon. Finally, placed in the south, it brought good luck to the house and its occupants, especially the female ones.

In the modern Craft the festival of May Eve or Beltane is a time for handfastings and the symbolic 'sacred marriage' between the Lord of the Greenwood and his Flower Bride. It is a time of mirth, joy and happiness because the Faith is 'a religion of love and light' [23]. It is the festival when the Lady or Maid is crowned as the May Queen, the Queen of Elfame or the Queen of the Sabbat with a circlet of wild flowers.

The God, represented by the stang garlanded with birch, hazel, hawthorn and willow, now relinquishes his dark winter aspect. He is no longer Arthur, but Robin, the Green Man and Lord of the Woods. In this form he will rule now through to the autumn. Basically the theme of Beltane is that the dark days are gone, and summer is a- coming in with the sun from the south and with oak, and ash and thorn.

Chapter Nine
The Goddess of the Land

In the folk traditions of the British Isles Midsummer or the summer solstice in June was a time to mark the longest day of the year when the sun rose in the sky to it zenith and was in its full power and glory. Contrawise, as befits a belief system with a dualistic character, it was also a mysterious, Otherworldly time with the smell of death in the air and omens of impending doom. The sun may be blazing high in the sky, but from midsummer the evenings gradually begin to shorten and we begin the slow descent towards the dark season.

When the Church took over the old rites to celebrate the midsummer season they chose June 24 as the Feast of St John the Baptist and it became Midsummer's Day. In the 12th century the bishop of Exeter denounced those who practised sorcery (in the archaic sense of casting lots) on Midsummer's Eve. This date was chosen for divining the future because it was one of the three so-called 'spirit nights' with May Eve and Hallows Eve. On these nights witches, ghosts and faeries were supposed to roam loose and the veil between the worlds was thin.

In order to protect themselves and their animals from the powers of darkness at midsummer superstitious people placed sprigs of St John's Wort over the doors of their houses, barns, stables and cow sheds. It was gathered at midnight on Midsummer's Eve, especially if it was also a full moon, when its magickal and healing powers were said to be at their height. St John Wort placed under the pillow on that night would not only protect the sleeper from evil, but also give them dreams of their future lovers.

At midsummer the Goddess is the Queen of Elfame or Faerie. It was believed that contact could be made with the Little People at the 'inbetween times' of dusk on Midsummer's Eve and the dawn of Midsummer' Day. In the famous story of *Puck of Pook Hill* by Rudyard Kipling the children accidentally awake Puck, the spirit of the land, in a faery ring on Midsummer's Eve. There are a number of places where the faery folk can be seen. These include along faery paths, at burial mounds and springs, near oak, ash and hawthorn trees, at crossroads and fords where several streams meet. near waterfalls, and at 'the bottom of the garden' where it is divided off from other land by a hedge or fence. In fact at any boundary point where Middle Earth and the Other are believed to meet. They are also likely to be the same places where witches like to gather for obvious reasons.

Midsummer was the one time of the year when human could communicate with the faery folk and curry favours. This was usually achieved by visiting a known haunt of the Good People at dawn on Midsummer's Day or the solstice and offering a libation. In olden times this may have been blood, but in later times it was the produce of the farm such as milk, cream, eggs, honey or fruit cake or mead and elderflower wine. As late as the 19th century in Staffordshire home-brewed beer and a cake were left out for the nature spirits. This was a bribe to stop them suckling the cows in the form of hedgehogs [1].

Faeries, devas, elementals and nature spirits seldom appear to the human eye as the gossamer-winged fancies of Victorian paintings - unless, of course that is how you really believe they look. They can manifest in many forms including points of light or as the traditional shapes of elves, gnomes and goblins of fairy tales, as the nymphs, dryads and satyrs of classical myth, as hybrid half- human, half-animal creatures, as eccentric life-size humanoids in old-fashioned Victorian or Edwardian clothes, or as the great 'Shining Ones' like the Tuatha de Danaan of Irish myth. Faery warriors, it is said, are tall and thin wearing bone armour and carrying weapons of bone, bronze, wood and stone [2]. It should always be remembered in dealing with the faery folk that they are amoral and not all of them are friendly or beneficial to humankind.

The connection between the faeries and the witches is a very strong one and is well established. It is often overlooked by modern Wiccans, some of whom do not even believe in faeries, and by folklorists. In both the European and British witch trials the female leader of the coven was often called the Queen of the Faeries or the Faery Lady. There are accounts of witches being taken into 'faery mounds' and taught the arts of seership and healing using herbs. For example, in the 17th century John Heyden, a London astrologer who foolishly predicted the death of Oliver Cromwell, was forced to flee for his life to rural Somerset. There he claimed to have met a lady dressed in a green robe near a 'fairy hill'. This faery lady took him into the mound where there was a glass castle and taught him wisdom. This experience sounds like a typical underworld initiation by the Goddess or Queen of Elfame.

Some country folk and traditional witches are of the opinion that the faeries are the spirits of the dead. To these witches Elfame is the place where the souls of witches go after death while they await reincarnation. A few advanced 'old souls' do not incarnate again on Middle Earth having been freed by successive incarnations from the cycle of death and rebirth. They become the Mighty Ones, or the Hidden Company, and act as spirit guides to their Craft brothers and sisters in incarnation [3].

The belief that faeries are descended from the forbidden mating between the Fallen Angels and human women is still found in the folk tradition and the beliefs of the old witch families. This belief is based on esoteric lore concerning such sensitive and controversial subjects as faery lovers and the physical and spiritual continuity of the 'witch blood' from ancient times, and the existence of a hybrid 'elven race' with special magickal and psychic powers as described by the traditional Cheshire witch in the last chapter.

It is a body of secret knowledge which has been hinted at in the fictional works of writers like Arthur Machen, H.P. Lovecraft and Dion Fortune, and it is also there for all to see in the folklore records of marriages between the faery folk and humans. It is not however widely accepted in modern neo-pagan and Wiccan circles. An American magazine recently ridiculed the idea that witches were 'a race apart' with special powers inherited through hereditary or soul incarnation. It was dismissed as a product of the popular Sixties television series *Bewitched* or the Hollywood movie *I Married a Witch*. Yet such a belief is held in the Traditional and Hereditary Craft today and is based on ancient wisdom teachings that have survived in folklore and fairy tales.

Robin Goodfellow as the god of the witches

Puck has been mentioned and it appears this Olde English folk character represents the faery aspect of the witch god. He is also known as Robin Goodfellow and was the son of Oberon, the name of the King of the Faeries in Shakespeare's *Midsummer Night's Dream*. Shakespeare borrowed Oberon from the Germanic myth of the elf king Auberon or Alberich, ruler of the earth gnomes or dwarves who guarded treasure and made the jewellry and weapons for the Gods. Alberich therefore has links with the blacksmith aspect of the witch god as Tubal Cain, Vulcan and Wayland the Smith. Today Oberon is still recognized by traditionals following the Elven system in Wales and the West Country In that tradition he has the title of 'High Lord of elves and humans' [4].

In folk tradition Robin Goodfellow was seen as a brownie or hobgoblin (spirit of the hearth) figure who attached themselves to households and did domestic chores. His real nature however is revealed in a 17th century illustration for a pamphlet. Robin is depicted in semi-human form, with ram's horns, pointed ears, shaggy legs and cloven hooves like Pan, an erect phallus, a broomstick over his shoulder and holding a lighted candle. He is surrounded by a double circle on the ground and a ring of dancing male and female figures. His credentials as the witch god are impeccable, even though he had become a debased figure in folklore.

Puck haunted hills and burial mounds and in the medieval poem *Piers Plowman* he is described as 'the prince of the world. This is an unusual name for a nature spirit or goblin, as it is usually a title given to Lucifer as the leader of the fallen angels or Watchers. The belief that Puck was also the 'spirit of the land' seems to have been independently preserved in the occult tradition. In 1942 a small group of occultists and ceremonial magicians invoked Puck as part of the war effort. Their idea was to contact the spirit of the land, symbolised by Puck, in a ritual to help defend England from the Nazis [5].

In British folk traditions and seasonal custom midsummer was a time for rituals dating back to ancient sun worship. A wooden wheel covered in twisted plaits of straw was set alight and rolled down a hillside. This was to mimic the motion of the sun in the summer sky. A very early reference to this practice is found in 4th century CE Gaul (France). After the blazing wheel reached the bottom of the hill its charred fragments were placed in a temple dedicated to the Roman sun god Apollo [6].

The traditional midsummer fires, which only died out in Cornwall and Scotland in the last century, may date back thousands of years to when Roman farmers lit fires in the fields to protect their crops from diseases in the summer. These St John fires were lit after dusk on Midsummer Eve and when they were blazing a bone was tossed into the flames. This was said to represent an unknown Christian martyr, but may have been a folk memory of ancient human and animal sacrifices. It was also believed that the smell of burning bones drove off dragons and other evil beasts. Hence we have the modern term bonfire or bone fire. An alternative meaning may derive from the Old Norse *buane*, meaning a beacon, or from banefire, indicating the banishing of evil.

Once the fire was well alight, St John's Wort was thrown onto it as a protective charm and the animals were led around the flames. Great care was taken that this was always done in a clockwise or sunwise way. In common with the ancient practice at Beltane, the livestock was also passed through the smoke. Torches were lit from the fire and the farmer and his workers circumbulated the fields, before visiting the byres and repeating the procedure so any pregnant cow had a healthy birth and a strong calf. As the fire died down, mothers passed their babies through the smoke to make sure they stayed healthy. In the Highlands women leapt the flames with their skirts up and their bodies exposed. This was supposed to make sterile women fertile and other women have big, bonny babies [7].

After the witch-hunting period there are instances where the midsummer fires were used to protect the farm from witches. In one case at St Clear in Cornwall a witch's pointed hat, besom and oak-handled ritual sickle were thrown in the flames [8].

Throughout the night people with torches and lanterns stayed by the fire to 'watch and ward' until dawn broke. Originally, in pagan times, the fires on midsummer Eve would have celebrated 'the splendour of high summer with the sun at the peak of its power and glory in the heavens, and providing ripeness to the maturing fruits and grains' [4]. The folk memory of this original purpose survived in the custom of spreading the ash from the midsummer fires on the fields to promote a good harvest.

At midsummer the Goddess is the Queen of Elfame, as we seen, and the Enchantress. Her symbols are the queen bee, the owl swooping down from the night sky on its helpless prey, and the lynx or wild cat who has always been independent and untamed. She represents the ageless femme fatale, the female sexual predator who chooses whatever man she wants to be her lover and makes him king. This is an erotic image of women and it is one that the patriarchy has always felt uncomfortable with. As a result it has reacted with fear, demonisation, repression and often violence.

The midsummer goddess is first and foremost Sovereignty, the goddess of the land and the kingmaker. She is also, as far as us lesser mortals are concerned, the White Goddess written about by the poet Robert Graves the muse and patron of poets, artists and writers. As the White Goddess she can inflame the artistic with the madness of inspiration, creative energy and genius. She also has the power to destroy, for those the Goddess loves may die young, as their creative fire flares and burns out prematurely under her touch.

The goddess of the land is not the gentle maiden of springtime or the nurturing mother of Yule. Her sacred weapon is the double-bladed axe and if threatened or crossed she adopts the persona of warrior woman or warrior queen. Like Boudicca or Maeve, she will fight to protect her young, her people, and vanquish the enemies of her land. She is both Queen and High Priestess, controlling the political rulership of the land and conducting the seasonal rituals that bind the people to it.

The Otherworld Castle

Sovereignty is, of course, the ancient earth goddess, sometimes known as the Earth Spirit in modern parlance. She is princess, queen and queen mother and the transformative nature of Sovereignty is, like the land or the seasons that change the land, a major feature of the hero's quest. She is beautiful and may bestow kingship on the hero, but she is likewise deadly, dangerous to the unworthy' [10].

In many of the ancient myths she becomes identified with the country in which she is revered and worshipped; as Erin, for instance, in Ireland, and Britannia in Britain or, on a wider level, in post-Christian times as the Virgin Mary who has been adopted by many European nationalist

As the goddess of the sacred landscape, she guards the waters of the holy wells and the fords in the shape of a hag. In Irish folklore she is the banshee or faery woman, the washer-at-the-ford who can predict the wyrd of kings and heroes, the guardian of ancient families and the messenger of death. The only man who can drink or cross her waters is the worthy man who will be king by virtue of wisdom. The foolish and unworthy will refuse to embrace her; the worthy will kiss and transform her, just as the land is transformed by a wise and just ruler.' [11].

In Ireland the story is still told to those who will listen of a king who had five sons and of the prophecy that one would become the High King ruling the whole of the island. It was also predicted that the son who would be king had to hunt down and catch a golden fawn. When this Otherworldly creature appeared all the sons chased after it. Only one, called Mac Niad, caught it. This is a version of the Chase of the White Hart (the Goddess) who is captured by the God at the spring equinox.

A snow storm began and the sons sought shelter in a house deep in the forest owned by an old woman. The first son demanded a bed for the night and the crone replied he could have one if he shared it with her. He refused and was told he had refused Sovereignty and would not be king. One by one the three other brothers went to the house and the scene was repeated.

Finally Mac Niad tried his luck and at her asking he told her that he had caught a strange golden fawn that day. When he made no objections to the bedtime arrangement, the old woman was transformed into the most beautiful young woman he had ever seen. She told the prince that she was the Sovereignty of Scotland and Ireland and that he would become the High King. She also promised that his son after him would win her favour and become king with the gifts of a druid, prophet and poet. In other words he would be given the mantle of kingship by the White Goddess of inspiration and wisdom.

A similar tale is told in the legend of Niall and the nine hostages. The hero meets a hideous old hag by a holy well and she demands a kiss from him. When he willingly gives it without pause, she changes into a young woman wearing a purple gown - the colour of kingship. In a saga about the hero Fionn, he is out hunting a doe when a beautiful woman invites him to stay in her Otherworldly house in the woods. As Fionn prepares for bed a hag appears dressed in a black and white dress. She tells him that she was the deer he was chasing and as a penance he must now marry her.

Fionn refuses and the hag goes berserk, killing many of his warriors and rampaging across the land until she is finally hunted down like an animal and killed. She dies cursing her father, a wizard who had put a spell on her that she would remain a hag until a great prince agreed to marry her. If Fionn had been wise enough to accept the offer of marriage she would have changed into her youthful self and borne him a son who would have ruled the world [12]. In this story the hag in black and white is the destructive side of the goddess of the land. She is the Dark Goddess unleashed when the Bright Goddess is unable to find a worthy man suitable to be her king and lover.

This destructive aspect of the goddess of the land has been recognized in the controversial quasi-Christian figures known as sheela-na-gigs. These are found carved on the outside walls and near the doorways of churches and castles. They are crude images of a hag-faced woman squatting with her legs apart to

140

expose her cunni. They have been said to be representations of the Cailleach or Old Hag as both the creator and destroyer of life. Their primary function seems to have been as objects to ward off evil forces and armed attack. These images have been described as 'territorial war goddess in her hag-like aspect, with all the strongly sexual characteristics which accompany this guise in tales' [13].

A possible clue to the identity of the sheela may be discerned from one found carved on a stone in the church of St Michael and all Angels at pennington in Cumbria. The stone was first found in the 1920s embedded in the church wall. It depicts a standing female figure with legs wide open and her fingers pointing to or holding open her labia. The stone was moved to the church porch until a few years ago when a new vicar, under the impression the figure was 'cursed,' gave it to the Kendal museum for safe-keeping.

Local tradition says that the sheela on the stone is in fact an image of the Norse goddess Freyja. It is seen as a classic example of how pagan beliefs were incorporated into the building of a church in the Middle Ages. It is also said locally that the vicar sent the stone to the museum because he objected to to the villagers using it as a focus for a 'festival'. When several local women became pregnant after the festival he decided the image of the fertility and witch goddess had to go [14].

In medieval Christian times the concept of the king wedded to the land appears in the Arthurian romances. It appears, in a sub-limated version, in the legend of the knight Gawain and the Loathly Lady. In order to save Arthur's life, his nephew Gawain agrees to marry Lady Ragnall, who is described as the most ugly woman in all the world. On their wedding night the old hag turns into a stunningly: beautiful woman. She tests Gawain by telling him that he can have her fair either by night or day, but not both. Faced with this dilemma, Gawain informs his bride that the choice must be hers. By giving her sovereignty the spell is broken and she remains young and beautiful all the time.

In one version of the story Gawain first meets the Loathly Lady when she is sitting 'betwixt an oak and a holly bush'. In another tale, Gawain is challenged by the Green Knight at Yule to a year-long quest and ritual game of beheading. Also Gawain's bride, after giving him a child, only lives for another year. This suggests she is a 'faery woman' who marries a mortal and then returns to the Otherworld when he has sired her changeling.

Gawain in facts fits quite neatly into the role of the sacred king. He is born out of wedlock and to conceal the event Arthur's sister decides to kill him. In different versions of the tale, the baby is either set adrift in his cradle, or handed over to merchants who take him abroad, or given to a knight who passes him to foster-parents. Eventually he ends up in Rome and is adopted by the Pope as his own kith and kin.

In all cases Gawain is unaware of his birthright and destiny as the noble relation of the king. He is eventually recognized and accepted by his parents and Arthur, but only after he is forced to combat the king. In the story of the Loathly Lady. he in fact saves Arthur's life when the king is threatened by a figure who represents the summer or Oak King.

The medieval courtly romances of the Arthurian myths, and the Marian cultus in the Roman Church, envisioned England as 'Merlin's enclosure' and 'Our Lady's Bower'. The goddess of the land who armed the young warrior hero and granted him kingship was represented in the Arthurian cycle as Argante, the Lady of the Lake. Her alter-ego or shadow aspect is the myst-erious Morgan Le Fay, the half-sister of Arthur who guards the Cauldron beneath the Hollow Hill on the Isle of Avalon.

Arthur has already shown that he is the rightful king by drawing the first sword from the stone anvil and indicating to the people that he is the God's representative on Earth. Merlin however, who is another aspect of the God in human form, guides him to his fateful meeting with the Lady of the Lake, sometimes presented as his faery foster mother, to receive Excalibur. After Arthur's death, when his body has been taken by the three queens on their barge to Avalon to await rebirth, and the dream of the Fellowship of the Round Table has been shattered, Excalibur is rightly returned to its guardian. The Lady of the Lake will look after it until a new sacred king is worthy to hold it or Arthur returns from his sleep in the underworld to reclaim it.

In Christian times Sovereignty became subconsciously associated with powerful queens like Elizabeth I, the focus for a cult of Diana-Artemis, and her cousin Mary, Queen of Scots. Mary is a rather tragic, Morgan Le Fay type figure, represented by her enemies as a sexual predator and 'dark queen' who had to be sacrificed because she tried to usurp the chosen representative of the Goddess. It has been claimed that Elizabeth I represented the Triple Goddess in her British form of Arianrhod, Brigid and Dana [15]. In modern times Princess Diana has taken this role.

Elizabeth was certainly known widely as the Virgin Queen, despite the many rumours about her sexual affairs, and it should be remembered that in the old sense a virgin was only an unmarried woman. Several occult secret societies of the Tudor period, such as the School of Night and the Dragon Society, deliberately identified the queen with Diana. There is even a dramatic portrait by Cornelius Vroom depicting Elizabeth as the moon goddess with a bow and a crescent in her hair. Some of this symbolism has been transferred in modern times to Princess Diana, who after her tragic and sudden death has become 'the Lady of the Lake'. Only time will tell if Prince Charles will 'sacrifice' himself for the good of the land and give way to the young 'sun king' born at the summer solstice.

The special relationship between the medieval English king and the Virgin Mary, as a Goddess substitute, is exemplified in the anonymous work of art known as the Wilton Diptych. This was painted in the late 14th century and is now exhibited, significantly, in the National Gallery in London. It is painted on three wooden panels and shows King Richard II, the Black Prince, kneeling in a wooded landscape to the Madonna and child. She is standing in a fenced off enclosure or garden, showing it is 'not of this world'. This is emphasised by the fact she is surrounded by a company or host of (feminine) angelic figures wearing flowery crowns. Richard's own semi-divine status is underlined by the fact he is flanked by three early Anglo-Saxon saints and kings. According to art historians, the king appears to be waiting for a sign of benediction from the Virgin, or her approval to rule over the land.

When the painting was cleaned and restored in 1993 it was discovered that the small orb on the top of the flag of St George held by one of the angels had a picture on it. This was revealed to be the image of a green wooded island with a white-towered castle on it. The island is floating in a dark sea which was originally painted silver. This painting within a painting conjures up visions of Shakespeare's description two hundred years later of Britain as 'this little world, this precious gem set in a silver sea'. It will also remind Crafters of Caer Sidi, the Spinning Castle of Arianrhod in Celtic mythology, or the Castle of Roses on the Island of the Dead beyond the setting sun. Art historians suggest the flag of St George is symbolic of the power of the land Our Lady is passing to the king so he can rule over the Blessed Isles with her blessing and protection.

In the symbolism of the Traditional Craft the flower of the Goddess at midsummer is the five-petalled Tudor rose, the Red Rose of England, and the full moon in June is called the Rose Moon. In that flower, which is at the centre of Craft symbolism, 'we see the cycle of birth, initiation, consummation, repose and death. This cycle sums up or manifests life and the cycle of the seasons, showing forth the feminine mysteries of creation and destruction in their yearly round. Seen as a token of everlasting-love, the rose hints at the transforming power of that force to conquer even death' [16].

As one traditional witch has put it, love is a lie 'because it creates inspiration - and from inspiration comes the thirst for wisdom, which can be both creative and destructive.' [17]. Life, love and death are, after all, the three aspects of the Goddess, and the beautiful, sweet smelling rose is surrounded by sharp thorns.

Midsummer, like Beltane, is a happy time for the celebration of life. There is much rejoicing for the benefits of the summer sun, for lazy days in the woods and by the river bank, resting before the hard work of the harvest to come. The solar disc stands high and proud in the blue sky of June, and the Sun King and the Rose Queen rule over the land in peace and harmony.

All, it seems, is well with the world, but the dark shadow of the reaper's scythe is already over the fields, the poppies red as blood are about to bloom, and the hungry land is demanding its annual sacrifice. As the storm clouds of late summer begin to gather, and prayers are offered to the Gods for good weather to gather in the harvest, Fate has already selected her victim. He who would be king must die in the corn and shed his blood for the folk and the land.

Chapter Ten

Corn Kings & Scarecrows

At the Beltane and Midsummer rites the Fate goddess, as the spring maiden and Sovereignty, captured the heart of the God, married him in the greenwood, and made him king to rule over the land with wisdom and justice. The final drama in this light half of the year is enacted at the Celtic festival of Lughnasadh or as it was known to the Anglo-Saxons, Lammas in early August.

In Celtic times Lughnasadh, or Lugh's Day, was the principal festival of the Irish god of light, Lugh. He was one of the Tuatha de Danaan and was nicknamed 'Lugh of the many skills'. His festival on August 1st was celebrated with pre-harvest games, horse racing, sports and general merry-making. Until fairly recently it coincided with the August Bank Holiday and was still a time of horse racing and country fairs.

In the North Country it marked the start of the Wakes weeks when all the factories closed down for the summer holiday. On the Isle of Man the rites of Lughnasadh survived in the custom on August 1st of young people climbing hills to indulge in riotous games and lovemaking. In the early 19th century the Church banned this practice. It was replaced by sedate family outings on the first Sunday in August to collect bilberries.

Lugh's 'many skills' was a reference to his adeptship of arts, commerce, and crafts. For this reason the Romans equated him with Mercury and Hermes, and with their sun god Apollo, husband of Diana-Artemis. The sacred bird of Lugh was the raven and some historians connect him to Woden or Odin, the Northern European version of Mercury [1]. Lugh's ravens also link him with the triple Irish war goddesses known as the

Morrigan. His other sacred bird is the goose and this again links him with the fate goddess/es.

His name means 'shining' or 'light' and he was the foster-son of the ancient earth goddess Tailltu. Her home was at the sacred omphalos or centre of Ireland, the holy hill of Tara, and it is said that Lugh founded his festival in her honour. Lugh's real mother was one of the faery race called the Formorians who had invaded Ireland before the Tuatha de Danaan. Folk tradition said they were the Nephelim, or 'mighty giants'. of Biblical lore who were the offspring of the mating between the Watchers and human women.

Lugh's grandfather was a monstrous one-eyed giant called Balor and he received a prophecy that he was to be killed by his future grandson. Balor took his daughter up into a tower on an island (note the symbolism) to prevent her from marrying and having a child. Unfortunately one of the Tuatha de Danaan breaches the defences of the island, enters the tower and carries her off as his bride. Balor threw the resulting child into the ocean, but he was rescued by the sea god Manaanan and fostered by Tailltu and the smith god Goibniu, the son of Brigid.

In the end Lugh is forced into battle against his demonic grandfather and he kills him. This resembles combat between summer and winter, light and darkness etc. In one version of the myth, it is Crom Dubh, the 'Black One' or 'Twisted One', the dark god of the harvest and summer's end that Lugh fights and slays. It would therefore seem the festival of Lughnasadh represented 'the mythic pattern of a God of Light and a God of Summer's End in combat for the Goddess of the Land' [2].

The Welsh version of Lugh was Llew Llaw Gyffes and he features in the fourth branch of *The Mabinogion*. Llew was the product of a virgin birth when his mother Arianrhod stepped over the magick wand of her brother, the wizard Gwydion. This was a test of her virginity by her prospective husband Math ap Mathonwy, the Lord of Gwynedd in North Wales. As she stepped over the wand Arianrhod gave birth to a golden-haired boy who she immediately abandoned. He was called Dylan, and with his mother's rejection he immediately jumped into the sea and swam away. Gwydion, unseen by anyone present, picked up Arianrhod's placenta and hid it in a chest.

One day the magician heard a voice crying from the chest. When he opened it he found inside a fully formed baby. The inference is that Gwydion created this homunculus by magick and the story is a blind to hide the fact that it is the result of an incestuous affair between the wizard and his sister [3]. The baby boy is called Llew and, like Lugh, he is fostered up until he was eight years old. Then he was returned to the court of Lord Math.

One day Gwydion set out to Caer Arianrhod to visit his sister. This castle or tower, also known as Caer Sidi 'has passed into the Mysteries of Britain as the magical tower of poetic initiation and also the Otherworldly Caer (castle) of transformation and death' [4]. It can be compared to the tower in which Lugh's mother was imprisoned, the glass tower where Merlin ended his days,and the castle turrets in fairytales where princesses sleep after being pricked by magical spinning wheels belonging to old crones. Arianrhod herself is 'an Otherworldly queen and has archetypal connections with Ceridwen as the mistress of initiation' [5].

The boy followed Gwydion and when they arrived at her castle Arianrhod enquired who he might be. The wizard replied that he is her son and is reproached by his sister for hiding him away for so many years. When she asked his name Gwydion replied again that he had none In response to this news, Arianrhod said that nobody would name him but herself. Brother and sister part on bad terms.

Gwydion made a magickal boat and he and the boy returned to the castle disguised as shoemakers. It is interesting that Lugh was the patron god of shoemakers and that his Greek counterpart Hermes owned a pair of winged shoes enabling him to fly. On this second visit Arianrhod saw the boy throw a stone and hit a wren - the sacred bird of the Holly King as the twin god of the waning year. She cried out that the fair boy had a skilful hand.

Gwydion then named him Llew Llaw Gyffes, which has roughly the same meaning in Welsh. Llew or Lieu can also mean 'lion' and refers to both his solar nature and his royal birthright.

Llew and the wizard then resume their normal forms and Arianrhod realises she has been tricked by the pair. She then laid a wyrd on her son that nobody would arm him but her. When the boy became a young man he sought a horse and weapons so he could become a warrior. Again he and the wizard assumed disguises, this time as bards, and made a visit to Caer Arianrhod. When they arrived the wizard summoned up a phantom fleet to attack the castle. Arianrhod armed herself and her female servants and then offered weapons to the bards to defend themselves. By doing this she unwittingly fulfilled her son's wyrd.

For the second time Arianrhod was angry at her brother for tricking her and she swore that Llew's destiny would be 'never to have a wife of that race that is now on Earth'. Gwydion and Math joined forces to create a wife for Llew from the flowers of the oak, broom and meadowseet. She was named Blodeuwedd, meaning 'flower face', but as an Otherworldly creature produced by magick she did not have the morals and loyalty of a human wife. While Llew was away at Math's court, a hunter passed by their home chasing a stag. He was called Gronw Bebyr and Blodeuwedd offered him hospitality as night was closing in.

The couple immediately fell in love and they spent the night together under Llew s roof in the marital bed. They then plotted how to kill Llew. When he returned from court Blodeuwedd asked him in what circumstances he could die. Llew replied he could only be killed by a special spear which takes a year to make working only on Sunday (the sun's day). He cannot be killed inside or outside, naked or clothed, on a horse or on foot.

In fact the only way Llew can be killed, the couple work out, is if a bath is made with a roof on it on a river bank. Then Llew can stand half-naked with one foot in the bath and the other resting on the back of a goat. Gronw made the spear and Blodeuwedd

149

lured Llew into showing her exactly how he could die. Gronw threw the poisoned spear, killing Llew, who shapeshifted into an eagle and flew away. Gronw then seized Llew's lands and took his flower bride as his own wife. Gwydion followed a sow, the sacred animal of the Dark Goddess, until it led him to the rotting corpse of the eagle high up in the branches of a tree. We can surmise that it was resting in the Night Mare's Nest made from the bones of dead poets, especially as the sow is feeding on the rotting pieces of eagle's flesh dropping from the branches to the ground. If it was also an elder tree then the symbolism would have been perfect. Gwydion struck the eagle with his wand and it was transformed back into the corpse-like body of Llew who is returned to Math's court to be restored to full health.

As soon as was recovered from his death and rebirth ordeal. Llew sought revenge on Gronw and his wife. Gwydion helped to hunt Blodeuwed and her female servants down. Her retinue were drowned in a lake fleeing from the wizard. When he catches Blodeuwedd he strikes her with his wand and she is transformed into an owl. Again this is a sacred bird of the Goddess in her dark, underworld aspect. Meanwhile, Gronw was anxious to save his own skin and he offered Llew his land back, plus a large amount of gold and silver in compensation for the grave wrong he has done him. Llew refused the offer and instead said that Gronw must return to the place where the murder took place and stand willingly while a spear is aimed at his heart.

Gronw reluctantly agreed to this arrangement, but as he was a coward fearful of losing his life, he asked his warband if any of them will take his place. In disgust they refused and he is left to face his wyrd alone. When they arrive at the place of destiny, Gronw asks if he can stand behind a standing stone by the river so it is between him and Llew. Knowing that his enemy cannot escape fate, Llew agreed. The spear was thrown and it travelled through the stone killing the usurper. Llew lived on to rule over his lands in peace and he later became the Lord of Gwynedd [6].

Llew's story is of the god or hero who, by prohibitions placed upon him by the Goddess, is refused three times the chance of sacred kingship represented by a proper name or title, weapons to defend the land and a bride to produce heirs. His Otherworldly bride made of flowers can be seen as a version of the spring maid, but the sun god and would-be Oak King is betrayed by the Holly King as Wild Hunter.

In the end Llew triumphs over both of them; his wife shows her true colours when she is transformed into an owl, the sacred bird of Lilith, and the Wild Hunter dies a ritual death, killed by the solar power of the spear of light which destroys his phallic power (the standing stone). Llew can then take back the land and become the rightful and worthy king who has died and been reborn.

In folk tradition Lammas Eve, also known as St Margaret's Day, was when a huge cartwheel was heated in a fire until it was red-hot. It was then rolled down a hillside and its smooth passage, or not, was regarded as an omen for the harvest. While the midsummer fire wheel symbolized the motion of the sun across the sky, the fiery wheel of Lammastide was the sun descending from the height of the sky into the underworld [7].

The purpose of the Lammas rites was to prepare for the harvest and perform rituals of sympathetic magick to promote a good crop and fine weather to gather it in. Three generations ago the witches of Buckinghamshire went out into the fields before the harvest was finished and sat astride a stang or horse-headed stave. They then 'rode' on their magickal steeds 'through thick (the uncut sheaves) and thin (the stubble)'. The purpose behind this was that the steps of the 'ride' were danced into the land in order to dispel and appease the old, the powers of decay, and thereby usher in the new, the powers of increase' [8]. In the Isle of Man in 1617 a woman and her son were burnt at the stake for performing such a fertility rite. They had been found in possession of a 'riding pole' with its head carved in the shape of a phallus [9].

Recent scientific research as shown that dancing, music and sexual activity in the vicinity of plants can induce extra growth.

Hence there is some logic behind Morris dancing, 'to awaken the Earth', the skipping and hobby-horse dances of folk culture, the 'riding' of broomsticks in the fields by witches, and the sexual rites of spring to stimulate nature and new life.

In 16th and 17th century Italy the Inquisitors uncovered a secret cult of 'night travellers' known as the *benandanti*. These cunning folk or white witches took part in 'ritual battles' in their dreams at harvest time to combat the evil actions of black witches and demons who attacked and destroyed the crops. It is possible this is a folk memory of pagan rituals carried out in former times to protect the crops. Under the influence of the Inquisition, who were dealing with a set of beliefs they could hardly comprehend, the cult of the *benandantis* and the witches eventually became combined in Satanic fantasies about the witches' sabbat created by the Church [10]. However the motif of witches as persons who could either bless or blast the crops had obviously survived from medieval times and resurfaced in these magical 'night battles' between good and evil magicians.

In the Christian Church, dating from Anglo-Saxon times, the Celtic Lughnasadh was Lammas or a mass to celebrate the gathering in of the 'first fruits' This was when the new corn was brought to the church to be blessed by the priest. This Christian sacrament was a sanitised version of the former blood sacrifices at this time for 'both the killing of the god and the sacred meal, which gave natural and supernatural strength from the partaking of his blood and body, were ritual acts with a mystical significance' [11].

The theological theory behind blood sacrifice, and especially human sacrifice, was that 'blood was thought to contain the essence of the life force, and by the outpouring of the divine victim's life essence, preferably directly on to the soil, the union of heaven and earth was perpetuated and the vital energies were renewed throughout the land' [12]. The blood sacrifice of animals or humans was seen as an act of life, not death, especially in the case of a human victim, whose soul was believed to go straight to Heaven or to the realm of the Gods. In some cultures to be

152

selected as the victim for sacrifice was regarded as a great honour because it bestowed divinity.

The extent of human sacrifice in pre-Christian times has been, and still is, a matter for hot debate and, like so many questions about pre-history, it may never be resolved. The Romans painted a sensational picture of the human sacrifices allegedly practised by the Celts, although some of it may have been political propaganda. It is known that the Celts were bloodthirsty warriors who executed their prisoners-of-war and collected their heads as trophies. These were either used as spirit oracles or placed upon gateways to their hill forts as warnings or to ward off evil.

One of the most sensational of all the claims made by the Romans concerned the so-called 'Wicker Man' allegedly used by the druids for mass human sacrifice. As the name suggests it was a giant wickerwork frame in the shape of a human figure and hollow inside. Into this frame the Romans say animals and humans were placed and it was then set alight so they were burnt alive.

Unfortunately, we have only one biased account by Julius Caesar of the Wicker Man in operation and it could therefore be just a crude attempt at anti-Celtic 'black' propaganda. Despite this it is a powerful image and one that still turns up in popular culture. It was the subject of a film in the 1970s called *The Wicker Man* and starring Christopher Lee, Edward Woodward and Britt Eckland.

The Roman writer Lucan also dramatically described a Celtic nemeton destroyed by the Roman army in southern France. He says that its altars were heaped with hideous offerings and every tree was sprinkled with human gore.

The most significant example of Celtic human sacrifice is probably the so-called Lindow Man or 'Pete Marsh', as he was so wittily nicknamed by the media. His preserved remains were found in a Cheshire peat bog in 1984 and were not far from the famous witches' meeting place of Alderley Edge. Lindow Man's body now rests, hopefully easily, in a glass case in the British Museum where he is gawped at by thousands of tourists every day..

Because of the problems with successfully carbon-dating the so-called 'bog bodies', estimates of Lindow Man's age range from the Ist century BC. to the very surprising late 6th century CE. These ranges make him either a Celt, a Roman Briton or even an Anglo-Saxon. However, the experts seem to have now agreed he was (probably) killed sometime in the Iron Age.

The problems with the carbon-dating process has led to some sensational speculation about the Bog Man. One, supposedly academic account, mixed archaeological fact with romantic fiction to provide him with a complete life history, and even a name, as a 'druid prince'. He was allegedly sacrificed at Beltane in 60 CE in a last magickal attempt to halt the Roman occupation [13].

From the evidence Lindow Man does seem to have been of aristocratic birth, he wore ritual tattoos and seems to have been killed in the ritual manner known as the 'triple death' - stabbing, hanging or strangling and drowning - associated with other similar bodies which were placed in pools and lakes. The fact that he was wearing an armband of fox fur may be significant. In some Celtic traditions of the Craft one of the marks of office of a Magister is a silver ring with a fox mask.

Lindow is not the only 'body in a bog'. Over the last fifty years over two thousand corpses have been found all over Western and Northern Europe. What they represent is matter for conjecture. There are some archaeologists who claim they are the remains of murder victims or criminals executed for adultery or homosexuality under the Celt's strict legal code. Because of their deposit in water, evidence of a triple death, the use of nooses and ritual binding, and in some cases staking down, most experts on the subject think they were victims of ritual murder or human sacrifice.

154

Some members of the modern Craft agree with the experts that the 'bog people' were ritually killed during fertility rites to the Mother Goddess. One Hereditary witch has claimed: 'the Old Religionists in Scandinavia and northern Germany wore neck collars or halters to acknowledge their sub-servience to the Goddess. Some male victims (in the bogs) were strangled or hanged. A noose or halter was placed around the neck of the male victim irrespective of the manner of death. The leather noose or rope halter was symbolic of the victim to the Goddess...Many women wore neck collars or hide collars when they were sacrificed to the Goddess' [14].

The bloody death of a victim sacrificed to the Goddess, especially in the role of sacred priest-king, is described in the following mytho-poetic account of the event.

First the victim is made drunk on mead, the nectar of the Gods, he is then led willingly into a ring of twelve standing stones arranged around an ancient oak tree. In front of the tree stands a stone altar and the tree has been lopped to represent the t-shape of a Tau cross. The victim is bound to it with willow thongs in the 'five fold bond', joining wrists, neck and ankles.

He is then whipped until he loses consciousness, flayed, blinded, castrated, impaled with a mistletoe stake, and finally his body is hacked into pieces on the, altar stone. The blood is collected in a bowl and is sprinkled on the tribe to make them virile and fruit-ful.

This gruesome account goes on to describe how the dismembered joints of the sacred king are roasted on twin fires made from the branches of the lopped oak. This bale fire has been lit using the sacred fire preserved from a lightning-blasted oak, or created by an alder wood drill in an oak log. The flesh of the victim is then eaten as a sacred meal, except for the sexual organs and head, and what is left over is burnt in the balefire. The head, or rather the skull, is either kept for use as a tribal oracle or with the phallus and testes, placed in an alder wood boat and rowed to an island in the river where they are buried [15].

The above account is an imaginative one, but it contains the essential elements of sacrifice and the partaking of the victim's essence which is later to be found in the Christian sacraments where the believer drinks the blood and eats the flesh of Christ in a symbolic manner. The ancient concept of the king wedded to the land also appears in a sublimated form as the 'divine right of kings', the anointing ceremony at coronations and the folklore belief in the 'King's touch' to heal the sick.

Discussing the nature of kingship in Anglo-Saxon England it has been said that in the English kingdoms 'the royal race - the *stirps regia* which sprang from its founder - provided the source from which the individual rulers were chosen.' In the case of the House of Wessex, from whom our present royal family claim bloodlinks, 'the earthly founder was the god who was the divine ancestor of almost every Anglo-Saxon royal house, Woden'.

Both the East Anglian royal dynasty and the royal house of Mercia also claimed descent from Woden. In 6th century Northumbria the name Oswald was chosen for many heirs to the throne. 'Os' was a divine prefix associated with Odin or Woden and his powers of communication and knowledge. Many of the Scandinavian kings traced their royal ancestry back to Freyr, brother-consort of the witch goddess Freyja, or to the war god Tiw or Tyr [16].

The concept of the sacred king in the Northern European religious tradition dates back to the combination of the spiritual and political in the German monarchy and the roles of tribal chieftain and priest. The title of king, according to the dictionary, is derived from the Old English *cyng*, meaning kin. It refers to a person who, usually by virtue of their hereditary position and birthright, is appointed or chosen to be the representative of their kin. As such the king was expected to be generous to his kin or people to the actual point of being willing to be sacrificed (i.e. 'made sacred') in order that the land and the crops should flourish and be blessed.

The king is therefore the charismatic embodiment of the 'luck' of his folk' ...the king 'does' his office as mediator between them (and the Gods), sacrificing for victory, for good crops, for peace, 'making the year' (17). However if this relationship breaks down, if the king fails in duty, and ignores his people he is said to have 'lost his luck'. In such a case the people will remove him from office, by violence if needed, and replace him with another. In this context 'luck' is not merely a matter of good or bad fortune. It is as much linked with the king's wyrd as it is with his personal qualities and alleged magickal powers over fertility.

Before the Viking period of emigration in Northern Europe the temples raised to the Powers were usually privately owned. In most cases the head of the household or family, the lord and lady if you will, acted as the family priest and performed the seasonal rituals and blots on behalf of the others. By the time the Norsemen had began their raids on the coasts of Western Europe 'the king had become the tribal high priest, 'the warden of the holy temple'... sacrificing for good crops, victory in battle, he assured plenty among his people, but when the Gods deserted him, and his luck no longer flowed from him, he could be deposed or even killed in time of tribal disaster'.

For instance, 'when bad harvests continued in Sweden under the Ynglingar king Donaldi, in spite of much sacrificing by the king, he was killed. His descendent, King Olaf Tretegia of Sweden, failed to make blot, neglected the rites necessary for good crops, so the latter failed; the Swedes, who 'used always to reckon good or bad crops for or against a king', buried the king in his house as an offering to Odin (18).

There is also the, possible legendary, tale of King Vikar, who was selected as a sacrificial victim by the casting of lots (the runes?) He was offered to Odin by the traditional method of stabbing with a spear and hanging from a tree. In fact 'ritual king slaying' in the north was not an uncommon occurrence as a means of dealing with tribal disasters when the 'luck' of the king had deserted the folk (19). Originally, especially in Sweden, the king was regarded as the human husband of Freyja. In later times this role was usurped by Odin and so it was to him the kings were offered as sacrifices.

The ritual sacrifice of the sacred priest-king, or God incarnate, survived in Christianity with the pagan elements surrounding the crucifixion of Jesus. In the Gospels there is an account of how a Roman centurion stabbed Jesus in the side with a spear while he hung on the cross. The resulting flow of blood and water from the wound was caught by Joseph of Arimathea in the cup used at the last supper and this became the Grail. The cup, it is said, was carved from an emerald that fell from the crown of Lucifer during the Battle in Heaven.

The weapon used by the soldier was no ordinary spear. It was the so-called Spear of Power or Spear of Destiny and was the official symbol of authority of the Jewish high priests and kings. It was forged from a fragment of meteoric iron by the divine blacksmith Tubal Cain [20]. The first blacksmith had survived the Deluge with his son and the ancient People of Cain, the Kenites, also known popularly as the Fire People, were said to be sacrificial priests of the Goddess. They were also known as Good Shepherds, a title used to describe Jesus and other Middle Eastern saviour gods such as Adonis, Attis and Tammuz who die, descend to the underworld and are reborn [21].

The Spear of Destiny, it has been alleged, is identical to the shining spear of Lugh, one of the Four Hallows of the Tuatha de Danaan or People of the Goddess. In the Grail legends it is the Bleeding Lance and it is the spear that pierced Odin on the World Tree and killed his son Baldur, the Northern god of light. This spear is a symbol of the ritual weapon used to send the sacred priest-king or sacrificed God to the Otherworld, where he encounters the Goddess and is reborn from her Cauldron or Grail in the underworld initiation [22].

Did this pagan concept of sacred kingship survive into Christian times as same speculative writers have suggested? There is a suggestion of it the murder of King Oswald of Northumbria in the 7th century. He was originally a heathen until he was

158

converted by St Alden. The king then invited Aidan to convert his subjects and the story is told of their visit together to a place where the native population worshipped a sacred spring. A church was built on the site by the king and the locals adopted him as their patron saint naming their village Kirkoswald or 'church of Oswald'

Oswald was killed in battle by the pagan king Penda of Mercia and after his death his body was dismembered. Parts of it were hanged from a tree and other parts scattered across the land. In pagan times the custom was to divide up the body of a sacrificed king and bury it in separate parts of the land to bring fertility and prosperity to the people. It is interesting that recent research suggests that King Harold was not killed by an arrow in the eye at Hastings as is popularly supposed. Instead it is believed his body was beheaded, disembowelled and castrated in a form of 'ritual death'

A cult of saintship grew up about Oswald immediately after his death and he was commonly called 'king, saint and martyr'. The plot of land where he had fallen in battle and was soaked in his blood stayed green while the rest of the killing field was trampled and Brown. Earth from the site was said to have miraculous properties and the water used to wash his bones was re-used for healing and exorcising evil spirits. When Penda himself died in battle 'the earth was watered with his blood' [23].

Several would-be kings of Anglo-Saxon England were murdered before they could take the throne in strange circumstances. One notable example was Prince Wigston of Mercia who was killed by having the top of his head chopped off with a sword. After his death several miracles were accredited to him and he eventually became St Wigstan.

King Edgar of Northumbria survived an attempt on his life before his coronation and also became a saint after his death. The son of the Mercian king Coenwulf became a saint after his death in 821, and another Northumbrian prince Eahlmud was murdered before ascending the throne and canonised. The East

Anglian King Edmund, murdered by pagan Danes in 870, briefly became England's patron saint. His death was a multiple one involving shooting with arrows and beheading. His head was thrown into a wood where his followers later found it, guarded by a wolf from other predators. The wolf is the totem beast of Woden.

There are ritualistic and pagan elements surrounding the deaths of most of the Anglo-Saxon kings who became saints. It is unlikely, as some speculative writers have suggested, that these elements survived the Norman Conquest, although the mysterious death of King William II (William Rufus) in the New Forest at Lammastide 1100 leaves many questions unanswered.

One interesting pre-Conquest example is King Edward the Martyr, who was killed at Corfe Castle in Dorset in 978. After his death Edward was made a saint and his demise came shortly after the Great Famine of 976 blighted the land [24] and during a period when the pagan Danes were invading England. It has been suggested that Edward took the old role of Woden-sprung priest-king as the Lord's Anointed, mediating between God and the people, for through him God's power flowed into the land [25].

Edward's father was King Edgar and it is alleged he killed his second wife's husband so he might marry her. She was called Aelfthryth and when Edgar died she plotted to put her own son, Edward's half-brother, on the throne. Three years later the plot succeeded when Edward was lured to his step-mother's castle by his dwarf jester. He was alone and without an armed escort as he rode to meet his wyrd.

The king was greeted at the castle gate, near a holy spring which had been sacred since Celtic times, by members of the old Queen's household. The king was offered a cup of wine, possibly poisoned, as he sat on his horse outside the castle and at its threshold. He was then shot with arrows and stabbed. He fell from his horse and died instantly.

The murderers panicked and they decided to hide the body by burying it an a nearby marsh. However a column of light was seen hovering above the burial place by some local men from Wareham. They recovered the body from the marsh and took it to the nearby church of the Blessed Virgin Mary. It was later buried in Salisbury cathedral and pilgrims visited the tomb to receive miracle cures.

On the way to the marsh the murderers stopped at the cottage of an old woman who was blind and she was instantly cured when she touched the king's bloody body. At the spot where the king's body was buried a spring with healing powers sprung up. It is also recorded that, in the pagan fashion, the king's body was dismembered and bones from it were scattered across southern England to create seven shrines in his memory. All were credited with healing powers and miracles.

According to one writer, Edward's death on March 18th, near the vernal equinox, was associated with *blot*s to a Saxon goddess called Hred or Hreda who was a deity of victory. Twenty-three years after Edward's death or martyrdom, this date was officially made the feast of St Edward. It has been suggested this was merely a cover-up of a transfer of a pagan festival to a Christian one [26].

Edward's wicked stepmother, the old Queen, allegedly killed the Abbot of Ely in a bizarre incident in 971. The unfortunate cleric was out riding in the New Forest when he discovered the queen beneath a tree engaged in the preparation of a magickal potion! She was apparently attempting to use her 'magic art' to shape-shift into the form of a horse so she might 'satisfy her burning lust, riding and leaping hither and thither with the horses and showing herself shamelessly before them' [27]. It is said that she did eventually confess to Edward's murder, founded two nunneries as penance and wore a hairshirt. Seemingly a small penance to pay for the killing of a king.

Except in a symbolic form, human sacrifice does not appear to have been a feature of historical witchcraft, despite the crude lies of the Church who accused witches of killing and eating un-baptised babies. A charge that had already been used against the Jews, Cathars and Knight Templars.

Writing of the early Pickingill Craft of East Anglia, which claims to date back to Saxon times and worshipped the fertility and earth gods of the Norse version of the pagan Old Religion, one Hereditary witch has said: 'The Vanir deities from earliest times had demanded both blood and sexual fluids to ensure the fertility of the fields. Fortunately the Pickingill tradition eschewed sacrifice and blood, as did most of the 'Viking' traditions in England' [28].

A possible symbolic substitute for the sacrificial victim in the old harvest rites was the scarecrow. In folklore they were called 'mommets', 'bogies' or 'mawkins'. Mommet referred to a night spirit, a bogey is a goblin and mawkin can mean a ghost or fetch. The scarecrow universally had a sinister image and at Lent, near the spring equinox, men, usually tramps, were pelted with sticks and stones if they appeared in the village. This cruel custom, mentioned in Shakespeare's *Merry Wives of Windsor*, was replaced in the 19th century by attacks on a puppet or scarecrow called Jack-a-Lent. Originally the scarecrow may have been placed in the field as a guardian to protect the crops from physical and psychic harm, as would the earthbound spirit of the sacrificial victim.

The scarecrow could also be an image of the corn spirit, Old John Barleycorn himself, the God sacrificed at Lammastide. This theme is explored in a modern folk song by June Tabor called *The Scarecrow*. It is basically a love song to the scarecrow, but on an inner level it describes the God's journey around the Wheel of the Year. Everywhere in folklore there is evidence linking the scarecrow with the spirits that haunt the cornfield. In 17th century Estonia, for example, a straw puppet was placed in a tree or on a fence to protect the cattle and sheep from wolves and to promote the fertility of the crops.

In North America the legend that the scarecrow came alive on Hallowe'en and joined with other night spooks and goblins to terrorise humans is commonly represented in popular culture. The American writer Nathaniel Hawthorne, author of the *Legend of Sleepy Hollow* based on the Wild Hunt, wrote a folk tale based on this belief which was common in his native Salem in New England. In the story a 17th century witch called Mother Rigby made a scarecrow from her besom and used a magical pipe to bring it alive.

The Dr Syn stories by the English writer Russell Thorndike also brought together witchcraft, the Wild Hunt and the sinister image of the scarecrow in a bestselling fictional format based on old folk tales and legends. In the stories Dr Syn is a respectable vicar by day. At night however he donned the mask and guise of the mysterious Scarecrow who rode the Essex marshes with his gang of smugglers known as the Night Riders. The smugglers disguised themselves as the Wild Hunt using masks and ragged clothes to frighten the locals away from their haunts.

It is very easy to adopt a high moral tone with respect to these accounts of human and animal sacrifice in the past. It should be remembered that they were widespread in ancient times and even in the Bible we can read of the 'burnt offerings' made to Jehovah. Even in the time of Jesus pigeons and doves were sold in the precincts of the temple in Jerusalem for sacrificial purposes. As we have seen, the Christian Mass is a sublimated version of the rites of human sacrifice which sometimes included the eating of the victim.

These blood sacrifices of the past pale into insignificance if they are compared with the atrocities humankind has perpetuated against its own kind and the animal realms. Thousands upon thousands of Jews, heretics, 'witches', Catholic and Protestants were murdered by the Church in the past. In our century we have seen the senseless slaughter of a whole generation of young men in the trenches of the Somme and Ypres, the death camps of the Boer War, Stalinist Russia and Hitler's Germany, the nuclear horrors of Hiroshima and Nagasaki, the killing fields of

Vietnam and Cambodia, the 'ethnic cleansing' in Bosnia and Kosovo, the genocide in Rwanda, and the millions of animals tortured and killed daily in vivisection laboratories all over the world.

Today, thankfully, we have evolved beyond the crude practice of offering the life force of a living creature, animal or human to the Gods of our people. If we feel the need to make offerings then we can light a candle or some incense, pour a libation of alcohol, or offer a coin, some clothing or jewellry or even something more personal to the Powers. The real sacrifice is ourselves on the Path and to the Gods and that is a daily one throughout the Wheel of the Year.

The cutting of the last sheaf of the harvest was surrounded by folk beliefs which are pretty obviously survivals of paganism. To the Anglo-Saxons the last sheaf gathered in was an important religious symbol representing the child of the corn goddess [29]. It was believed to be the dwelling place or embodiment of the corn spirit, who could be in male, female or animal form. In European countries the spirit of the corn took animal form as a sow, frog, mare, fox, goat, hare, goose, cat or wolf. These creatures have been linked with deities of the harvest including Dionysus, Attis, Osiris, Adonis and Demeter [30].

The festival of Harvest End or Harvest Home coincided with the autumn equinox in September when the days and nights were equal. It was the time of the Zodiac sign Virgo, the corn maiden or goddess. At this period there was a feeling in the air that autumn was when the Bright Goddess of spring and summer handed over to the Dark Goddess of winter. The last sheaf was significantly called the Old Woman, the Old Witch, the Queen, the Old Sow, the Mare, the Bitch, the Hare, the Gander and the Maiden. In Scotland two corn dollies made from the last sheaf were called the Cailleach and the Maiden. They were dressed accordingly in handmade clothes and were the harvest of the past year and the year to come.

164

In the Scottish Highlands the last sheaf was called the Maiden before Samhain (November Ist) and the Cailleach afterwards. 'this (sheaf) was thought to contain the spirit of the grain goddess, so the 'maid from the farm ran to the farmhouse with it, where it was fashioned into a corn dolly and hung up over the hearth for winter. The Cailleach presided over the home, and was taken out and scattered on the fields prior to sowing time in the spring. This was the cycle of the Earth Goddess complete' [31].

The corn dollies were given evocative names such as the Harvest Queen, Corn Babies or Ivy Girls. The women who were selected to take the dolly back to the farmhouse were called the Queen of the Harvest or the Queen of the Feast. They were carried home in a harvest wain or cart that was decorated with flowers and boughs of oak and ash. This wagon was drawn by four or six carthorses garlanded with flowers and with gleaming horse-brasses on their collars. The reapers sat on top of the wagon blowing horns and singing bawdy songs, while the other workers walked behind. Sometimes the waggoner wore a woman's dress' [32]. It is tempting, if speculative, to compare this sight with the procession of Nerthus or Freyr's wain through the countryside in pagan times.

The (usually) male farmworker who cut the last sheaf by throwing his scythe at it was given the title of Harvest Lord, and the female worker who brought the corn dolly safely back from the fields was his Harvest Lady. They ruled over the traditional Harvest Supper, sometimes called the Feast of the Maiden. When these rites of Harvest Home became too riotous and rowdy in the 19th century the more sedate Harvest Festival of the Church became popular when the fruits of the crop were offered

The person who cut the last sheaf was sometimes roughly treated by the other workers. If the farmer and his wife entered the reaping field on the last day of the harvest they were often threatened or they had a cord tied around their arms and were bundled into sheaves. In some European countries if a stranger walked onto the threshing floor they were bound with a flail and a rope made from twisted corn was placed around their necks. It seems 'the person who cuts, binds and threshes the last corn is treated as an embodiment of the corn spirit by being wrapped in sheaves, killed in mimicry by agricultural implements and thrown into the water' [33].

In the Craft the period from Lammastide to Harvest Home is 'the time for thanksgiving, the time of mature contemplation for the past year's work. The seeds of that working should be looked at, and thanks given for whatever has been achieved. It is also a time of sorrow, for the season of growth is over and the year must surely die' [34].

That is the inner meaning of Lammas and Harvest Home. On the practical level the Gods will be thanked for the harvest and the story of the death of Old John Barleycorn will be re-enacted. As the fall comes, the leaves begin to flutter down from the trees, the mist rises from the empty fields and the first frost makes hedgerows white, the reign of the bright Summer Goddess comes to an end. She must become the Wise Crone, the Dark Queen and the Destroying Hag.

She is now the Winter Goddess of the waning and dark moon whose gifts are visions of the future and the release of death. The spring maiden and the summer enchantress hide their beautiful faces behind the grim visage of the winter Hag. She is the Old Queen who rides out from the faery mound at the head of the Faery Host at midnight on Samhain Eve. Beside her rides the dark and sinister figure of the Wild Hunter with his stag skull mask and antlers. The dark season has begun and once more the goblin dead haunt the spirit paths waiting to be invited in.

Chapter Eleven

A Winter Night's Dream

In Anglo-Saxon times early November was the time when the surplus cattle, sheep and pigs were brought in from their summer pastures and slaughtered so their meat could be salted for the winter. Writing in the 8th century CE the Venerable Bede said the pagan Saxons called November *Blodmonath* or blood month. In a religious sense it was when the *blot* was performed - the pre-winter sacrifice of animals to the Gods in the hope the weather would not be bad and not too may of the tribe would die before spring.

To the Celts November 1st was Samhain (Sow-an) or 'summer's end' In Wales it was *calan gaef* or the first day of winter, while Hallowe'en was *nos calan gaef* or winter's night. Despite the modern custom of Wiccans and pagans to treat Samhain as the Celtic New Year, there is little evidence to support this idea. In fact it seems to have been a myth that developed during the Celtic Twilight of the last century [1].

In 835 CE the Church decided to move the Festival of All Saints from May 13th to November Ist. A century later November 2nd was made All Soul's Day when it was the custom for Christians to pray for the dead in Limbo. It is possible, as some contemporary writers have suggested, that these Christian festivals associated with saints and the dead influenced the folk celebrations of All Saints' Eve or All Hallows Eve (Hallowe'en). However, Samhain and Winter's Night were already marked by our Norse and Celtic ancestors as a festival for the dead. It was a special time when summer gave way to winter and supernatural forces were believed to be on the loose.

Hallowe'en, with May Eve and Midsummer Eve, was one of the three 'spirit nights' of the year when the veil between the worlds was thin In the old days it was when people gathered around the open fire to frighten each other with ghost stories, relate local legends and divine the future. A door or window was left open for the dead to enter and a special meal, known as the Dumb Supper, was prepared and left out for them.

Outside, in the countryside, all hell had broken loose as the spirits of the underworld roamed abroad scaring travellers. The Wild Hunt led by the King: and Queen of Elfame rode the night sky, along with witches on broomsticks on their way to the Grand Sabbat presided over by the Devil. Churchyards, cross-roads and stiles were crowded with the dead and their whispers 'buzzed like bees'. In Wales the White Lady and the Old Black Sow, representing the Dark Goddess, could be encountered in dark lanes by any mortal daft enough to be out and about on Winter's Eve.

As late as the end of the 18th century gangs of men in Montgomeryshire on the Welsh Border dressed up in masks and ragged coats or sheepskins at this time of the year. They roamed the street attacking passers-by and were commonly known as 'Hags'. In Lancashire, in a combination of pagan and Christian practice, people met together to light bonfires at Hallowe'en and pray for the dead.

Hallowe'en bonfires were usually lit at dusk and the reason behind them was to scare away the powers of darkness with light. As the days grew longer the sun was sinking in the sky and so it was believed the dark powers were in ascendant. In post-Christian times popular beliefs associated witches with these powers of darkness. The cry went up "Burn the Witch' when more peat and wood was thrown on the fire.

In recent years it has been said that the modern secular celebration of Hallowe'en, which is a commercial travesty, is becoming combined with Bonfire Night or Guy Fawkes Night on November 5th. The two festivals have become blurred in popular cultural terms and folklorists suggest the burning of effigies, whether of Guido Fawkes or an unpopular government minister, is a folk memory of ancient human sacrifices at the beginning of winter.

In rural Derbyshire in the 1950s this type of folk memory survived in the treatment meted out to the guy on Bonfire Night. He was called the Lad, an old name for the Devil, and was carried deosil around the fire. Sometimes he was decorated with greenery and had a noose around his neck. the children used to make strangling gestures or 'stab' the guy with a stick, before throwing him on the fire. After the fire died down a large oatcake was broken up and placed in a tin box. The person who selected the burnt piece had to 'jump the bonfire'.

One of the local people who attended this event as a child said he felt the burning of the guy was done to appease 'what was out there' in the darkness. Even as a small child he felt the burning of the effigy was nothing to do with an historical event in the 1600s, but everything to do with the woods and moors in the dark around the bonfire [2].

Samhain was and is first and foremost a festival of the dead and they were believed to be able to return to the world of the living for a brief time at this period of the year. In Celtic mythology the abode of the dead was either underground, under water, in a hollow hill, or on an island in the western ocean 'beyond the setting sun' or rather these were the entrances to the underworld, the liminal places where contact could be made with the ancestral dead. In the Iron Age Glastonbury Tor, which was then an island surrounded by marshes and the sea, was regarded as hollow and an entrance to the Otherworld. It was the dwelling place of Gwynn ap Nudd, the Welsh version of the leader of the Wild Hunt, and of Morgan Le Fay and her nine maidens who guarded the Grail.

The Island of the Dead and the Hollow Hill, the womb-tomb of the ancient earth goddess, are probably pre-Celtic concepts. The Hollow Hill and a castle on an island in the sea, a lake or a river stil survives in the Traditional Craft. One modern traditional witch has said this Castle of Roses is 'located on the horizon of western sea and sunset..It can be seen out at sea and where the water and the sky meet and merge' [3].

Describing the journey of the soul to the Rose Castle this same source says the journey takes it 'along the path through the underworld to the banks of the timeless river that is the boundary between this world and the next...far out in the river..is the island on which stands the triple-towered castle. It is perched on a rocky outcrop with a snaking path leading up to its gale from a desolate path covered in stunted bushes', The soul is carried across the River of Death (Styx) by a hooded ferryman (the God) and as he or she begins to walk towards the castle the wasteland blooms with roses. Then the soul 'instinctively knows that the Goddess has gathered it home again' [4].

The Queen of the Rose Castle is the triple goddess of life, death and wisdom. As a poet once said, describing this pale-faced goddess in lunar symbolism: 'the new moon is the White Goddess of birth and growth, the full moon is the Red Goddess of love and battle; and the old moon the Black Goddess of death and divination' [5]. As our old friend Diana-Artemis she is 'the goddess of the wild, virgin nature, all the inviolate places of the Earth where humans dare not enter'. She is also the 'immanent presence of the whole of nature as a sacred reality' [6].

As Artemis, the Greek version of Diana, she is very ancient for 'the Old European Bear Goddess, Bird Goddess and Weaving Goddess of the spindlewhorls can be rediscovered in the stories and images of her and in the kind of festivals held in her honour' [7]. Her priestesses were called 'she bears' and wore bear masks when they danced in sexual ecstasy before her images. She was one aspect of the triple moon goddess as the new moon, with Selene as full and Hecate as the dark moon.

Artemis was no modern 'pretty moon goddess in a Laura Ashley frock and glitter in her hair'. She demanded sacrifice and when the human hunter Actaeon crossed her path, and dared to gaze on her nakedness while she was bathing, he met his doom. Artemis transformed herself into a stag and, in a version of the Wild Chase, enacted at Samhain, lured him to his death. For this reason her priestesses also wore the masks of the goddess' hunting dogs.

As we saw in the end of harvest rites, the summer goddess has changed into the dual-faced Crone/Hag. Now the harvest is over the wheat has been separated from the chaff, the initiates from the cowans, those awake from those still asleep in the dreamless slumber of the profane. In the old Welsh legend, the witch Ceridwen has become a hen and swallowed poor little Gwion who had become a grain of corn. 'Now we see the Goddess changing over from the bountiful mother into the owl, then the sow of the Crone, for it is on the threshing floor with the flail of life's experiences and the airy knowledge that the wheat and the chaff are divided' [8].

The transfer of the power from the Summer Queen to the Old Hag of winter is described in an Irish legend about Pope Boniface and how Samhain became the Feast of All Saints. It is said that on Winter's Night in Rome the boys played a board game featuring the figure of an old woman and a young woman at different ends. The old hag sent a dragon to destroy the young woman, but she responded by sending a lamb to subdue it. Then the old woman let loose a lion, but the young girl made it rain and the lion retreated and so on.

The Pope stopped the boys from playing the game, but they protested and said it had been taught to them by the prophet Sibyl (one of the names for the witch goddess in southern Europe). Probably this legend of the mysterious board game had nothing to do with the Pope or Rome. Instead it sounds like a symbolic battle between Brigid and the Cailleach at the beginning of winter [9].

The motif of the Castle and the Rose appears dramatically in popular European fairy stories such as *Sleeping Beauty* and *Snow White* and it identifies them as disguised myths about the witch goddess. In *Snow White*, for instance, we see a jealous stepmother who is often represented as a witch figure. She is the dark destroyer, the dark aspect of the Goddess (Holda), who seeks to kill her stepdaughter, the princess, or the spring goddess (Freyja). The stepmother commands a huntsman or woodsman to do the dreadful deed and he takes the girl into the woods. He is so captivated by Snow White's innocence and beauty - the shining face of the Bright Goddess - that he cannot kill her. Instead he kills a boar or a stag and presents its heart to his evil mistress as proof of the girl's death.

Once the stepmother looks in a magick mirror, realises Snow White is still alive and the huntsman has tricked her she tries

The Dark Goddess as the fairytale wicked stepmother

herself to bring about the girl's death. She dresses up as an old woman (the Hag) and visits Snow White in the woods with a poisoned apple - the underworld fruit of immortality. When Snow White dies she is laid to rest in a glass coffin in a sacred grove on top of a hill.

Snow White is guarded by an owl, a raven and a dove. All sacred birds of the Goddess in both her dark and bright aspects. She is also guarded by the seven dwarves who are skilled in metalcraft and work in the caves. They are representatives of the faerie realm of Oberon the King of the Faeries, who is also Robin Goodfellow or Puck, the faery aspect of the god of the witches in English folklore. The glass coffin is symbolic of the Glass Tower or Spinning Castle and the prince whose kiss brings Snow White back to life is none other then the young Horn God who awakens the spring maiden from her winter slumber when she dreams of being the Hag.

In the tale of Sleeping Beauty or Briar Rose the old witch lore of the Northern European tradition is even more evident in the story. Twelve wise-women, faery godmothers or gossips are invited by the king and queen to attend their daughter's birthday. The godmothers shower the princess with gifts and blessings. Then a thirteenth godmother, who has not been invited, turns up. She is called Held (Holda) and curses the princess with death at the age of fifteen after pricking her finger on a spinning wheel. Luckily, one of the godmothers commutes this death sentence into a sleep or trance which will last a hundred years. The predicted event comes to pass, eventually a prince fights his way through a barrier of thorn bushes around the castle and awakes the sleeping princess with a kiss. The thorns immediately turn into roses.

In this fairy tale the thirteen wise-women represent the thirteen moons of the lunar year. Holda is the thirteenth moon, the dark moon ruled by the Three Fates, the Three Spinners, the Three Ladies or the three Wyrd Sisters. The spinning wheel, weaving the fate of humanity and the Web of Wyrd, is their primary symbol. The castle of Sleeping Beauty and the rose garden

173

represent the underworld realm of the Goddess where souls come to rest before rebirth. the barrier of thorns is the boundary between this world and the next as previously described.

The sleeping princess motif connects with the Arthurian legend of the 'once and future king' asleep in a cave. As in the German legend of Brunhilde, who falls into a deep sleep after pricking her finger on a thorn, the princess will awake when she is needed. The prince who does so with a kiss or 'the breath of life and is the God who joins in the sacred marriage with the spring goddess. In some versions of he fairy tale not only Sleeping Beauty but the castle's inhabitants are placed under the sleeping spell of the faery godmother or Dark Goddess. Truly then it becomes the 'enchanted Castle of the Otherworld'.

In the Briar Rose version of the legend the princess climbs higher and higher into a tower until she reaches the attic. This is symbolic of the Tower of Babel which is regarded as significant in those branches of traditional witchcraft influenced by Freemasonry. The Tower of Babel was an ancient ziggurat temple that represented the sacred mountain. The Great Rite or sacred marriage was performed on an open air altar on its top level by a high priest and priestess taking the roles of the sun god and moon goddess. It is in the attic that the princess meets the old woman with the spinning wheel who is her nemesis. She is 'the dangerous and malign aspect of the Great Mother, the Great Spider. This fearsome magic web, always present in the images of spinning and weaving, is associated with the web of life, the binding to life and, again, with the threefold lunar symbolism of past, present and future, which introduces the element of time and is connected with the Mother Goddess and the Fates in their malefic, destructive aspect' [10].

The image of the princess held captive in the tower, as in the fairy tale of Rapunzel and Rumplestiltskin (a phallic fertility figure) is also associated with the theme of the sacred marriage and the crafts of spinning and weaving. The long hair of the princess features in these stories and this has always been a sign of the witch or goddess figure. Spinning and weaving are the magickal crafts of the witch goddess, just as smithcraft is usually associated with the God as Tubal Cain, Vulcan and Weyland and with the masculine mysteries of the Craft. It is an older woman (the Crone) who initiates the younger woman (the Maiden) into the feminine mysteries and this initiation represents the annual transition or transformation between the twin aspects of the Bright and Dark Goddess in the spring and autumn.

At the beginning of winter the God passes through the portals of the dolmen into the burial mound or Hollow Hill and descends to the underworld. Pagan burial mounds were still being used for Christian internments as late as the time of the Emperor Charlemagne, who issued an edict banning their use. The wights, or earth spirits, that haunted these places were ruled by Odin. On Winter's Night blots were made at burial mounds, especially if a king was buried there, for the fertility of the folk and the land.

The October full moon was and is still popularly known as the Hunter's Moon. This name reflects the importance that hunting once held in human life as a means of providing the tribe with fresh meat. Today, at least in Western civilised cultures, most humans do not hunt down their daily meal. Hunting is reserved as a 'sport' for pleasure and even then it faces opposition from those who evolved beyond this stage. Some anglers, poachers and blood sport followers eat what they catch, but in most cases hunting is a leisure pursuit, and not a matter of life and death for the hunter.

On a spiritual level 'our understanding of the hunter has evolved from a physical function of a food provider, to a more subtle one of guardian, guide and shadow within' [11]. In the Craft the Wild Hunter's role is as a psychopomp, or guide to the dead, whose Wild Hunt gathers up the souls of the dead and takes them to the spirit world. As the Hunter of souls, Old Hornie has a dual function 'as a guide of the dead and second as a Guardian of the Gate that initiates seek to pass when they wish to enter the psychic realms' [12].

The Wild Hunt usually rode along the spirit paths and across the night sky between Hallows and Candlemas. According to a member of one of the old family traditions in Derbyshire: 'January was when the God, the Old One, Woden, or whatever name you want to call him, took his hounds and rode through the sky. It was the hardest time of the year when most of the old and weak died, and it was believed the God was active and about chasing his human flock' [13].

It is interesting that British emigrants took the legend of the Wild Hunt across the Atlantic to Canada and the United States. In the mythology and folklore of the Old West it lived on in the legend told by cowboys about the 'ghost riders in the sky'. These were spectral cowboys condemned to driving a ghostly herd of cattle across the sky. In fact this myth became the subject of a pop ballad that reached the the U.K. hit parade in the 1950s.

Samhain is a Celtic festival and the transformation of the Bright God of summer into the Dark God of winter is described in the First Branch of the Mabinogion. This tells the story of Pwyll, the prince of Dyfed in West Wales, and his fateful meeting with Arawn, Lord of the Underworld, while out hunting. The story is a solar myth and begins with Pwyll hunting in a wooded valley called Cwm Cych. There he encountered another huntsman with his pack chasing a stag across a ford in the river Cych. Pwyll intervened in the chase and set his own hounds upon the animal.

The grey-cloaked hunter riding a grey horse arrived on the scene and he chastised the prince for his action. To make amends for the slight, Arawn demanded that the prince fight the underworld lord's enemy, Hafgan. In Welsh *haf* means 'summer'. To do this Pwyll had to change places and bodies with Arawn for a year and a day, and kill Hafgan with a single blow.

The prince agreed to this and, disguised as the lord of the underworld, arrived at the court of the spirits where he was warmly welcomed back from his hunting trip in the world of mortals. Pwyll even slept in the same bed as Arawn's wife, the queen of the underworld, but he never had marital relations with her. At the appointed time, the prince fought and killed Hafgan. Once the year and a day were up, the prince and the king of the dead exchanged bodies once more and returned to their respective worlds. They became close friends and Pwyll was given the honourary title of Pen Annwn, or chief of the underworld [14].

In a second tale concerning Pwyll, the prince consummates his relationship with the queen of the underworld. The story says that one day Pwyll was at his court in Narberth and he was sitting on a mound near his palace. As he sat there a veiled woman rode by on a white horse. Pwyll was intrigued by this and sent his men after her, but she rode away too quickly. Three times this happened and in the end Pwyll chased after her himself, but however fast his horse went she eluded him. Eventually he shouted out for her to stop and she did willingly. The woman told the prince that her name was Rhiannon, that she was secretly in love with him and had been trying to get his attention.

Rhiannon and Pwyll get married and they rule together as king and queen over Dyfed for three years. However the queen fails to produce any children and the people turn against her. In the fourth year of their reign she finally has a child. When it vanishes from the bed chamber and the nurses cannot find it they kill a puppy, smear its blood on Rhiannon's face as she sleeps and strew its bones around the room. They then falsely accuse the queen of killing and eating the baby in case they are blamed for its disappearance. Rhiannon is forced to undergo penance for seven years for her alleged crime and becomes the queen mourning for her lost or dead child.

Meanwhile, in Gwent, a farmer owned a mare which gave birth each May Eve. Just as regularly the resulting foal vanished from the stable. When she was due to give birth again the farmer stood guard and he saw a monstrous claw come through the window to seize the newly born foal. He chased the monster off and when he returned to the stable the foal had changed into a golden-haired boy.

The farmer and his wife pretended the baby was their own and became his foster-parents. The boy grew up very fast and showed an uncanny ability with horses. One day the farmer heard the sad story of Rhiannon and recognized her likeness in the boy. He handed him over to his real royal parents and the boy, named Pryderi, grew up to be the next ruler of Dyfed [15].

Both these tales about Pwyll have underworld themes. They are also linked to the Mythic Theme in this book of sacred kingship, the goddess of the land, the ritual battle between the summer king and winter king, and the descent of the God to the underworld. This is very obvious in the first story where Pwyll confronts the Wild Hunter at a ford - a liminal crossing point between this world and the Other. Arawn makes him his champion to defeat the summer king with a single blow. It should be remembered that Sir Gawain in the Arthurian legend had to kill the Green Knight with a single blow, as a second would bring him back from the dead. Arawn is none other then Gwyn ap Nudd, who each May Day until the end of the world has to fight a rival for the hand of a lady - the Oak King and Holly King in ritual combat for the favours of the Goddess.

In the story of Rhiannon and Pwyll the mound at Narberth, which now has a graveyard on its slopes, is another boundary or threshold place where humans and Otherworlders can meet and communicate. The veiled Lady on a white horse is the ancient horse goddess known to the Celts as Epona. Her dramatic image is carved on the hillside at Uffington in Berkshire. It is adjacent to Bronze Age burial mounds indicating the site was in use in Celtic times. Below it is a large mound known as Dragon's Hill and nearby is the prehistoric burial chamber called Wayland's Smithy.

Rhiannon is the ancient Mare Goddess who rides between the worlds' [16]. The white horse is a symbol of Sovereignty and Rhiannon, Epona is a goddess of the underworld. In the ancient coronation rites of the Irish kings the new ruler was obliged to have intercourse with a white mare. It was then killed, cooked in a cauldron and the flesh eaten as a sacred meal. The king also had to take a ritual bath in a broth made from the horse's flesh. This primitive and grisly ritual was a debased version of the granting of sacred kingship to a human candidate by marrying the goddess of the land.

In the Welsh story when Rhiannon finally gives birth she is falsely accused of of its murder. She takes on the role of the mourning mother and the Devourer, the Great Sow Goddess who is said to eat her own children' [17]. The claw that carries off the foal each Beltane is the Dark Goddess demanding her annual sacrifice. Pryderi, raised by foster-parents like Lugh, Llew and Arthur, is destined to replace his father as sacred king. His love of horses means he will also become the husband of Sovereignty.

In some traditions of the Craft the Holly King of winter is mythically portrayed as Arthur, the once and future king. Why should this be? In the early Welsh poem *The Spoils of Annwn* it is said that Arthur descended to the underworld to rescue a youth. In the poem Annwn, or the underworld, is depicted as Caer Sidi, the spinning or turning castle of Arianrhod. It is described as 'the four-square Caer, four times revolving' and it stands on the Island of the Strong Door' [18].

Once in the underworld Arthur finds a cauldron rimmed with pearls and guarded by nine maidens, or aspects of the Goddess. This is the same cauldron of Avalon guarded by Arthur's half-sister Morgan and her nine priestesses, and it is to Avalon that Arthur's body is carried after his final battle. We have previously seen that Caer Sidi is the Tower of Glass, the Spiral Castle of the Otherworld where the dead are imprisoned, according to mortal opinion, but where they learn the wisdom of the initiating Goddess according to esoteric lore' [19].

Arthur is a human, possibly super-human, representative of the sacred king, and therefore of the God. He passes from being King of Britain to being King of the Underworld, the inner guardian of the Hallows, which he guards for the next Pendragon when he shall come' [20]. The prophecy remains that one day when he is needed Arthur will return to save his land from its enemies.

Although this prophecy has been misused for political purposes, it remains a powerful one and has been grafted on to other British folk heroes. When Lord Kitchener died in the First World War it was popularly believed he was not dead at all, but sleeping an enchanted sleep in a cave and would return like Arthur.

King Arthur's 'enchanted sleep' became the motif for several folk tales from those parts of the country where the king was said to have lived or done battle. One version, based in the Eildon Hills of the Scottish Border country was the subject of a romance by the 19th century writer Sir Walter Scott, In this story a horse-dealer is led into a cave in a hillside by no less a person as Thomas the Rhymer. Inside he sees a group of sleeping knights in black armour. On an 'antique table' or altar is a sword and horn.

Thomas tells the horse-dealer that whoever blows the horn and draws the sword will become the king of Britain. Unfortunately the man bungles it by blowing the horn before he draws the sword, not realising that there is a special sequence. A ghostly voice condemns him as a coward for doing the ritual incorrectly.

In an early 19th century Welsh version the entrance to the cave is concealed in the roots of a large hazel tree. It must be a large tree, hut then we remember that we are dealing with the entrance to an Otherworldly place and the normal laws of physics do not apply! Inside the cave are resting Arthur and his knights, plus a pile of gold. A passing traveller stumbles upon the cave and tries to make off with the gold. At the entrance he accidentally touches a bell which awakens the sleeping warriors. When he is unable to give the correct answers to their questions, the man is violently ejected from the cave and finds the gold he has packed into his pockets has vanished. It is after all faery gold.

In a Northumbrian version of the legend, the cave is under a castle and a beautiful maiden is present as well as the enchanted warriors or knights. In this account the ritual test the mortal

180

intruder has to pass involves a choice between a jewelled sword and a ivory horn belonging to Merlin. He therefore has the choice between sacred kingship, represented by the Sword of Power, or the magickal powers of the faery-born wizard [21].

The Merlin/Woden figure of the magician or wizard appears in one of the most famous versions of the legend known as The Wizard of Alderley. This is based on a folk tale of a mysterious wizard who guards a mysterious cave under Alderley Edge in Cheshire. This cave contains a white horse and some sleeping warriors, usually identified as Arthur and his knights.

In the story a miller or farmer sells his horse to a mysterious stranger dressed in a monk' habit. This figure leads the miller to an iron gate in the hillside which is the entrance to the cave where the warriors sleep. The miller is given treasure in exchange for his horse and leaves. When he returns later on his own and tries to find the iron gate it is no longer there [22].

The wizard of Alderley Edge is none other than Merlin and is the guardian of the Otherworldly cave and its sleepers. He has to venture out into Middle Earth now and again to buy horses for the time when Arthur returns. The gate to the cave is made from iron because that is the metal used by warlocks and magicians to bind and control the faery folk. It prevents psychic contamination which would disturb the warriors' enchanted rest.

Alderley Edge is not far from where the Lindow Man was found sacrificed in a peat bog. It is also an area associated with witchcraft, ancient and modern. At least one traditional coven has met at the Edge for the last hundred years. A so-called 'druid's circle' of standing stones erected in the last century has been used for witch rites since the last war. Today the Edge is a victim of its own publicity, but it still retains an aura of mystery.

We have come across the motif of the Sleepers before; in the folk story of the warriors sleeping under the Rollright Stones and guarded by a witch or wise-woman who can grant kingship, and in the fairy tales of Sleeping Beauty and Snow White. The sleeper can be female and she is 'allied to the creatures and to the powerful faery and underworld contacts'. In the story of Snow White, as we have seen, 'she is associated with the Guardian, who takes the form of a man or a stag, and he protects her through sacrifice' [23]. He is, of course, the Horned God.

In a meditation on an ancient king buried in a prehistoric tomb on Jersey in the Channel Islands, a modern writer has described the mystical role of the sacred king as the human representative of the God, and the esoteric symbolism of his ritualistic death. On death the king successfully merges with his environment, while his spirit remains earthbound as a 'sleeper' so he can still communicate on this plane with those who seek him out. In fact, the most important feature of the Son of Light is that he mediates between humanity and the supernal or infernal powers' [24].

The king has the after-death name of 'Stone King' or 'Earth Man' and these names, or rather titles, emphasis his connection with the physical landscape in which he is buried. During his life he was responsible for communicating 'earth peace' to his people. This was achieved by merging with the environment (the land) and emerging on the Other Side as '"aentity of wholeness or integration', able to link and mediate through various stages of human and non-human evolution.

The work of the sacred king was to achieve the mystical integration of the 'blood and the land', which is so misunderstood nowadays, and then achieve other levels of awareness involving contact with non-human entities. The burial mound in which the king was interred is symbolic of the womb of Terra Mater or the Mother, and a 'guardian' was placed to ensure the king's physical remains were not disturbed before his 'new birth'.

Unfortunately, the guardian in this case was no Otherworldly wizard. Instead a human volunteer was ritually killed. They were then psychically bound to 'watch and ward' over their king's body until he successfully merged with the Other. Once this stage had been reached, the spirit of the human guardian could be released in a ritual of exorcism and joined the ancestral dead in the the spirit world (35).

In Scottish folklore elements of the God's descent to the underworld and the 'underworld initiation' can be found in the ballad of Thomas the Rhymer. He was a 13th century aristocrat called Lord Learmont of Ercledoune. Thomas was widely renowned as a prophet and he served William Wallace (Braveheart) and Robert the Bruce as a seer in the nationalist cause against the English. These powers of seership were rumoured to have been the result of an underworld initiation gained by his relationship with the Queen of Faerie.

In the story Thomas was sleeping one day under a hawthorn tree when a lady dressed all in green rode up. She was riding a pure white horse with silver bells at its bridle. Thomas at first believed this shining apparition was the Virgin Mary, but of course she is the witch goddess in her summer aspect as the Faery Lady. They 'embrace' beneath the May tree and she invites him, or commands him, to return to her realm for seven years. This is the period traditionally served by the sacred king before his ritual death. Thomas eventually returns to Middle Earth but after his death, like Tannhauser, he returns to the Hollow Hill. There he becomes one of the Hidden Company and is a guide to those who would follow his path to the world of faerie.

In some versions of the Traditional Craft today, two circles are cast at Hallows. One is for the living and one is for the dead. Using a circle or the act of circling to make contact with or enter the spirit world has always been a prominent feature of folk ritual and folk magick. It is a ritual act associated with nocturnal visits, usually at the witching hour of Bull's Noon or midnight on the full moon to prehistoric burial mounds, crossroads, ancient standing stones or churchyards built on pagan sites.

Once there the brave dance or walk three, seven or nine times widdershins, backwards or forwards or deosil around the hallowed ground. This magickal action prompts visions of the future or a manifestation of the Devil (the Horned God), 'a lady

Thomas the Rhymer with faery harp

on a white horse', spirits who are guardians of treasure, faeries or long-dead pagan priests who will reveal secret knowledge.

In all cases the act of circling is a ritual metaphor for gaining access to the Other, crossing the boundaries of this world into the next and making contact with supernatural forces or beings. Circling rituals were also found in rural funerals in bygone ages. The funeral party often followed an old 'corpse way', a church road or spirit path that went across country, often in a straight line and ignoring new roads. The procession paused along the way to circle a pile of stones (sometimes of pre-Christian origin) and sometimes the coffin was placed on the stones while the bearers rested. When the coffin reached the church they often circumbulated the churchyard before entering the building.

The Spiral or Maze dance is also performed at Hallowe'en as it was at Beltane, but for a different reason. When it is danced at the beginning of the dark season it is a dance of death performed northways or widdershins. It is danced by the coven with the Master or Magister standing in the centre. He is stag-masked as Herne, with his arms crossed on his chest in the traditional sign of the skull-and-crossbones.

At Hallows the spiral dance is symbolic of the journey of the initiate or the God to the Castle of Glass ruled by the Dark Lady. In one family tradition the ritual of the Wild Chase is enacted at this festival to challenge the guardianship of a piece of land such as a woodland, perhaps to be, used as a working site. Three times the challenges have to be made and if it fails then the Gods may demand their own price in full.

The ritual involves the preparing of mandrake (bryony), yew, stinging nettles, oak leaves and belladonna in the cauldron. This is lit, along with three black candles, and both are dedicated to the Wild Chase and Herne the Hunter. A cup of red wine is dedicated to the Morrigan or any other hunting goddess such as Diana-Artemis, and is added to the fire.

It is said that at this point in the ritual a vision of the Wild Chase will appear in the steam rising from the cauldron. If it does then the challenger has to run around the boundary of the land and it will be granted to them. If you actually see the Wild Hunt then you will ride with it after death. Also you are then entitled to ask the faery folk residing on the land to come to your aid and also all wild creatures. This is a serious ritual that should not be practised lightly. Once the guardianship of the land has been granted by the Powers the responsibility of holding it can never be given on [26].

Hallowe'en is the Great Assembly of the year. This is when the alder bridge to the Other Side is opened and the ancestral dead are invited into the circle to join in the celebrations. It is a special time when the Hidden Company draw near and can be often felt or even seen outside the circle. They are the discarnate

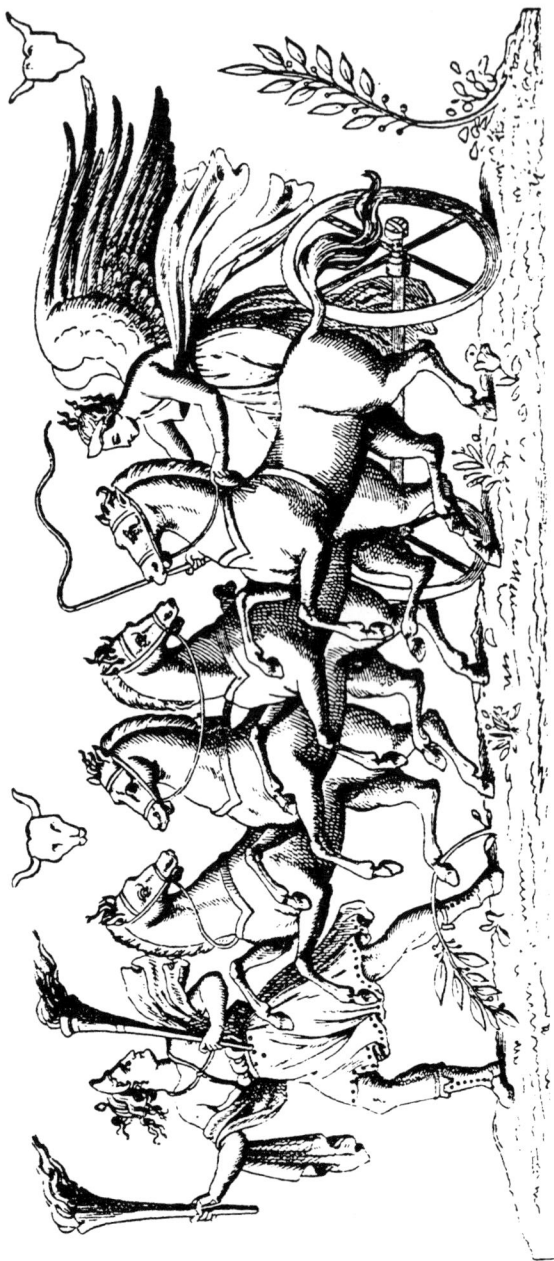

Eos or Aurora - goddess of the Dawn with Lucifer

spirits of witches who have gone before and now return to act as spirit guides to the living.

To those of the Craft the dark season that commences on Winter's Night is a time for planning, consolidation and peaceful contemplation. It culminates at Yule or the winter solstice when the sun appears to stand still in the sky and the world ceases to spin. This is the 'time between time' when we should take a spiritual rest before the Wheel of the Year turns anew and the 'stag and the old woman' welcome in the New Year, so that the cycle can begin anew.

In this process of contemplation followed by rebirth the archetypal image of the Wild Hunter is important because if we can face him 'who carries much of our shadow and allows the dark wisdom within to teach us then we can go quietly into the underworld over the winter months' [27]. By confronting our natural fear of death and the dark inherited from our ancestors, and overcoming our Christian conditioning that darkness equals evil, we can discover what the Dark God and Goddess have to teach us.

By turning inwards at this time we find that the 'Interior Castle, where if we can enter and ask and answer questions, the pale-faced Goddess of Wisdom will serve us from her cauldron which leads to healing wholeness and rebirth' [28].

This then is our own personal underworld initiation at Hallows and our own quest for the vision of the Grail granted to those who are worthy in heart and spirit. It is the vision of the Grail which is in the gift of the Dark Lady and it is into her realm that we must descend at this time to cain that sight at her hands.

Chapter Twelve

Making Traditional Magick

It has often been said that the Craft is divided into two separate, yet complementary and often overlapping, areas of belief and practice. These have been called 'ritual witchcraft' and 'operative witchcraft' The former covers the 'religious' aspect of the Craft i.e. the annual cycle of seasonal festivals and the worship of the Old Gods. The operative aspect deals with the 'magical' side i.e. spells, charms. healing, cursing and hexing, familiars, divination, astral travel, communing with the spirit world etc. In ancient times magick and religion were basically the same and it is true to say that witchcraft could be described as a 'magical religion'.

Because magick and religion were two sides of the same coin these two aspects of the Craft are not mutually exclusive. It could even be said that a modern Christian clergyman who performs Mass and does exorcisms, for instance, is combining the duties of a priest and a magician - although they would be horrified if you suggested it. Some witches may be worship or mystically orientated, while others may be more attracted to the magical arts. Some traditional witches concentrate on the use of their psychic and magical powers and indeed may do so under an outwardly 'Christian' veneer. These practitioners have more in common with the old-time cunning folk than with modern neo-pagan Wiccans.

Witches throughout the ages since the days of classical Rome and Greece have always been eclectic. They have drawn on whatever sources gave them inspiration or, more importantly, achieved the end results. It is therefore not surprising to find that in the past witches borrowed from the grimoires of medieval magick, or that the village wise-woman and rural sorcerer combined homespun folk magic with the more sophisticated arts of astrology and making planetary talismans. Having accepted that fact, it is therefore not surprising to find a rural Lincolnshire cunning man in the early 19th century using a system of geomantic divination that seventy years later was being practised by the middle-class occultists of the Hermetic Order of the Golden Dawn [1].

It has been claimed that 'divers cunning men and fortune-tellers had borrowed sigils and 'barbarous words' from grimoires to counter 'witchcraft'. Their clients were impressed by this hocus-pocus and readily believed that this superior 'magic' would overcome the curses of malevolent witches. The village cunning man often doubled as the Magister of the local coven' [2]. Another source states: 'The solitary ceremonial magician, often a man of letters, has served as the Man in Black for covens of the Traditional Craft...' [3].

In fact it would be a mistake to believe, as many modern Wiccans do, that the old cunning folk and witches were illiterate peasants who could not read and had no written materials on magick. Several rural cunning men and women ordered manuals of magick and books on the occult from London booksellers. There are also claims that several homegrown grimoires were in circulation among the cunning community, such as *The Devil's Plantation*, *The Secret Granary* and *The Book of Cain*. In 1791 *The Conjuror's Magazine* appeared in print with articles on ceremonial magick, astrology and alchemy [4].

This mixture of witchcraft, paganism and occultism was not a new process. By the late Middle Ages the divisions between pagan survivals, folk magick and Christian demonology were already becoming blurred. In fact they were combining to form a hybrid form of magical practice. One example of this is a medieval exorcism ritual involving an invocation to the Holy Trinity and the saints to banish elves from a patient's body because they were believed to be causing an illness.

The idea that elves can cause illness goes back at least to Saxon times when superstitious people thought they had been shot by elf bolts or poisoned arrows by the elves. In the medieval ritual the exorcist called upon Herdiana, who is described as 'the

Mother of elves', to depart from the possessed person's body. From her name, Herdiana is obviously a form of the witch goddess [5].

In the 15th and 16th centuries Renaissance magicians like Mersilio Ficino, Giovanni Pico della Mirandola, Giordano Bruno and Dr John Dee, combined classical paganism, the Jewish Cabbala, folk magic and even necromancy in their magical practices. This was the period of *magia naturalis,* or natural magick, using herbs and flowers, incense and candles, gems and crystals, and astrological correspondences. Some of these practices were adopted by the village witches and cunning men. In the late 18th century and early 19th century they received fresh impetus from the works of Ebenezer Sibley, a well-known London astrologer, and his pupil, the magician Sir Francis Barratt who started his own magical school in 1805.

Although so-called 'high magick' was regarded as the pursuit of the intellectual and the academic, the magician in his study, magical ideas about the attainment of 'gnosis' or self-knowledge and the use of the magical arts for self-transformation had filtered down to the cunning men and rural sorcerers. However, because they were consulted for their services, they restricted their public work to spells for love, health and money and countering the effects of so- called 'black witches'.

The old folk magic still retained some of its original atmosphere, for 'the Old Magic works equally well in otherwise unremarkable fields, woods and hedgerows, particularly in relation to certain types of tree. The origination of oak, ash and thorn in Kipling's children's tale *Puck of Pook Hill* can open the inner eye and ear to much imagery that leads to revelation' [6].

In early medieval Norse society we find a form of women's magick called *seidr.* Although its dictionary definition is a spell or enchantment, the word means 'seething' and it refers to the raising and projecting of psychic energy in an enraged or emotional state, often associated with a condition of sexual arousal or excitement.

It has also been associated with the boiling or seething of narcotic plants, possibly in a cauldron, to induce a state of trance. In practical terms the practice of *seidr* magick covered the foretelling of personal destiny, necromancy, summoning elemental spirits and bringing death and illness.

One important aspect of *seidr* was that it was a form of sex magick. The 'seething' was the lighting of 'the 'sacred heat', usually expressed through an individual's libido' (7). Seidr was associated with the seer-priestesses of the witch goddess Freyja and it may have included certain 'Western-tantra' practices such as prolonging intercourse without reaching orgasm, the use of multiple orgasms to project psychic energy and bring magical desires into physical manifestation, and the sublimation of the sexual force so it can be used for magical purposes (8). It is said that Odin was taught *seidr* by Freyja, even though any man who studied or practised it was condemned in Norse society as effeminate or homosexual because this magical art advocated so-called 'unnatural practices'. In other words it was ancient women's magick which no real man would want anything to do with in a patriarchal: society.

If *seidr* was woman's magick, then blacksmiths were commonly believed to practice a masculine form of the magical arts. A 12th century prayer to St Patrick includes the words: "Against the spells of women, of smiths and magicians protect us". The blacksmith was surrounded by myth, folklore and superstition and his reputation as a magician dates back to the Bronze Age, when the first metals were smelted. The worship of the old smith gods like Tubal Cain, Goibnui, Vulcan and Weyland became deeply associated with the male mysteries of the Traditional Craft and the old Horned God. It has been said the association of smiths and horned gods is as ancient as Tubal Cain, the Kenite goat god' (9).

The early smiths were nomadic travelling folk who took their trade from settlement to settlement in ancient times. When this mysterious stranger appeared he was treated respect and some awe; not only because he controlled fire and smelt metals, but

191

also because of his uncanny power over the sacred horses of the Indo-European tribes. As the controller and ruler of fire, the forger of metal and the tamer of horses the smith appeared to hold sway over the animal world and the forces of life and death. This potent combination of practical skill, physical strength and supernatural power singled out the smith as a natural magus. It

Witch anointing herself with the sabbat ungenti or flying ointment

is therefore not surprising that the tools of the smith have become incorporated into the symbolism of some traditional covens.

Because of the reputation of the smith as a magician, they were widely consulted by country people who wanted to protect their homes from evil spirits and black witches. It was believed that witches stole horses at night to ride to the Sabbat. They were returned at dawn 'hag ridden', exhausted, sweating and with their manes tangled in knots. To prevent this happening the smith recommended chalking crosses or pentagram over the stable doors. A magical charm called a hag-stone was also placed around the horse's neck. This was a flintstone with a natural hole in its centre and was said to represent the all-seeing eye of God. Horse- shoes were also nailed up over the stable door to keep evil away. It is paradoxical that the hag-stone and the horseshoe are both symbols of the Goddess.

The hammer and tongs and bellows of the blacksmith are sometimes found among the ritual tools of the Traditional Craft. They are symbols of the magical or spiritual transformation represented on the Gundustrup cauldron found in a peat bog in Denmark. On the cauldron a line of warriors is being dipped head first into it by a divine figure. This is the higher gnosis of magick represented by the smith figure who brings fire down from heaven and transforms it into metal. Sacred objects made from meteoric iron were highly prized in ancient times. In another form this is a magical process of spiritual alchemy where lead is turned into gold. This is a physical metaphor for the transformation of matter into spirit.

The female mysteries of the Craft are exemplified by the traditional 'Drawing Down the Moon' ritual performed at full moon. In modern Wicca this is the invocation of the Goddess who then 'possesses' and speaks through the High Priestess. In the traditional circles of the Craft it takes a rather different, and more literal form.

In the traditional ritual, the Lady holds up a small mirror to catch the reflected rays of the moon and project them into a bowl or cup of wine. While she does this the other coveners pace around her nine times in a moonwise or widdershins direction. Then the Master steps forward, holding a lighted lantern in his left hand and the ritual wand or knife in his right.

Certain words are exchanged then the Magister ritually sharpens the knife (if it is used) on a whetstone, and plunges it into the cup or bowl. The wine is stirred three times and drops of it are splashed around the four quarters. The Master then kisses the Lady, they drink in turn from the receptacle, and it is passed around the circle for all to partake. The traditional honey or oat cakes follow [10].

In an alternative form the witch or witches meditate on the full moon reflected in a pond, lake or even the cauldron filled with water, until they achieve a trance state. Cornish witches sat on a cliff-top at full moon and gazed at the 'moon path' across the sea until they entered a trance. and were able to communicate with spirits and the Old Ones.

Female witches were highly regarded for their alleged ability to control the weather. In sea ports there was always some old beldame who would be willing to 'whistle up the wind' for a few pennies. This was often done by knotting a cord or thread which was then sold to the sailor. Once at sea he undid each knot depending upon the strength of the wind required. Kites were also used to conjure up storms and it was said the witches were sometimes in league with smugglers and pirates. They conjured up the storm and when ships were driven on the rocks they shared in the spoils with the wreckers.

Divination was a magical art practised by male and female Crafters. Today this will include the use of the tarot cards and runes, but in earlier times it was playing cards, crystal balls, pendulums - a ring or crystal suspended from a thread, or a hair - and, of course, scrying in the mirror and the traditional palmistry and tea leaves.

If a mirror was not available a bowl of ink or water was used instead. Ordinary looking glasses were also used and these appear in folk magical rites where young ladies sought to discover their future lovers or husband~ The serious witch, however, made her own special 'magic mirror' or speculun out of black-painted glass. Often each coven selected its most psychic member to be the coven seer, scryer or oracle.

Trancing was often used to induce a state of mind where the future could be divined or the spirit world contacted. A maze etched or drawn on a flat stone or piece of slate was used for this purpose and were popularly known as Troy stones. The trance state was gained by either concentrating on the symbol or slowly tracing it with a finger. One of these stones could be seen on display in the witchcraft museum at Boscastle, North Cornwall and used to belong to a famous Manx wise-woman.

Healing has always been an important part of the white witch's work. This could be done by the simple act of laying on of hands' or by absent healing. This was the projection of the healing force to the patient who may be some distance away. Before they became a New Age fad, crystals were also used. Water, usually gathered from a holy well at dawn, was poured over a crystal to 'charge" it and then collected in a bottle. Herbal or flower tinctures might be added to this liquid to make a 'healing elixir'. On the night of the full moon it was left in the moon's rays and then given to the patient to drink

Welsh witches diagnosed illnesses by 'taking the measure'. This has nothing to do with initiations, but involved two lengths of scarlet wool or thread. One was bound around the wrist and ankle of the patient. The other was worn by the witch. After a few days if the thread was removed and it had shrunk the person would live. However, if it was larger and slacker then recovery would either be very slow or the person might even die.

Healing was often carried out using plants and herbs. The poisonous foxglove for example was widely used for sore throats and sinus trouble It could also be useful for sores, swellings, burns and water retention A Shropshire wise-woman told Dr William Withering in the 18th century that foxgloves were also good for heart disease. As a result digitalis was discovered and digoxin and both are still used in the treatment of heart disorders.

Plants that were natural hallucinogenics were used by witches to open the Third Eye and gain the Sight. One of the most powerful, and poisonous, is *amanita muscaria* or fly agaric, the red capped toadstool with white spots which is always associated with elves and goblins in the illustrations to children's storybooks. White Bryony, the English version of mandrake, was also used to induce trance and psychic vision. It was only used in small does because it was so toxic and wrong use could send the person involved straight to the spirit world.

Mandrake grew, it was said, under gallows where its seeds were fertilized by the ejaculations of hanged men at death. This folk tradition links it with Odin who hung for nine days and nights on the World Tree to gain the knowledge of the runes. Witches said that mandrake also flourished on patches of ground where a male and a female witch had both urinated.

The Devon witches had a special potion to gain the Sight called a Faery Cup. This was used at either Beltane or Midsummer to facilitate communication with the Little People. Among its more common ingredients were rosebay willow herb, the purest honey from wild bees and, of course, 'magic mushrooms'. Anyone who took this concoction in the right ritual conditions was guaranteed to become 'enchanted' and find the faerie realm.

In the old witch trials it was said that each witch was given a familiar spirit at her initiation by the Devil. This was a confused notion associated with the techniques taught to real witches when they entered the Craft to obtain elemental servitors, conjure up elementaries or thought forms, and work with spirit guides from the Other Side. In some cases these 'familiars' were merely domestic pets the witch had trained and had a psychic bond with as a result.

Alternatively, the familiar could be a fetch - the spirit body of the witch clothed in animal form when she astrally projected. There are plenty of folk stories about phantom animals, especially hares, who are wounded or killed by huntsman. Shortly afterwards an old woman reputed to be a witch is found dead or with similar injuries to the hunted animal. It was commonly believed such a creature could only be killed with a silver bullet or they would still roam the countryside after death as a werebeast.

In many of the trials the witches are said to have shapeshifted into the form of animals. This may be a description of the witches assuming an animal disguise as a fetch, or where they link consciously with the mind of a trained pet. However, certain dances, like the Wild Chase, do involve the wearing of animal masks or costumes. In the surviving Cochrane tradition the most important spirit masks are the stag, raven and squirrel. The stag mask is worn by the Magister who opens the circle and leads the dance as the representative of the old Horned God. Raven is the trickster and 'taker of souls', while Squirrel is the coven seer and the 'messenger of the Gods' [11].

Earlier we discussed healing and it is a fact, acceptable or not, that witches can cure or curse. The majority of the cases during the Persecution in England and Wales involved accusations of bewitchment. The anti-witchcraft laws here where always more concerned with the alleged powers of the witch to kill and injure people, harm livestock and destroy crops then with the Craft as a so-called Satanic heresy. To what extent the power to curse has survived today is difficult to know, except that there is evidence of some people claiming to be witches who use malefic magic to harm others.

The early Wiccan revivalists in the 1950s had an ambivalent attitude to the subject. In public they always claimed that they did not do rituals to harm anyone. However, in private, so-called 'binding rituals' were carried out using a poppet or wax image. In one case an image was bound with cords to stop a blackmailer. It is said that the person concerned was in such a rage that the other members of the coven had to prevent him causing magical

Wax images at Castle Rising (1963)

harm during the ritual. Modern Wiccans will often quote the 'ancient' maxim 'An ye harm none. Do What Thou Wilt' which probably dates from the time of Gardner.

The traditional witch is more likely to view this as New Age nonsense promoted by someone who has never been in a decent magical punch-up. "You leave me and mine alone or else" seems more appropriate. They are the sort of people who go into heelbars to buy a bag of hob nails, though they may not bother using a wax doll as an intermediary" (12). This may be an amusing and tongue-in-cheek view, but it does have some basis in fact.

To judge from some of the exhibits in the Witches House museum in Boscastle a few years ago, there is a thriving modern tradition of malefic magick used to kill and injure operating at a common level in the West Country. This usually involves neighbourhood disputes and family feuds. Some of the magick is crudely home-made, but in more serious cases the services of a genuine grey or black witch have been employed. These beldames, known as Aunt Bettys or Aunt Mays or just Aunties, have been described as acting like a psychic version of Murder Inc.

One ancient form of cursing dates from Norse usage and is called the Niding Pole. This was a staff carved with an appropriate curse in runic letters. The top was either carved with a horse s head or surmounted by an actual horse skull. This represents the Night Mare, the dark aspect of the Goddess, who carries the curse to its victim. The pole was placed in th ground and its face was pointed towards the direction where the victim lived. This was usually done within sight of their house, when he or she was deep in sleep in the dreaming stage in the early hours of the morning, and when the moon was either waning or dark.

The usual methods of bewitching or cursing were the physical glance of the Evil Eye, the Witches Ladder and the poppet or wax image. The traditional stance for projecting the Evil Eye was to stand on on leg, point the hand using either the forefinger or the Horned God sign with two fingers, and have one eye closed. Anyone who had only one eye, like Odin, or had a squint or lazy eye' was regarded in ancient times as having the power of the Evil Eye.

The so-called Witches' Ladder was a three-stranded cord or thread with a noose at one end to resemble a hangman's noose. At regular intervals goose, crow or black hen feathers were knotted into the cord and bound with candlewax and drops of blood from the witch. The witch muttered her curse or spell as she wove and knotted the cord. If a dove's feathers were used then the Ladder could be used as a let spell. The object was then placed in a secret location within the victim's house or its vicinity and left to do its work.

Wax images have been used in malefic magic since the days of the Ancient Egyptians. In the early 1960s the wax images of a man and woman were found nailed to the door of the ruined Castle Rising, near Kings Lynn in Norfolk. They had been pierced with thorns and also nailed to the door was a sheep heart with thirteen thorns in it. Over the next few weeks similiar finds were found in local ruined churches. According to a local folklorist, the images were part of an involved ritual carried out by a witch who was being employed by a young woman wronged in love and seeking revenge [13].

It should be clearly stated that cursing or banishment is a rare event in modern traditional witchcraft. It is not something to be treated lightly or for 'a bit of a giggle'. When such rituals are performed they are done with a serious and deadly intent and with the full knowledge of the responsibility and consequences that could follow.

The curse is there in the magical box of tricks of the witch as a last resort. As one modern traditional witch says: 'Just as life is not all sweetness and light, neither is the Faith. The ability to take magical revenge on the enemies of the coven is an intrinsic part of the Craft'. He adds: the formal cursing is a weapon in the armoury of the Faith, but one that should be rarely ever used in defence of ourselves' [14].

If curses are a fact of magical life, then the poor victim must also resort to magick for psychic self-protection and defence. This was where the cunning man or warlock came into the picture. Protection against 'owl blinking' or cursing in popular folk magick included the use of horseshoes, twigs of birch or rowan placed over liminal boundaries such as doors and windows, a runic pattern of nine interlocked crosses chalked on the doorstep, windowsill and gate, or pentagrams carved on the trees near the house.

Protective measures often began when the house was being built. The pagan custom of foundation sacrifices survived into the Middle Ages and beyond. There are frequent reports of mummified cats, dogs and some times birds being found walled up in old houses [14]. In rural parts of England and Wales the skulls of horses have been found buried under the floors of farmhouses and even chapels as protective objects. The pagan idea behind these burials was to ensure that the spirit of the animal would remain earthbound as a house guardian to 'watch and ward' over the building.

Shoes, representing wealth, were also embedded in walls or in the chimney breast as a lucky charm. More formal talismans, inscribed with magical sigils, and probably supplied by the local witch or warlock are also known. Today traditional witches still make clay or wooden poppets to act as guardians for new houses. These images are imbued with a thought form and placed out of sight on top of a roof beam or under the tiles [16].

Thatchers also still make special effigies of squirrels, cats or birds at the gable ends of roofs for similar protective purpose. These seem to be a modern, more humane, version of foundation sacrifices and enslaving animal spirits to protect the home.

Once the house was built and inhabited, other magical pre-cautions could be taken. These included nailing horseshoes above the front and back doors, points upward to stop the luck 'running out'. A rowan tree planted near the front door and an elder at the back entrance warded off evil forces. A holly or thorn hedge

201

around the property was a protective psychic device and on the physical level also deterred burglars.

Inside the house the coloured fishing floats, sometimes called 'witch balls', can be employed. Like feng shui mirrors they reflect back evil forces. Ordinary mirrors coated in silver paint or decorated with magical sigils have a similiar effect. They are the opposite to the black-coated witches' mirror which attract spirits from the Otherworld. Various types of spirit traps, like bottles filled with coloured beads or marbles, or devices similar to the popular Native American 'dream-catchers' modelled on spider's webs can be used to get rid of unwanted elementals, poltergeists and other troublesome household spooks.

If all else failed of course the local cunning man or white witch was called in. This usually happened if the house was badly haunted or if its occupants believed they were under psychic attack. To break a curse the witches' bottle was employed. This was a glass bottle or a pottery or stoneware jar which was filled with the urine of the victim, a lock of hair, nail parings and bent pins. The bottle was then tightly corked or sealed and boiled on a fire. When it broke or exploded it was said the witch would appear and beg for mercy. The spell would then be broken. In some cases it was said the witch suffered injury or even died as the curse rebounded [17].

Cecil Williamson, the founder of the Boscastle museum, has described a modern version of the witch's bottle still practised by the Aunties in the West Country which he witnessed. The ritual is known as 'the Boiling' and it involves the stewing of groundsel, dandelion, verbena and cabbage in a cast-iron pot. When this came to the boil, a tightly sealed bottle of the victim's urine was placed in the pot. When this bottle eventually exploded in the heat the spell was said to have been broken. The key to the operation is that the spellcaster is informed beforehand that the Aunties are working against them so its effect is partly psychological warfare [18].

If talk of cursing is likely to make the average modern Wiccan have palpitations, then any discussion of necromancy is likely to send them to an early grave (Pun intended). We have seen earlier how the Celts used skulls as oracles and in folklore there are the famous 'screaming skulls', who seem to act as house guardians. In East Anglia it has been alleged that a sinister secret society known as the Order of Bonesmen exists and still practice necromantic rites. It is said they are the ones responsible for obtaining horse skulls for use as protective charms in houses. They also have the power to call up the dead using tunes played on a bone flute [19].

The Bonesman may be related to the Traditional Craft who have also been reputed with knowledge of necromantic, rituals. At the full moon in March 1963 a bizarre ritual was held at the ruined church of St Mary's at Clophill in Bedfordshire. The skeleton from an 18th century grave was removed and the skull surmounted on a metal spike. The bones, of a young apothecary's assistant called Junny Humberstone, were arranged in a ritual pattern on the altar. On the wall a 'Celtic' equal-armed cross had been painted in red. When the police arrived the remains were handed over to the rector of the local parish church for a secret re-burial.

The initial reaction to the incident from the police and the media was predictably sensational, There was talk of a 'Black Mass', even though the use of human bones is historically unknown in such a ceremony. The Celtic Cross was mis-identified as the so-called 'Mark of the Beast' used by Aleister Crowley and this confirmed the popular belief that Satanism was involved. An interview was even published in *The News of the World* with a Satanist allegedly present at the ritual. Rather unconvincingly, he said that the original plan was to use a naked woman on the altar. However, because it was so cold (it was one of the coldest winters on record) they unearthed a skeleton from the church-yard instead. This seems highly unlikely.

Despite the lurid stories of 'black magic' that have surrounded Clophill over the years, it has been rumoured that the event in

1963 was in fact a traditional necromantic ritual. Its purpose, it is said, was to contact the spirit of a long-dead witch and open up a gateway so the soul could come into incarnation again. An alternative theory is that the skull was being used in the ancient way as an oracle.

Graveyards, those that are on former pagan sites, are frequently used in traditional witchcraft, as are ruined churches that once stood on pagan shrines. A few years a traditional group from Windsor was actively using a ruined church at Henley-on-Thames for rituals. Unfortunately they were disturbed one night by a local farmer and the matter reached the ears of the local press. A sensationalist story was published about 'black magic rites' and car chases along country lanes at night, thus rendering the site unusable.

One traditional witch has published an account of how a human skull can be used in necromancy. He has emphasised that the rituals connected with this object are in no way an attempt to call up the dead by incantation or to bind that soul or spirit into the service of the group. 'Any contact made from the Other Side will be on the basis of a willing and mutual acceptance of each other's world....' [20].

It should be clearly understood that some traditional witches find such literal rituals to be atavistic and not in keeping with the modern ethos of the Craft. While the human skull is an important symbol in the circle, if only as a symbol of the Horned God in his winter aspect, there is no suggestion that real skulls are obtained by desecrating graveyards or by any other illegal or improper means.

Chapter Thirteen
A Lantern in the Dark

In 1951 Parliament repealed the old Witchcraft Act which had made it illegal to call yourself a witch or claim to be practising witchcraft. This breakthrough followed years of campaigning by Spiritualists outraged at the imprisonment of medium Helen Duncan under the Act in 1944. Duncan was jailed because the government believed she had exposed wartime secrets as a result of information received during a seance with the spirit of a dead serviceman. This is possibly the only time the government recognized the validity of psychic powers. At the time of writing a campaign has been launched to get Duncan's conviction quashed and a pardon issued.

The repeal of the Witchcraft Act meant that in theory anyone claiming to be a witch could come out into the open and publically proclaim their beliefs. In practice this is what happened in 1953 when Gerald Gardner published a non-fiction book on witchcraft. As a result of the book and the publicity it created, Gardner says he was contacted by other witches from all over the country. As early as 1951 Cecil Williamson had taken advantage of the new atmosphere by opening his Museum of Superstition and Folklore on the Isle of Man, which he later sold to Gardner. Williamson had also organised a Witches' Convention and he noted that the other witches present disagreed with the version of the Craft promoted by Gardner. They also disagreed with any attempt to bring the Craft out into the open or publicise it. It has even been said that some traditionals did not want the old Witchcraft Act repealed because they foresaw the problems ahead [1].

These problems quickly surfaced in the 1950s with a series of sensationalist newspaper articles linking the revival of modern witchcraft with Satanism and black magic. These stories began

205

with a fairly tame magazine interview with members of Gardner's New Forest coven in 1952 [2]. It ended in 1959 with an expose of Gardner's London coven which was described as 'a repulsive sect' practising 'sex worship' [3].

It was not until the early Sixties, and the death of Gardner in 1964, that a few people claiming to be traditional witches came out of the broom closet and began to state their views and beliefs in public. This was precipitated by the foundation of the Witchcraft Research Association in the summer of 1964. Its stated aim was to bring together the revivalists and the traditionalists in what was optimistically described by its organisers as 'kind of United Nations a of the Craft'.

The claim made by the WRA, in the pages of its official newsletter *Pentagram*, was that witchcraft had survived the Persecution and that the traditional groups now emerging from the shadows represented a genuine link with the past. One article in the first issue claimed the Old Religion had survived under the cover of witchcraft. It had been 'carried on in secret by groups of loyal adherents who perpetuated their knowledge hereditarily and in this way the old teachings were carried down to the present day' [4].

One of the founder members of the WRA was Doreen Valiente. She had been Gardner's High Priestess during the 1950s, but left the coven in a dispute over his publicity attracting antics. She later worked with the famous traditional group founded by the late Robert Cochrane in the early 1960s. In both her books and a talk given at the Pagan Federation Conference in November 1997 she has praised Cochrane's traditional way of working.

At a dinner given to fifty members of the WRA in October 1964, Valiente also linked the survival of the pagan Old Religion from ancient times to modern traditional witchcraft. She told her audience: '*Pentagram* is now contacting surviving traditions from covens which have never been in any way connected with Gerald Gardner. In fact it is becoming increasingly clear that the Old Craft has survived in fragments all over the British Isles. Each has its own version of the tradition, in its own words; and each has its own ideas of practice and ritual' [5]. This is, I believe, the first time the term 'Old Craft' was used in public to describe traditional witchcraft.

In the third issue of the newsletter the editorial stated: 'A number of groups exist who claim to enshrine the traditions and teachings of bygone ages - and can prove it to their own satisfaction'. Two groups who claimed just that were represented in *Pentagram* by articles on their version of the Craft. One was a writer using the nom-de-plume of Taliesin and he claimed to be the member of a Celtic hereditary group in the West Country. The other one was Robert Cochrane, who said he could trace his family tradition back to the 1700s. He was described as an 'editorial consultant' to the newsletter.

Both men had known each other since at least 1962 when they (allegedly) placed an advertisement in *The Manchester Guardian* seeking responses from people interested in Robert Graves book *The White Goddess*. Both men were fiercely critical of Gardner and modern Wicca, but Cochrane took a more radical approach. He believed that the Traditional Craft must be modernised if it were to survive in the 20th century. However he also staled that 'The value of the Old Craft today is that in it lie the seeds of the old Mystery Tradition' [6] and he suggested this was not true of modern Wicca.

In the fifth issue of *Pentagram*, the last one to be in newsletter format and deal exclusively with Craft matters, the widening divisions between the traditionalists and the Wiccans came out into the open in a series of bad tempered exchanges. That issue contained an open letter from Arnold Crowther, the High Priest of a Gardnerian coven in Sheffield, attacking those who advocated 'cloak-and-dagger methods' and he criticised the editor for 'publishing petty insults from non-entities'.

This verbal attack was defended by Taliesin who proceeded to launch his own onslaught on those Wiccans who wrote articles for women's magazines and allowed film crews into their rituals.

(Nothing changes!) This was a direct reference to the publicity activities of Arnold Crowther and his partner Patricia who had always had a high profile in the public eye.

In the same issue Gerald Gardner was defended by the High Priest of a Wiccan coven who claimed 'secret knowledge of the Old Faith as had been handed down to me from two distinctly separate family lines of Suffolk and Irish witches'. Taliesin responded to this in scathing terms and accused Gardner of inventing Wicca based on the theories of Dr Margaret Murray and Idries Shah regarding historical witchcraft.

The WRA did not survive these tensions and emotional conflicts between its warring members. *Pentagram* limped on until 1967, publishing a couple more times in a glossy magazine format and with articles on occultism and magick. Its editor then ceased publication claiming, rather feebly, that there was nothing more that could be written on witchcraft! The true reason was that the arguments in the newsletter had publically exposed the major differences in approach and ambience between modern Wicca and modern traditional witchcraft.

Sadly this dichotomy still exists today. In recent years it has been publically expressed in the relationship between the Pagan Federation, founded by a Gardnerian witch in 1971 and now with a current membership of several thousand, and the much smaller Association of Hedgewitches, who claim to represent solitary witches and includes members who are allegedly Old Craft. In private the differences between the two groups have led to allegations of expulsions, the refusal to publish advertising, the making of false accusations and claims that Wiccans in the PF will not recognize any other forms of the Craft or those not initiated into the Gardnerian or Alexandrian branches. Recently these allegations have boiled over into the public arena which is why they are mentioned here. Thankfully, at the time of writing the PF and AHW have called a truce, but suspicions still exist on both sides.

Over thirty years ago the situation in *Pentagram* did have some positive effect in highlighting the fact that there were genuine seekers looking for something different and deeper then what was currently on offer. In an open letter several readers collectively expressed their discontent with what they had been offered by a Gardnerian coven 'whose 'elders' appeared to be disinterested in learning - and had precious little to teach' [7]. It is a sad fact that little has changed since then and these remarks are typical of people since who have sought contact with traditional forms of the Craft having become disillusioned with the popular neo-pagan and Wiccan scene.

However it would be another ten years before interest in the Traditional and Hereditary Craft was revived again in the public arena. This was in the early 1970s when a series of articles were first published in *The Wiccan* (then the name of the Pagan Federation's newsletter) and then continued in the independent Craft journal *The Cauldron* in the 1980s and 1990s.

The articles appeared first under the reference of 'well wisher' and later under the nom-de-plume of 'Lugh'. He was an Englishman who had emigrated to New Zealand in the early 1960s, but now lives in Queensland, Australia and is called E.W. Liddell. He has since claimed that the information and views expressed in the articles were not his, but those of various Elders and coven leaders representing the Hereditary Craft in East Anglia today. The articles were very controversial and they made several contentious claims about the 19th century cunning man George Pickingill and his alleged influence on the formation of the Golden Dawn, Aleister Crowley, Gerald Gardner, and the creation of modern Wicca. Most of these articles have now been published in book form by Capall Bann [8]. Critics of the Lugh material, including Mike Howard who published many of the articles in his magazine *The Cauldron* and edited the book, have pointed out that in the more than twenty years since it began to appear no independent or documentary evidence has been forthcoming to support its claims,

In the 1980s and 1990s articles on various aspects of the Traditional Craft by other writers began to appear in magazines like *The Cauldron*. Several books were also published by writers such as Marian Green, Ruth Wynn Owen, Evan John Jones, Nigel Jackson, Paul Huson, Andrew Chumbley, Paddy Slade, Rhiannon Ryall and Nigel Pennick who all claimed insider knowledge of different forms of hereditary and traditional witchcraft.

Three Gardnerian High Priestesses also came out in public claiming to have had contact with traditional witches and groups. Doreen Valiente, Lois Bourne and Patricia Crowther have all written about their experiences with pre-Gardnerian Traditional Craft (see Bibliography). Despite this, ignorant and ill-informed writers still claim that modern witchcraft only started with Gardner. This interest has in turn led to a renewal of 'older' versions of the Craft and even the formation of new groups reconstructing traditional or historical forms.

As we have seen throughout this book, the Mythic Theme has been an important aspect of the mythos of modern traditional witchcraft which has been its subject. It is broadly based on the agricultural cycle and the solar-lunar pattern of the year. This Mythic Theme can be confusing to newcomers and, as we noted before, the God and Goddess of the witches are shapechangers who can show their dark and bright sides at the same time. This is especially true at those festivals which mark boundary or crossing over points between summer and winter when the dark and bright powers are changing over. There is also the mystery at Yule when the Crone becomes the Mother and gives birth to the Horn Child.

Probably the best way to understand the Mythic Theme is to meditate on the mytho-poetic Journey of the God given in Chapter Two. This follows the path of the God from birth at the winter solstice, to manhood and warriorhood at the spring equinox, his marriage as the Heron King to the Hawthorn Queen at Beltane, his rulership of the land as sacred king at midsummer with the Queen of Elfame, his ritual death at

Lammastide, his descent to the underworld at the autumnal equinox to face the Dark Lady, and his emergence at Hallows as the Wild Hunter and Lord of Death, leading once more to the rebirth of the Sun Child at Yule. As we follow the God's path through the year, and his relationship to the Goddess, we can see its symbolism mirrored in the seasonal cycle, the natural world and the changing patterns of sun, moon and stars.

It must be asked what relevance does this Mythic Theme have to life at the end of the 20th century and to the average person in modern society. It is true that since the Industrial Revolution most people in this country have not earned their living from agriculture. In fact we are in a situation today where the seasonal production of food has become meaningless with imports from abroad filling the shelves all year around. Some inner city children today believe that milk is produced in a factory along with frozen peas and baked beans.

Few modern witches make their livings today from the land, by working on farms, following rural trades like black-smithing or professions like vets, or even producing country crafts if only for the tourist market. Some do but they are firmly in the minority and the average pagan or witch is more likely to live in a large town or city and earn a living from computers.

It has been said that there has been 'no case for a fertility religion in Europe since the advent of the countershare plough in the thirteenth century, the discovery of haymaking, selective breeding of animals etc.' [9] This may be true as today we have the Common Agricultural Policy, pesticides and butter mountains. This is why many Wiccans, and some progressive traditionalists, support environmental causes instead and concentrate on the destruction of Mother Earth and her endangered species, including humanity. Many others are involved in animal welfare and stopping cruelty to animals in vivisection labs, factory farms and circuses.

In the post-modern world therefore the traditionalist has to look at the Mythic Theme expressed through the festivals of the

Wheel of the year in wider terms then fertility rites. The emphasis remains on the welfare of the land, but by observing and celebrating the passing of the seasons and the natural cycle of growth, decay and renewal we link ourselves to the natural world and the cosmos. That is just as important, if not more important, in this age for our psychic wellbeing as it was in the 13th century.

We are reminded almost daily by the pundits. self-styled experts and 'talking heads' that many of humankind's problems are linked with our disassociation from nature and this has led directly to the destruction of the environment. Industrial pollution, the careless disposal of radioactive and other waste, the burning of the tropical rain forests, acid rain and global warming are all human created factors which are degrading our natural habitat. In turn humans are suffering the consequences in the increase in heart disease, stress, cancer, asthma and the spread of new illnesses like AIDs, CJD and E-coli.

While the destruction of the planetary biosphere is a serious one and is aggravated by our modern technological and consumer society, those who profess to be 'pagans' leading a 'pagan lifestyle' have no reason to be smug or self-righteous about following an 'earth religion' which respects the sacredness of all life on Mother Earth' etc. Despite their reverence for nature spirits and nature gods, it was our Neolithic ancestors who first used the crude 'slash- and-burn' method of clearing forests for agricultural use. It is even possible that the 'sacred fires' of Beltane, Midsummer and Hallowe'en, with their purification of the land from evil and the spreading of the ashes on the fields to bring fertility, were a folk memory of the methods employed by the Neolithic, Bronze and Iron Age people to clear the land for planting. The great herds of animals, like the mammoth, the Great Elk, the bison and the woolly rhino, that used to roam the world were also hunted into extinction by our ancestors before the days of agriculture. The hunters may have been following a 'pagan lifestyle', but they had no thoughts about preserving or protecting 'endangered species'.

Where does the traditional witch come into this gloomy picture of modern environmental rape and destruction? It is true to say that they have a realistic approach to nature as 'red in tooth and claw' They recognize that the natural world works on the Darwinian principle of the survival of the fittest and that Mother Nature can be both capricious and cruel. While they actively support measures to save the countryside, they take a more real view then the 'fluffy bunnies' of the bambi school of neo-paganism.

This links with their belief in a Dark God and Goddess whose aspects are often ignored today. In fact in some polite circles any mention of the Dark Goddess or the Horned God is likely to lead to whispered allegations of Satanism. In reality the Dark God is the Lord of Death and we must all face him eventually. The Dark Goddess is the destroyer, the Black Mother who eats her own children. Both these aspects of Divinity represent our own dark, shadow sides and the untamed forces of elemental nature which have to be faced and accepted as part of human existence on this unpredictable planet.

Ever since ancient times humans tried, and failed, to tame and control Mother Nature. Today they are trying to do it by raping and abusing the environment in the name of progress and profit or by playing at Goddess with genetic engineering, organ transplants and test-tube babies. Natural forces can be destructive, but the Goddess cannot be blamed if ignorant or arrogant humans build houses below sea level, on flood plains, on geological fault lines, or in the shadow of active volcanoes. She will willingly, and violently, take revenge on those of her children who foolishly ignore her natural laws of creation and destruction.

Many modern Wiccans and pagans have embraced the theories of Dr James Lovelock. This proposed that the Earth is a self-regulating organism that is 'alive' and conscious. Unfortunately, few have read his book expounding the theory and have only encountered it in second-hand New Age versions. What they therefore ignore, or do not know, is that Lovelock believes Gaia, as he has termed the organism from the Greek name of the earth goddess, is capable of adjusting the biosphere to deal with any threat to the planet's survival.

It is therefore possible that at some point in the not-too-distant future Terra Mater may decide that the human race is a parasite or virus that is endangering the future of life on this planet. When that happens Gaia will destroy us and once again the Goddess will eat her children. It is quite possible that AIDs is the first attempt by nature to fight back against what she regards as a threat to the biosphere's future.

Having said this, the traditional witch, as much as anyone else, respects and loves nature in a sacred sense for 'the Goddess in all her manifestations was the symbol of the unity of all life in nature. her power was in water and stone, in tomb and cave, in animals and birds, snakes and fish, hills, trees and flowers. Hence the holistic and mytho-poetic perception of the sacredness and mystery of all there is on Earth'. This was written in the past tense to describe an ancient view of the Goddess, but the words are just as meaningful in today's world. (10)

As far as the traditional witch is concerned 'the Earth Goddess was out there in the land and she was also within the inner landscape she was the focus of the individual's relationship between themselves and the forces of the universe that gave them life, nurtured and sustained them, and finally brought this incarnation to an end' (11).

Witches have always been the human guardians of sacred sites. It has been claimed that the old-time witches used these sites, and the natural energies, for healing the land. This was done by dancing in circles or spirals and 'tapping into' the positive leys that intersect at standing stones, burial mounds, old trees and crossroads. All the places we have seen are associated in folklore with witches and the faeries. These old style witches 'could turn and bend the forces of nature because they knew how to manipulate and direct natural energies' (11).

One writer has remarked about the difference between the 'invisible world', as he calls it, and the physical landscape marked out by the Ordnance Survey map. He says: '..whilst the Ordance Survey marks the location of stones, hills, springs, woods, and paths, it does not show that these, and other, material features have life and relationship. A map to accompany a walk 'through a nature reserve may represent the animals, plants and birds that can be encountered an route. A child's map is perhaps more likely to animate the trees and rocks as well s illustrating people and other living things.' [12]. To the witch the landscape is sacred, for it is the physical manifestation of the inner landscape or the 'enchanted land' - the Otherworld haunted by normally invisible guardian spirits, the Gods and Goddesses of nature and the shades of the dead.

Describing ancient paganism one contemporary writer on the subject has said: 'the whole pagan world is different from our own. It has a totally different definition of reality, one that makes little sense in terms of our religion of 'science' [13]. However, he tries, to understand the pagan world view and to bring it in to modern society, 'The key point seems to be the pagan view of the 'spirit' of place, the genius loci' [14].

He concludes: 'We're not looking at the past for its own sake; the past is gone. Our aim should be to learn from the past, to put our studies to practical use, to understand the pagan world view in terms of its practical relationship.' [15]

If the past has really gone as this writer says, and it does not linger on in the shadows of the Other, then we can still learn from it to build on the future. As far as our history and ancient heritage is concerned, as George Orwell said in his prophetic book *Nineteen Eighty Four* - those who control the past, control the future. It is the future of the Craft which we must now discuss and the different futures that are thrown up in such a discussion.

The Traditional Craft is firmly rooted in the Earth and the 'spirit of place' yet it also recognizes the importance of contact with the

Other. Its teachings and beliefs are, it is claimed, based on eternal truths dating back to the earliest beginnings of human consciousness on the planet. While the traditional witch's feet walk the woodland path, her eyes are also on the stars.

It is often said by those that give media interviews and connect with the High Street that modern paganism is 'today's fastest growing religion'. No evidence is ever offered to support this statement and compared with Buddhism or Islam it seems unlikely. Also if you discuss the future of modern paganism with any Wiccan or neo-pagan type the response will be along the lines that eventually it will become an established religion with an professional priesthood, public temples in every city and mass televised rituals at Stonehenge.

This may be all dreams, but when traditional witches are asked the same question they tend to be a little more reserved and conservative in their answer. Some of them sincerely believe that the present atmosphere of religious fundamentalism and intolerance will get worse before it gets better. Some even talk of the Craft going underground again in the future to avoid organised persecution. Few want anything to do with the media or the High Street, and the thought of the Craft turning into an established religion fills them with horror.

Even some of the progressive traditionalists, who want a more open and public face for the Traditional and Hereditary Craft, fear a return to the persecution of the past. They view with distrust the 'interfaith' policy of the Pagan Federation for more links with so-called liberal Christians. They point out that the Church has always been the natural enemy of the Craft through the ages. Recent pronouncements by a Christian minister that witchcraft should be outlawed and witches face the death penalty, and the warnings from the Vatican of the dangers of dabbling in paganism and astrology only reinforce this view.

Despite this pessimistic and gloomy outlook, as we approach the next century, and the dawning of the Aquarian Age, there is a widespread feeling that change is in the air. With any change, especially major ones, comes fear of the future and this is understandable in a transition period between Zodiac Ages when everything we believe in is challenged and often found wanting. Many people see this time as a turning point when in the words of one modern witch '..the present-day revival of interest in witchcraft, magic and the occult generally is all part of the onset of the Aquarian Age' [16]. She goes on: ' Slowly, but surely, humanity is rediscovering the Old Gods..the Old Gods themselves are returning actively to human consciousness' [17].

The same writer also claims '..the Old Religion of the past is growing and turning into the new religion of the future'.

Modern witches were not the first to regard the pagan way as the religion of the 21st century. In the 19th century Old George Pickingill recognized that belief in orthodox religion was collapsing. He allegedly calculated that the 'sixth sub-division of the Piscean Age commenced in 1808 and would end in 2116. The last cycle of the Piscean Age, the seventh sub-division, would end in 2424. Only then would the Aquarian Age truly dawn' [18].

Pickingill also allegedly worked out that the mid-point between 1808 and 2424 was 1962. He correctly predicted that a Craft revival for the New Age would be activated around that date. Coincidentally, that year saw a Grand Conjunction of planets in Aquarius which many astrologers believed heralded the dawn of the Aquarian Age.

This may be all fantasy, but the fact remains that there is a debate in the Craft today about whether the Aquarian Age will see the Old Ways established as a new religion, or whether it will be the start of a new dark period in Craft history with the return of persecution and repression. Whatever the answer, there are many following the Traditional Craft today who believe it offers access to an ancient heritage of wisdom and knowledge. As such it is very much a light from the shadows and a lantern in the dark to those seeking the Mysteries in our modern world.

Notes & References

Chapter One
(1) Aldcroft Jackson (1994:2)
(2) 'What is Traditional Craft' Andrew Chumbley in *The Cauldron* # 81
    (Lammas 1997)
(3) Gray (1975:166)
(4) *The Sufis* Idries Shah (Octagon Press 1964:210)
(5) Murray (1921:112-113)
(6) Duer (1985:46,24243-245)
(7) Ahmed (1936:47)
(8) Williams (1959:16-17)
(9) Luck (1985:5)
(10) *Pagan Cornwall:Land of the Goddess* by Cheryl Straffon (Meym
    Mamvro Publications 1993:102)
(11) *The Folklore of Herefordshire* by Ella Mary Leather (Sidgwick &
    Jackson 1912)
(12) Liddell & Howard (1994)
(13) Ibid (158)
(14) Ibid (150-157)
(15) *Ritual Magic in England* by Francis King (Neville Spearman
    1970:141)
(16) Day (1996:11)
(17) *A Field Full Of Folk: A Village Elegy* by Charles Moseley (Arum
    Press 1995)
(18) Pennick (1995: 9)

Chapter Two
(1) *The Ritual & the Castle* by Evan John Jones in *The Cauldron* no. 80
    (1996)
(2) *The Women's Encyclopedia of Myths & Secrets* by Barbara Walker
    (Harper & Row USA 1983:826)
(3) Crowley (Thorsons 1997:89)
(4) *Aspects of Occultism* by Dion Fortune (Aquarian Press 1962:5)
(5) *Pagan Dawn* no. 126 (Imbolc 1998)
(6) Personal communication 14.8.93
(7) *The Mystery of the Crystal Skulls* by Chris Morton and Ceiri Louise
    Thomas (HarperCollins 1997:259)

(8) *The Witches God* by Janet & Stewart Farrar (Robert Hale 1989:35-36)

(9) *Aradia: the Gospel of the Witches* by Charles Leland (1899)

(10) 'The Wish Maid' by Jack Shackleford in Talking Stick XV (Summer 1994)

(11) Valiente (1989:124) (12)

Chapter Three

(1) *The Festivals of the Year* by Ronald White (Privately printed 1965)

(2) *The World of Witches* by Julio Baroja (University of Chicago Press USA 1964:65)

(3) Valiente (1962:40)

(4) Leland (1899:102)

(5) Ginzburg (1990:101)

(6) Henningsen & Ankarloo (1990:195-215)

(7) 'Frau Holda , Venus Mountain and the Night Travellers' by Nigel Aldcroft Jackson in *The Cauldron* no. 59 (Winter 1991)

(8) 'The Goddess Holda' by Jack Gale in *Talking Stick* XX (Winter 1995/96)

(9) 'The Winter Goddess' by Lotte Motz in *Folklore* Vol 95:11 (1984)

(10) *From the Beast to the the Blonde* by Marina Warner (Chatto & Windus 1994)

(11) Gale (1995/96)

(12) Motz (1984)

(13) *The Mysteries of the Runes* by Michael Howard (Capall Bann 1994:155)

(14) *The Cat in Magic* by M. Oldfield Howey (Bracken Books edition 1993* 59)

(15) 'The Pickingill Craft and the Northern Tradition' by E.W. Liddell in *The Cauldron* #76 (Beltane 1995)

(16) Letters on Demonology and Witchcraft by Sir Waiter Scott (1831)

(17) R.J. Stewart

(18) *Celtic Gods, Celtic Goddesses* by R.J. Stewart (Blandford 1990:11)

(19) 'The Ritual of the Castle' by Evan John Jones in *The Cauldron* # 79 (1996)

(20) 'The Spirals of Existence' by Evan John Jones in *The Cauldron* # 83 (Candlemas 1997)

Chapter Four

(1) Aldcroft Jackson (1994:87)

(2) see Green (1991:64-66) and 'The Witches Stang' by Evan John Jones in *The Cauldron* # 68 (1993

(3) Jones (1993)

(4) 'The Magic Staff in Norse Tradition' by Alby Stone in Talking Stick
XVII (Winter 1994)
(5) Haunted East Anglia by Joan Forman (Fontana 1975) and 'The Witch
Sticks of Finchingfield' by Carole Young in Ash f 16
(6) Buckland (Llewellyn USA 1991:76)
(7) Pennick (1995: 100)
(8) Celtic Folklore: Welsh & Manx Vol i by John Rhys (Oxford University
Press 1901: 295)
(9) Aldcroft Jackson (1994:88)
(10) The Ancient British Goddess by Kathy Jones (Ariadne Publications
1991:106)
(11) Evan John Jones (1997)
(12) 'The Witches' Esbat' by Robert. Cochrane in New Dimensions
(November 1964)
(13) See Evan John Jones (1990: 134--46)
(14) Julia Day (1996:61)
(15) Liddell & Howard (Capall Bann 1994:61)
(16)Jones (1990:96-97)
(17) 'The Athame in Myth, Magick and Practice' by Rowan in White
Dragon (Imbolc 1996)
(18) Maple (1962)
(19) Valiente (1962: 37)
(20) Huson (1972:215)
(21) Liddell & Howard (1994:25)
(22) Aldcroft Jackson (1994:83)

Chapter Five
(1) 'the Faith of the Wise' by Robert Cochrane in Pentagram # 4 (August
1965)
(2) 'A Wood in the West Country ' by Taliesin in Pentagram # 4 (August
1965)
(3) Huson (1972: 19-21)
(4) 'Welsh Witches & Wizards' by Gareth Lewis in The Cauldron # 69
(1993)
(5) 'What is Traditional Craft' by Andrew Chumbley in The Cauldron
#81 (Lammas 1997)
(7) Ibid (57)
(8) The Discovery of Witchcraft by Reginald Scot (1584)
(9) Liddell & Howard (1994: 56-58,60-61)
(10) Green (1991:170)

Chapter Six
(1) The Lost Gods of England by Brian Branston (Thames & Hudson
1974: 41-45)

(2) Fletcher (1997:387)
(3) Ibid (407)
(4) Ibid (408)
(5) Cheney (1970:27)
(6) Harley MS 1585 in British Museum
(7) Howard (1995:47-48)
(8) *The Mound People* by Dr P.V. Glob (Faber & Faber 1974:150)
(9) Clarke (1995:159-161)
(10) Janet & Colin Bord (1982:45)
(11) Clarke & Roberts (1996:15)
(12) Ibid (45)
(13) Howard (1995:50)
(14) Murray (1921/1967: 109-111)
(15) Bottrell (1996:5)
(16) Clarke & Roberts (1997:55-59)
(17) Day (1996:9)
(18) *'The Regency'* by Ronald White in *The Cauldron* # 16 (Halloween 1979
(19) Cochrane (1965)
(20) *'Seasonal Changes'* by Peter Larkworthy in *The Cauldron* # 42 (Summer 1986)
(21) Huson (1972: 236) (22) Ibid (237-238)
(23(Howard (1995: 9)
(24) *'Breaking the Circle'* by John Matthews in *Voices from the Circle* (Aquarian Press 1990: 131)

Chapter Seven
(1) Not all historians and folklorists agree that all folk customs represent survivals of pre-Christian beliefs. See for instance Hutton (1991 & 1996)
(2) Baring & Cashford (1991:98)
(3) For more information on megalithic stellar lore see *The Stars and Stones* by Martin Breenan (Thames & Hudson 1983:10)
(4) Hutton (1997:1)
(5) Baker (1974:83)
(6) Pennick (1995:84)
(6) Howard (1995:24-25)   '
(7) *The Goddesses of the Northern People'* Part II Monica Sjoo in *Arachne* # 3 (March 1982)
(9) Howard (1995: 134-135)
(10) *The Goddesses of the Northern People'* Part I by Monica Sjoo in *Arachne* # 2 (December 1981)
(11) Ibid
(12) Baker (1974:85)

(13) *The Sun Gods of Ancient Europe* by Dr Miranda Green (Thames & Hudson 1991:125)

(14) Howard (1995:40)

(15) Liddell & Howard (1994:125)

(16) Howard (1995:54-55)

(17) *Earth Light* by R.J. Stewart (Element 1992:105)

(18) *The Silver Bough* Vol II by F. Marian McNeill (William Macllelan 1959:20-21)

(19) Jones (1990:158)

Chapter Eight

(1) The Spring Moon by F.P. in Ophir (March 1992)

(2) Howard (1995: 58-59)

(3) *The Leaping Hare* by George Ewart Evans and David Thomson (Faber & Faber 1972:135)

(4) St Leger-Gordon (1965:45-46)

(5) *Wheel of the Year: Living the Magical Life* by Pauline and Don Campanelli (Llewellyn USA 1989)

(6) *The Egg at Easter* by Yenetia Newall (Routledge & Kegan Paul 1971: 1-47,45-60,62-98)

(7) *Where is St George?* R.J. Stewart (Moonraker Press 1977:66)

(8) Baring & Cashford

(9) Howard (1995:63)

(10) Stewart (19~7:66)

(11) Glob (1974:153)

(12) See *The Twelfth Zodiac* by James Vogh (Hart-Davis, McGibbon 1977)

(13) 'She of Many Names' by Beth Neilson and Imogen Cavanagh in *Voices From the Circle* (Aquarian 1990:115)

(14) *Earth Mysteries* by Michael Howard (Robert Hale 1990:142)

(15) *The Life and Times by a Modern Witch* by Janet and Stewart Farrar (Piatkus 1987 (32-34)

(16) F.P. (March 1992)

(17) Howard (1995:87)

(18) Murray (1931:41)

(19) Howard (1995:81-82)

(20) Graves (1948:398)

(21) Baker (1974:115)

(22) Graves (1948:176)

(23) Matthews (1990:136)

Chapter Nine

(1) Baker (1974:71)

(2) Stewart (1992:37)

(3) Aldcroft Jackson (1994:50-52)
(4) Pennick
(5) *The Faeries of Olde England* by Margaret Pemberton in *The Cauldron* # 86 (Halloween 1997)
(6) Hutton (1991:327)
(7) Howard (1995:97)
(8) Straffon (1993:91)
(9) *'Cornish Midsummer Bonfires'* by C. Noall (Federation of old Cornwall Bonfire Societies 1963) quoted in Straffon (1993:9)
(10) *Arthur & the Sovereignty of Britain* by Caitlin Matthews (1989:151:
(11) *Ladies of the Lake* by Caitlin & John Matthews (Aquarian 1992:188)
(12> Ibid (210-215)
(13) Dr Anne Ross

(15) *The Virgin Ideal* by Peter Dawkins and Thomas Bokenham (Francis Bacon Society 1982:21)
(16) *'7he Midsummer Moon'* by F.P. in *Ophir* (June 1992)
(17) Robert Cochrane

Chapter Ten
(1) Ross (1967:321)
(2) Matthews (1989:151)
(3) *Mabon & the Mysteries of Britain* by Caitlin Matthews (Arkana 1987:79)
(4) Ibid (86)
(5) Ibid (79)
(6) *The Mabinogion Translated and Introduced* by G. Jones and T.Jones (Everyman 1970:6F75)
(7) Howard (1995:103)
(8) *'A Scattering of Dust...'* by Andrew Chumbley in *Talking Stick* XX (Winter 1995/96)
(9) Gardner (1953:31)
(10) For a full account see Ginzburg (1983)
(11) *The Arrow and the Sword* by Hugh Ross Williamson (Faber 1952:20)
(12)Janet & Colin Bord (1982:157)
(13) See *The Life and Death of a Druid Prince* by Dr Anne Ross and Dr Don Robins (Rider 1989)
(14) Liddell and Howard (1994:44-45)
(15) Adapted from Graves (1948:125-126)
(16) Cheney (1970:7.19)
(18) Ibid (12)
(19) Ibid (115)

(20) 'The Grail Mysteries' by Michael Howard in Talking Stick XIX
(Summer 1995)
(21) Walker
(22) Howard
(23) Angels and Goddesses by Michael Howard (Capall Bann 1994: 120-
121)
(24) Cheney
(25) Murder or Sacrifice? - St Edward, King and Martyr by Rachel Lloyd
(privately published 1978:9)
(26) Ibid (46)
(27) Ibid (50)
(28) 'The Pickingill Craft' by E.W. Liddell in The Cauldron # 76
(Beltane 1995)
(29) Cheney (1970:89)
(30) The Golden Bough Sir James Frazer (McMillan edition 1922:447-
463)
(31) The Earth Goddess by Cheryl Straffon (Blandford 1997:78)   (32)
Howard (1995:118)
(33) Frazer (1922:431)
(34) Jones (1990:179)

Chapter Eleven
(1) Hutton (1997:363)
(2) Clarke and Roberts (1996:123-124)
(3) 'The Rose Beyond the Grave' by Evan John Jones in The Cauldron
#78
(Halloween 1995)
(4) Ibid
(5) Graves (1948:70)
(6) Baring & Cashford (1991:321-323)
(7:) Ibid
(8) 'The Hunter's Moon' by F.P. in Ophir (September 1992)
(9) Matthews (1989:242-243)
(10) 'Fairy tales: Allegories of the Inner Life' by J.E. Cooper (Aquarian
1983:100-108)
(11) F.P. (1992)
(12) Ibid
(13) Clarke and Roberts (1996:112-113)
(14) Jones and Jones (1970 edition:3-9)
(15) Ibid (9-24)
(16) Jones (1991:45)
(17) Ibid (56)
(18) Translation by Matthews (1987:109)
(19) Ibid (110)

(20) Ibid (112)
(21) 'King Arthur' s Enchanted Sleep' by J.R. Simpson in Folklore
(1986:II
(22) This folk story forms the basis for the famous children's story The
Weirdstone of Brisingamen by Alan Garner (Collins 1960)
(23) Power Within the Land by R.J. Stewart (Element 1992:88) (24)
Stewart (1990:104)
(25) Stewart (1992:152-156)
(26) 'The Wild Chase' Anon. in White Dragon (Samhain 1994)
(27) F.p. (1992)
(28) Ibid

Chapter Twelve
(1) The Flying Sorcerer by Francis X.King (Mandrake 1992:42-43)
(2) Liddell & Howard(1994:151)
(3) 'The Sabazina Torch' by Andrew Chumbley in The Cauldron # 73
(1994)
(4) Pennick (1995:48) and Jones (1998)
(5) Magic in the Middle Ages by Richard Kieckhefer (Cambridge
University Press 1989:73)
(6) The Secret Tradition in Arthurian Legend by Gareth Knight
(Aquarian 1983:164)
(7) The Rune Mysteries by Nigel Jackson and Raven Silverwolf
(Llewellyn USA 1997: 160)
(8) Pennick (1995:69)
(9) Graves (1948:401)
(10) Valiente (1989:123)
(11) For a full and comprehensive account of ritual guising and mask
magick in the traditional Craft today see Sacred Mask, Sacred Dance
by Evan John Jones and Chas Clifton (Llewellyn USA 1997)
(12) Day (1996: 10)
(13) For a fuller account see 'Witchcraft in Kings Lynn' in Fate
(April 1965)
(14) Jones (1990:116,119-120)
(15) See The Archaeology and Ritual of Magic by Ralph Merrifield
(Batsford 1987: 116-136)
(16) Pennick (1995)
(17) see Merrifield (1987:163-175)
(18) 'A conversation with Cecil Williamson' in Talking Stick VII
(Summer 1992)
(19) Pennick 1995 (62-65)
(20) See Jones (1990: 134-146)

Chapter Thirteen

(1) This claim was made by Doreen Valiente during her talk at the Pagan Federation Conference in November 1997.

(2) *Illustrated* magazine 1951

(3) *Sunday People*

(4) '*Is the Craft Betraying its Heritage?*' by Ariel in *Pentagram* no 1 (August 19;4)

(5) '*Fifty at Pentagram dinner*' in Pentagram 2 (November 1964)

(6) '*The Craft Today*' by Robert Cochrane (in Pentagram 1 2 (November 1964:

(7) An Open Letter in *Pentagram* 5 (December 1965)

(8) See Liddell & Howard (1994)

(9) Cochrane (November 1964)

(10) *The Language of the Goddess* by M.Gimbutas (Harper & Row 1989:321)

(11) '*Secrets of the Nine Covens*' by E.W. Liddell in *The Cauldron* # 89 (August 1998)

(12) '*Gods and Hedgehogs in the Greenwood: Contemporary Pagan Cosmologies*' by Dr Graham Harvey in *Cosmos* 9 (1993)

(13) *Needles of Stone* Tom Graves (Turnstone Press 1978:3)

(14) Ibid

(15) Ibid (49

(16) Valiente (1978:13)

(17) Ibid (132)

Glossary of Terms

AMBER — Fossilised tree resin traditionally used for ritual necklace worn by the Lady or High Priestess

ADEPT — Person skilled in the magical arts

ALEXANDRIAN — Modern Wiccan following the tradition founded by Alex Sanders (1926-1988)

AMULET — Charm to ward off evil or bad luck

ANNWN — The underworld in Welsh Celtic mythology

ARADIA — Wiccan name of choice for the witch goddess. In Italian witchcraft the daughter of DIANA and LUCIFER who incarnated on Earth in human form.. See also DIANA

ARTEMIS — Greek goddess of the moon, hunting etc

ASTRAL TRAVEL — The projection of the spirit from the physical body

ATHAME — Ritual black-handled knife used in modern Wicca and now adopted by some traditionals

AURA — Life force or energy field around all living things

AVALON — Popular Celtic name for the underworld located at Glastonbury in Somerset.

AZAZEL — Leader of the Watchers or Fallen Angels. Witch god in some traditional groups.

BALEFIRE — Special fire lit for ritual purpose

BAN — To banish or curse

BANE — A destructive or poisonous thing

BELTANE — Celtic seasonal festival on May Ist

BESOM	Traditional witch's broomstick
BID	A witch's familiar spirit
BIDDING	Praying to a God or spirit
BIND	To cast or seal a SPELL
BIND-RUNES	Two or more RUNES combined to create a SPELL project negative thought forms or energy at an enemy
BLASTING ROD	Blackthorn wand used for above.
BLOT	Norse term for a sacrifice or offering
BOLLINE	Ritual dagger curved like a sickle and used to gather herbs
BONESMAN	East Anglian necromancer
BOOK OF SHADOWS	Handwritten book of rituals, spells etc kept by Wiccans. A term now adopted by many traditionals. Nowadays the original can be held on computer disc.
BROWNIE	Domesticated household spirit. See also HOBGOBLIN
BULL'S MOON	Archaic term for midnight
BURIN	Ritual white-handled knife used for practical purposes.
BURNING TIMES	Popular, emotive and inaccurate term used to describe the period of the witch-hunts by modern Wiccans
CANDLEMAS	Celtic festival on February Ist
CASTLE	Alternative traditional name for circle
CASTLE OF THE ROSES	Underworld home of the Dark Goddess
CAKES & WINE	Symbolic ritual meal at end of full moon or seasonal festivals
CERNUNNOS	Popular name in modern Wicca for witch god
CHALICE	Cup used for libations and CAKES & WINE

THE CHARGE	Address by the Goddess through her priestess in a Wiccan coven. Possibly 19th century origin.
CHARGING	Consecrating or blessing rituals tools, amulets, talismans, crystals etc.
CHARM	Words or object with magical power
COMPASS	Traditional name for circle
CONE OF POWER	Psychic energy raised in a a circle for healing, blasting etc.
CONJURING	Summoning a spirit or SHADE
CONJURING STICK	Traditional wand
CORN DOLLY	Image of the Goddess made from last sheaf of harvest
COVEN or COVINE	Group of witches traditionally numbering seven or thirteen.
COVENDOM	Area of a league (three miles) radius of a COVENSTEAD
COVENSTEAD	Regular meeting place of COVEN
COWAN	Unintiated person or outsider
CRAFT	Generic name for witchcraft and its followers
CRONE	1. Wise Old Woman or Grandmother aspect of the witch goddess. 2. Female ELDER over sixty years old.
CUNNING MAN	Male witch or WIZARD with knowledge of spells, herbcraft, magick, exorcism, healing etc. See also WARLOCK
CWN ANNWN	'Dogs of the underworld' in Celtic Welsh myth
DAME	See LADY
DEOSIL	Sunwise or clockwise
DEVIL	Archaic name for MAGISTER. Possibly from Romany for 'little god'
DIANA	Classical Roman goddess of the moon and hunting.

DIVINATION	Foretelling the Future
DRAWING DOWN THE MOON	Wiccan ritual to channel Goddess through the HPS
DWARVES	Elemental earth spirits
ELEMENTAL	Nature spirits
ELEMENTARY	Magically created thought form
ELDER	Senior member of coven or tradition. Usually somebody over fifty years old with at least twenty years experience in the Craft.
ELFANE/ELFAME	Old English term for Faeryland
ELF FIRE	Flame used to light BALEFIRE without metal
ELVES	Faery beings. In Norse mythology they are 'bright elves' and 'dark elves'
ELVEN RACE	Hybrid human descendents of mating between the Watchers and the daughters of men
EOSTRE	Germanic goddess of light and the dawn
ESBAT	Modern term for full moon meet.
EVIL EYE	Superstitious belief people can injure or kill by a glance or stare
EVOCATION	The conjuration of spirits or orf SHADES
FAMILIAR	1. Spirit, thought form or elemental servitar used by witch for magical purposes 2. Small animal kept as pet by witches.
FETCH	1. Projected spirit body of witch, sometimes in animal form. 2. Totem animal 3. Personal spirit guide or guardian in human or animal form.
FIREDRAKE	Elemental fire spirit
FIVE-FOLD KISS	Ritual salute in modern Wicca. Possibly of Arabic or Sufic origin.

FLY AGARIC	Red-capped, white-spotted toad-stool used to contact spirit world by traditionals.
FLYING OINTMENT	see SABBATI UNGEUNTI
FOUR WAYS	Crossroads
FREYJA	'Lady'. Norse witch goddess.
GARDNERIAN	Modern form of Wicca created by Gerald Gardner (1884-1964)
GLAMOUR	SPELL of illusion of fascination.
GEOMANCY	Divination using earth forces.
GOOD PEOPLE	Popular name for faeries
GOOD WOMEN	Early medieval name for witches
GREAT RITE	The 'sacred marriage' of the HP and HPS in Wicca.
GREEN MAN	Summer aspect of the witch god.
GREY WITCH	One who can cure or curse.
GRIMOIRE	Book of magical SPELLS and rituals.
GWYNN AP NUDD	Welsh Lord of the Wild Hunt.
HAEGESSA	'Hedge-rider'. Saxon term for witch.
HAG	Elderly aspect of the Dark Goddess.
HALLOWE'EN or HALLOWS	October 31st
HANDFASTING	Wiccan version of marriage service.
HARVEST HOME	Autumn Equinox (September 21st/22nd)
HEREDITARIES	Natural born witches belonging to a family tradition.
HERODIAS	Wife of King Herod and medieval name for witch goddess in southern France.
HERNE	Saxon name for Horned God. See WODEN.
HERTHA	Germanic earth goddess and alternative name for witch goddess in Saxon tradition
HEX	1. Curse 2. German name for witch.
HIDDEN COMPANY	Discarnate witches who act as spirit guides

HOBGOBLIN	Hearth spirit.
HOLDA	'Bright One'. Central European winter goddess and female leader of Wild Hunt.
HOLLY KING	God of the Waning Year from Hallows to May Eve. See also OAK KING
IMP	Archaic name for FAMILIAR
INCUBUS	Male elemental spirit or human fetch of sexual type. See SUCCUBUS.
IRMINSUL	Saxon name for Cosmic World Tree
LADY	1. Name for the priestess in Traditional Craft. 2. Title for the witch goddess.
LAMMAS	Celtic festival on August Ist.
LILITH	Sumerian/Hebrew goddess of the dark moon. Aspect of witch goddess in some traditional groups.
LOKI	Norse fire/trickster god worshipped in some traditional groups.
LUCIFER	'Lightbearer' Solar aspect of the witch god.
MAGISTER	'Master' The priest and representative of the Horned God in traditional covens.
MAGUS	Male practitioner of magical arts. See WIZARD.
MAID or MAIDEN	Assistant to the LADY. In Hereditary groups she may be her daughter or niece.
MAN IN BLACK	Archaic name for MAGISTER.
MEAD	Traditional sacred drink with apples and honey.
MIDGARD	'Middle Earth'. The material world.
MIDSUMMER	Summer solstice (June 21st/22nd)
MIGHTY ONES	1. The Watchers 2. The Ancestral Dead 3. The elemental guardians of

	the quarters of the circle. 4. The Hidden Company.
MOLE COUNTRY	Rustic traditional name for spirit world.
MORRIGAN	Triple goddesses of death, war, fate and sexuality in Irish mythology.
NECROMANCY	Evocation of the dead.
NERTHUS	Germanic earth goddess
NEMETON	Celtic name for sacred grove.
NIDING POLE	Horse headed staff used for cursing.
NORTHERN TRADITION	Generic term for Celtic and Norse spirituality in ancient Northern Europe.
NORNS or NORNIR	Triple Norse goddesses of fate and destiny.
OAK KING	God of the Waxing year from Beltane to Hallowe'en.
OLD PEOPLE	Folk name for Bronze Age and Neolithic people.
OLD RELIGION	Generic name for the pre-Christian pagan religions and beliefs.
ORACLE	Person in Traditional coven who divines the future for the group.
OTHERWORLD	1. The spirit world 2. The Faerie realm 3. Archetypal world 4. Other dimensions.
OVERLOOK	Cast the Evil Eye an somebody.
OWL BLINK	See above.
PAN	Greek goat-foot god.
PENDRAGON	Ritual title of sacred king married to the goddess of the land.
PENTACLE	Wooden or metal disc representing the element of earth.
PENTAGRAM	Five-pointed star representing the four elements and spirit.
PHILTRE	Archaic name for love potion.
PICKINGILL CRAFT	East Anglian witch tradition containing Norse, Saxon, French and Gnostic elements.

POPPET	Wax image.
PUCK	Old English 'spirit of the land'.
QUEEN OF ELFANE	Traditional title of witch goddess in her faery aspect.
ROBIN GOODFELLOW	Hobgoblin and degraded version of witch god.
ROBIN HOOD	Historical version of Woden as witch god.
RUNES	1. Norse or Germanic alphabet. 2 Generic term for any magical alphabet.
SABBATI UNGUENTI	Flying ointment made from narcotic plants.
SABBATS or SABBATHS	The eight seasonal festivals of the year.
SAMHAIN	'Sow-in' Celtic festival on November Ist.
SCOURGE	Small whip used in some Wiccan and Traditional Craft circles to raise power and gain the Sight.
SCRYING	Foretelling the future or contacting the spirit world using a crystal, mirror, candle flame or bowl of water as a focus.
SEAL	A magical symbol representing a spirit or angel used in CONJURATION
SEER	Coven member with the Gift, Power or SIGHT.
SEITH or SEIDR	'seething' Norse form of witchcraft
SHADE	Earthbound human spirit.
SHIMMERING	Shapeshifting.
SKYCLAD	Ritual nudity. Term borrowed from Tantra.
SORCERY	Archaic term for magick, often malefic.
SPECULUM	Magick mirror.

SPELL	Magical ritual or act designed to create changes in material world or influence events and people.
SPOOK	1. SHADE. 2 Nature spirit or elemental.
SPRING EQUINOX	March 21st/22nd.
STANG	'Pole' Norse name for forked staff.
SUCCUBUS	Elemental female spirit or human FETCH of sexual type.
SUMMERLAND	Popular Wiccan name for spirit world.
SUMMONER	Male officer of traditional coven
SWASTIKA	Cosmic or solar symbol of the universal life force.
TRADITIONAL	1. Witch belonging to a group or tradition claiming historical continuity from before the 20th century revival. 2. Coven or solitary witch following Craft in a traditional or historical way.
THEBAN	Medieval magical script.
THURIBLE	Incense-burner
TALISMAN	Object empowered to attract good luck, wealth, health, love etc.
TUBAL CAIN	The first blacksmith.
VAMPIRE	1. Predatory SHADE. 2. Person who takes energy from other living things.

Bibliography & Further Reading

The Historical Background

Ankarloo B, and Henningsen G. *Early Modern Witchcraft* (Clarendon 1993)

Baring A, and Cashford J *The Myth of the Goddess* (Penguin 1991)

Billington, S and Green, M *The Concept of the Goddess* (Routledge 1996)

Briggs, R *Witches and Neighbours: The Social and Cultural Context of European Witchcraft* (Harper Collins 1996)

Cheney,W *The Cult of Kingship in Anglo-Saxon England* Manchester University Press 1970)

Ewen, C. L'Estrange *Witch Hunting and Witch Trials* (Kegan,Paul, French & Trubshaw 1929)

Fletcher, R. *The Conversion of Europe from Paganism 371-1386 AD* (Harper Collins 1997)

Ginzburg, C. *The Night Battles: Witchcraft and Agrarian Cults in the Sixteenth and Seventeenth Centuries* (Routledge & Kegan Paul 1983)

Ginzburg, C. Ecstasies: *Deciphering the Witches Sabbath* (Radius 1990)

Guilley, R.E. *The Encyclopedia of Witches and Witchcraft* (Facts on File 1989)

Hutton, R *The Pagan Religions of the Ancient British Isles* (Blackwell 1991)

Jones, P. and Pennick,N. *A History of Pagan Europe* (Routledge 1995)

Lavack, B.P. *The Witch Hunt in Early Modern Europe* (Longman 1987)

l.uck, G. *Arcani Mundi: Magic and the Occult in the Greek and Roman Worlds* (Crucible 1985)

Maple, E *The Dark World of the Witches* (Robert Hale 1462)

Maple, E *Magic, Medicine & Quackery* (Robert Male 1968)

Mayr-harting,B.T. *The Coming of Christianity to Anglo-Saxon England* (B.T. Batsgord 1982)

Murray, M. *The Witch Cult in Western Europe* (Oxford University Press 1921)

Murray, M. *The God of the Witches* (Sampson,Low,Martson & Co 1931)

Murray, M. *The Divine King in England* (1952)

Purkiss, D *The Witch in History* (Routledge 1996)

Russel, J.B. *A History of Witchcraft, Sorcerers, Heretics and Pagans* (Thames & Hudson 1980)

Sharpe,J. *Instruments of Darkness: Witchcraft in England 1550-1750* (Hamish Hamilton 1396)
Summers, M. ed. *Malleus Malificarum* (Pushkin Press 1929)

Mythology & Folklore
Baker, M. *Folklore and Customs of Rural England* (David & Charles 1974)
Branston, B. *The Lost Gods of England* (Thames & Hudson 1977)
Clarke,D. and Roberts, *A Twilight of the Celtic Gods* (Blandford 1996)
Clarke, D. *A Guide to Britain's Pagan Heritage* (Robert Hale 1995)
Davidson, H.E. *Roles of the Northern Goddess* (Routledge 1998)
Duerr, P. *Dreamtime: Concerning the Boundaries Between Wilderness and Civilisation* (Blackwell 1985)
Frazer, Sir James. The Golden Bough (MacMillan 1923)
Glob, P. *The Bog People* (Faber & Faber 1969)
Glob, P. *The Mound People* (Faber & Faber 1974)
Graves, R. *The White Goddess* (Faber d(Co 1948)
Howard, M. *The Sacred Ring: The Pagan origins of British Folk Festivals and Customs* (Capall Bann 1995)
Hutton, R. *The Stations of the Sun: the Ritual Year in Britain* (Oxford University Press 1996)
Jones, K. *The Ancient British Goddesses* (Ariadne Publications 1991)
Jordan, M. *Gods of the Earth: The Quest for the Mother Goddess and the Sacred King* (Bantam 1992)
Ross,A. *Pagan Celtic Britain* (Routledge & kegan Paul 1967)
Walker,B. *The Women's Encyclopedia of Myths and Secrets* (Harper & Row 1983)

Wicca & Neo-Paganism
Bourne, L. *Dancing with Witches* (Robert Hale 1998)
Carr-Gomm, P. ed *The Druid Renaissance* (Thorsons 1996)
Crowley, V. *Wicca: Old Religion for a New Age* (Thorsons 1989)
Crowley, V. *Principles of Wicca* (Aquarian 1992) *Principles of Paganism* (Thorsons 1996)
Crowther, P. *One Witch's World* (Robert Hale 1998)
Day, J. *A Patchwork of Magic* (Capall Bann 1996)
Farrar, S. *What Witches Do* (Peter Davis 1971)
Gardner, G.B. *Witchcraft Today* (Rider 1952)
Gardner, G.B. *The Meaning of Witchcraft* (Aquarian Press 1959)
Glass, J. *Witchcraft, the Sixth Sense - and Us* (Neville Spearman 1965)
Harvey,G. and Hardman,C ed. *Paganism Today* (Thorsons 1995)
Harvey, G. *Listening People, Speaking Earth: Contemporary Paganism* (Hurst & Co 1997)

Jordan, M *Witches: An Encyclopedia of Paganism and Magic* (Kyle Cathie 1996)
Lurham, T. *Persuasions of the Witch's Craft: Ritual magic and Witchcraft in Present-day England* (Blackwell 1989)
Moorey, T. *Paganism: A Beginners Guide* (Headline 1996)
Moorey, T. *Wicca: A Beginner"s Guide* (Headline 1996)
Valiente, D. *Where Witchcraft Lives* (Aquarian Press 1962)
Valiente, D. *The Rebirth of Witchcraft* (Robert Hale 1989)
Starhawk *The Spiral Dance* (Harper & Row USA 1979)

Traditional Craft and Folk Magick
Botrell,W. *Cornish Witches and Cunning Men* (Oakmagic Publications 1996)
Buckland, R. *Scottish Witchcraft* (L1Llewellyn USA 1991)
Chumbley, A. *The Azoetia: A Grimoire of Sabbatic Craft* (Xoanon Press 1992)
Gwernan, G. *Introduction to Witchcraft* (Quest Publications n.d.)
Jackson, Nigel *Call of the Horned Piper* (Capall Bann 1994)
Jackson, Nigel *Masks of Misrule* (Capall Bann 1996)
Jackson, Nigel *Compleat Vampyre* (Capall Bann 1995)
Jones, E.J. *Witchcraft: A Tradition Renewed* (Robert Hale 1990)
Jones, E.J. *Sacred Mask, Sacred Dance* (Llewellyn USA 1997)
Jones, K. *Cornish Witchcraft* (Sir Hugo Books 1995)
Jones, K. *Witchcraft in Cornwall* (Oakmagic Publications 1995)
Jones, K. *Cornish Charms & Cures* (Oakmagic Pubs 1997)
Jones, K. *Folklore and Witchcraft of Devon and Cornwall* (1997)
Jones, K. *Seven Cornish Witches* (OakMagic Publications 1998)
Pennick, N. *Secrets of East Anglian Magic* (Robert Hale 1995)
Ryall, R. *West Country Wicca* (Capall Bann 1994)
Slade, P. *Seasonal Magic Diary of a Village Witch* (Capall Bann 1997)
St. Ledger-Gordon, R. *The Witchcraft and Folklore of Dartmoor* (Robert Hale 1961
Thomas. J. *Witches Stay Away From My Door* (Wolfe Publishers 1967)

FREE DETAILED CATALOGUE

A detailed illustrated catalogue is available on request, SAE or International Postal Coupon appreciated. **Titles can be ordered direct from Capall Bann, post free in the UK** (cheque or PO with order) or from good bookshops and specialist outlets. Titles currently available include:

Caer Sidhe - Celtic Astrology and Astronomy by Michael Bayley
Call of the Horned Piper by Nigel Jackson
Celtic Lore & Druidic Ritual by Rhiannon Ryall
Earth Dance - A Year of Pagan Rituals by Jan Brodie
Earth Magic by Margaret McArthur
Enchanted Forest - The Magical Lore of Trees by Yvonne Aburrow
Familiars - Animal Powers of Britain by Anna Franklin
Healing Book (The) by Chris Thomas
Handbook For Pagan Healers by Liz Joan
Healing Homes by Jennifer Dent
Herbcraft - Shamanic & Ritual Use of Herbs by S Lavender & A Franklin
In Search of Herne the Hunter by Eric Fitch
Magical Guardians - Exploring the Spirit & Nature of Trees by PHeselton
Magical Lore of Cats by Marion Davies
Magical Lore of Herbs by Marion Davies
Patchwork of Magic by Julia Day
Psychic Self Defence - Real Solutions by Jan Brodie
Sacred Animals by Gordon MacLellan
Sacred Grove - The Mysteries of the Forest by Yvonne Aburrow
Sacred Geometry by Nigel Pennick
Sacred Lore of Horses The by Marion Davies
Secret Places of the Goddess by Philip Heselton
Talking to the Earth by Gordon Maclellan
Taming the Wolf - Full Moon Meditations by Steve Hounsome
VORTEX - The End of History, by Mary Russell

Capall Bann is owned and run by people actively involved in many of the areas in which we publish. Our list is expanding rapidly so do contact us for details on the latest releases.

Capall Bann Publishing, Freshfields, Chieveley, Berks, RG20 8TF